DARKNESS FALLS

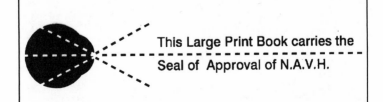

This Large Print Book carries the
Seal of Approval of N.A.V.H.

DARKNESS FALLS

KYLE MILLS

THORNDIKE PRESS
A part of Gale, Cengage Learning

Detroit • New York • San Francisco • New Haven, Conn • Waterville, Maine • London

GALE
CENGAGE Learning™

LIBRARY OF CONGRESS CATALOGING-IN-PUBLICATION DATA

Mills, Kyle, 1966–
    Darkness falls / by Kyle Mills.
      p. cm. — (Thorndike Press large print basic)
    ISBN-13: 978-1-4104-0677-4 (alk. paper)
    ISBN-10: 1-4104-0677-6 (alk. paper)
    1. Large type books. I. Title.
PS3563.I42322D37 2008
813'.54—dc22
                           2008001032

Published in 2008 by arrangement with Writer's House LLC.

Printed in the United States of America
1 2 3 4 5 6 7 12 11 10 09 08

DARKNESS FALLS

PROLOGUE

She'd hoped for snow, but not like this.

The flakes seemed to have merged into a single sheet, billowing around her, getting into her nose and mouth, robbing her of her balance. The wind subsided for a moment, but she could hear it building again in the distance, bearing down on her like a train and nearly sending her careening across the tundra.

Jenna Kalin blamed her nausea on the vertigo caused by the swirling snow, but knew that she was lying to herself. She'd spent years in the Alaska wilderness and had suffered through far worse storms. There had even been a time when she'd enjoyed the majestic fury of them, a reminder that, despite the growing influence of man, some aspects of nature couldn't be tamed.

She struggled to pull her boot free from the snow that had drifted around it and shone her headlamp behind her, illuminating a kaleidoscope of white flakes before being swallowed by the surrounding blackness. The rope extending from her waist began to sag, and she watched as the outline of her companion gained detail.

He had been confident to the point of dismissive ten hours ago, certain that his natural strength and fanatical commitment would make him more than a match for both her and the Alaska winter. But now his breath was coming out in ragged jets of steam and he was beginning to stumble with almost every step. Normally, she would have offered a few words of encouragement, but Jonas Metzger wasn't a man who evoked compassion or sympathy. In the time they'd worked together, the warmest feeling she'd ever had for him was vague discomfort.

Jenna had begged to come alone but they wouldn't let her. Michael Teague made a great show of concern for her safety but, as usual, that concern had an artificial ring. More likely he was worried she'd chicken out.

Jenna began fighting her way forward again before Jonas could reach her, concentrating on the endless darkness beyond her headlamp and trying to forget him. For some reason, the fact that he was there made her feel dirty. Criminal. Which, she supposed, she was.

It took more than an hour to cover the last mile, the tug of the rope at her waist becoming more frequent as her companion found it increasingly difficult to keep up. It wasn't until the blackness ahead began to turn gray that she realized she was grateful for the delay. Her nausea worsened when a recognizable shape formed in the distance, a giant tombstone defacing what had once been untouched wilderness. A tumor on what was supposed to have been protected forever.

As she got closer, the oil rig came into focus: the towering web of steel girders hung with lights, the swooping cables, the blackened snow piled up as a windbreak. Her queasiness was soon overshadowed by the anger she felt at the sight of the compound and the sounds of drilling carried on the diesel-scented wind.

She dropped her backpack in the snow and detached a smaller pack from it, slipping it over her shoulders as Jonas came even with her.

"Wait here," she said, turning off her headlamp and then reaching out to do the same to his. It was doubtful that anyone from the rig could see them through the storm, or even that they'd be watching at this hour, but there was no point in taking the risk.

She couldn't see Jonas's face, but the thick hood surrounding it moved slowly from side to side.

"I was told to come with you."

The words were nearly unintelligible, garbled by his thick German accent, the wind, and now the ugly grinding of the rig.

"You *have* come with me," Jenna said, taking a hesitant step toward him and leaning close enough that she didn't have to shout. "This is my responsibility and I need to move faster than you'll be able to."

He didn't agree or disagree, but just stood there, motionless except for the clenching and unclenching of his gloved hands.

It wasn't the solemn moment Jenna had fantasized about. She should have been standing there alone, remembering the years she'd spent in Alaska sleeping out under the stars, reveling in the almost comforting loneliness and silence. In a world of seven billion people, it was almost surreal to stand with nature instead of being one of the anonymous masses lined up against it.

She thought about Erin Neal — something she still did way too often. What would he say about what she was about to do?

"Wait here!" she repeated, unclipping the rope connecting them and then taking off at a pace she knew he couldn't match. When she finally glanced back, there was nothing. Just the darkness.

It took a good fifteen minutes to reach the steep snow bank that surrounded the drilling area and another two for her to climb to the top of it. She lay on her stomach, feeling the cold that had been numbing her face and hands leech into her torso and cause her teeth to begin to chatter. The scarf over her mouth was deflecting her breath and fogging her goggles so she pulled it off, giving the frozen air a direct path to her lungs.

The area below had been plowed flat to house not only the rig but also the men and machinery servicing it. The place was littered with tracked vehicles, stacks of equipment and supplies, as well as a few heated trailers that would be full of sleeping roughnecks right now. It was 2:00 a.m. but spotlights still illuminated every corner of the complex, robbing it of shadows in a way that made it look like an overexposed photograph. She remained motionless, moving only her eyes as she searched for signs of the nighttime skeleton crew she knew was there somewhere.

Nothing.

She continued to wait, but felt herself getting colder and colder. From experience, she knew it would be only another five minutes before her ability to move efficiently began to diminish.

"Now is not the time to start soul-searching," she said aloud. She'd made her decision a long time ago and now there was no going back.

Jenna pushed over the crest of the bank, slithering down on her stomach, counting on her white clothing to act as camouflage. The shouts and sound of running feet she'd half expected didn't materialize, and once she reached the base, she ran crouched toward a pyramid of rusting barrels.

The high berms surrounding the area completely blocked the wind, but it was still audible over the sound of the machinery, screaming through the top of the rig, furious at being blocked by something so trivial and short-lived as humans.

She crept forward, adrenaline drowning out cold, doubt, fear. Less than a minute later, her foot was on the first step of a set of metal stairs. A layer of ice made them difficult to climb, but it muffled the normal clang of boot against steel.

At the top, she found what she was looking for: a series of vats filled with what looked like muddy water but was actually a meticulously engineered fluid that was pumped around the rig's drill bit to lubricate it and keep the dirt and rock flowing up out of the hole.

Dropping to her knees on the catwalk, she removed her pack and dug two large plastic bags from it. When she stood again, she found herself staring down into the vats, unable to move.

No one would be hurt, she told herself for the thousandth time. The oil companies would whine and complain and eventually get the government to give them yet another subsidy to supplement the billions in profits they racked up every month. And, of course, the American people would engage in a brief display of self-pity before forgetting all about it. In the end, the only effect of her actions would be to ensure that some of the most pristine wilderness left in the world would be safe. Forever.

She looked at the ice-covered pipes and girders, at the well-lit compound, and finally at the expanse beyond. Sometimes things got bad enough that responsible people had to act to try to change things. The hard part was knowing when that moment had come.

She opened the bags and dumped a white

powder into the churning fluid, watching it disappear so quickly she could almost pretend that she hadn't done it. That the contents of those bags had never really existed.

It seemed impossibly anticlimactic. There was no explosion, no grinding of gears and ensuing silence, no sudden darkness as the lights died. She didn't know whether to feel relieved or cheated as she shoved the empty bags into her pack.

"Hey! Who the fuck are you?"

She spun around, reaching for a slick railing to prevent herself from falling. The rig worker was running at her with speed and grace that bespoke a life lived on frozen catwalks.

She ran for the stairs, half falling, half sliding down them until she slammed into the snow. The footsteps were audible behind her as the roughneck shattered the ice coating the steps and generated a dull ring that seemed impossibly loud.

Tripping over her bulky boots, Jenna pushed herself to her feet and sprinted back the way she'd come. The glare of the lights made her feel as if she were beneath one of the magnifying glasses that had so fascinated her as a child.

"Stop, goddamnit!"

The door of a trailer to her right opened and she saw a man wearing only a pair of greasy jeans peer out and then disappear for a moment before reappearing with a pair of boots in hand. He jumped to the ground and began pulling the boots on while yelling back through the open door.

She didn't look back, already certain that the man following her was gaining. She'd covered so many cold, hard miles that night and her legs just wouldn't respond. Or maybe it was more than that. Maybe somewhere deep inside, she wanted to be caught.

With an audible grunt, the man dived toward her, slapping the back of her foot and sending her face-first into the hard-packed snow.

Their slide was stopped abruptly by a stack of tires, and by that time, the man had a hand tangled in her pant leg. She flipped on her back and kicked weakly at him, sinking a boot through his thick beard and miraculously connecting with his chin.

She wasn't strong enough to hurt a man his size, but she did force him to let go and use both hands to ward off the second kick he was expecting. Instead, she pushed herself to her feet and started running again, struggling for traction and gripping a rusty snowcat for balance. The shouts audible from behind probably came from two or three men, but her mind multiplied them into an angry mob, and finally her legs responded. Her balance returned and she could feel the bitter cold of the air against her face as her speed increased.

She was almost to the snow bank when a figure stepped out from behind a pile of scrap and pointed a gun at her. She tried to stop, but her momentum carried her forward, bringing her so close as to make her impossible to miss. At that moment, though, she realized the gun wasn't aimed at her, but past her.

"Jonas, no!"

She threw herself forward, managing to deflect the German's arm just as he fired. The crack of the pistol was followed by a loud ricochet and not the soft thud she imagined a bullet impacting flesh would make.

When she looked back, the man chasing her was skidding on his back in the snow, trying to reverse himself. A moment later, he was running toward the relative safety of the rig along with the men who had spilled out of the trailers.

"Are you crazy?" she said, shoving Jonas back hard enough to nearly send him sprawling into the metal debris behind him.

"You could have killed someone!"

He didn't answer, instead grabbing her by the back of the neck and dragging her toward the wilderness they'd come from.

1

"Stupid piece of crap!" Erin Neal shouted, throwing his screwdriver and rolling out from underneath his perpetually jammed solar array. He gave it a hard kick before remembering he was wearing sandals, then limped off across the dusty wasteland that passed for his yard.

He'd spent the last three days using everything short of a cutting torch to get the panel tracking again, but it had been a waste of time. So now he was living his life at the evil whims of a glitchy solar panel and a windmill that sat dead in the still air. Building his house ten miles from the nearest paved road — too far to practically connect to the grid — didn't seem quite so smart now. At the rate his batteries were draining, his freezer would soon be dead, and he would lose the elk he'd bagged that fall.

He stepped up onto the wide porch that

wrapped around his house, escaping the Arizona sun that was doing nothing for him but deepening the red of his back, and slammed through his front door. It was time either to break down and call a professional or to go buy the diesel back-up generator he'd been resisting for so long.

The water in the sink was lukewarm, but he scooped some on the back of his neck anyway. Not as satisfying as a handful of ice, but since he couldn't open his goddamn freezer, it was the best he was going to get.

Erin grabbed a dirty drinking glass from the counter and spun, throwing it through the kitchen door and hitting the fireplace that dominated his small living room. It shattered spectacularly, and watching the shards scatter across the floor made him feel a little better. It always did.

The house wasn't large — an open living area built around the glass-strewn fireplace that supported a spiral staircase leading up to a loft and down to a basement, and a narrow hallway that led to a bathroom and an unused office. He'd built the structure himself out of old tires packed with sand and then covered it with white adobe. The materials not only created elegant curved lines that he probably wouldn't have thought of on his own but had the added benefit of covering up his mediocre carpentry skills. Despite a few things he wished he'd done differently, and the fact that he was starting to suspect that his solar panel was possessed, he couldn't really complain about how it had turned out. The orientation was perfect for passive heating and cooling and, with the exception of the last few days, the electrical system he'd designed kept him in the twenty-first century.

Erin splashed some more water on his neck and grabbed a dustpan from beneath the counter. The broken glass would at least force him to pick up a bit. By necessity, he didn't have many possessions, but somehow they always seemed to scatter themselves across the floor when he wasn't looking.

The ring of the cell phone startled him — not only because of the self-imposed silence around him but because no one really ever called him. Sometimes he wondered why he even had it.

The sound was slightly muffled, suggesting his phone had worked its way between his sofa cushions again, and he dug around until he came up with it.

"Hello?"

"Erin?"

"Who wants to know?"

"Ah, I see you haven't changed. It's Rick

Castelli. How you doin', man?"

Erin flopped down on the couch and propped his feet on a table he'd artistically welded together out of pieces of an old pickup.

"Rick? It's been a long time. Since that oil spill off the coast of California, right?"

"Yeah, we appreciated all your hard work on that cleanup, Erin. If I hadn't put you in charge of that thing we'd still be out there scrubbing rocks."

"So you're still at Exxon?"

"Nah. I hung out my own shingle a while ago. Mostly doing government consulting work now."

"Cushy," Erin said.

"Yeah, it's not bad . . ." His voice trailed off.

"So what do you want, Rick? I assume you're not calling to catch up."

"Not entirely. See, it's like this. The Saudis are having some production problems and I think it's something you'd be interested in."

Erin crossed his eyes and watched a bead of sweat slide down his nose. "I can guarantee you that I won't be."

"I haven't even told you anything yet."

"I'm retired."

"You're fucking thirty-seven years old."

"So?"

"Are you telling me you've got something better to do?"

"Than go to Saudi Arabia? Are you kidding me? Shit's blowing up over there and I hear they get double points for Americans."

"That's just media hype."

"Media hype," Erin repeated skeptically. "What, five bombs in the last two weeks? And how many people dead? From what I hear, the royals are working on an exit strategy."

"You know the fucking towel-heads," Castelli said. "All we ask them to do is stand there while we pump cold, hard cash down their throats, and they can't even handle that."

"You're still full of shit, aren't you, Rick?"

"What are you talking about?"

"Could it be that while we jump up and down squealing about democracy we're supporting a bunch of kleptomaniacal monarchs who use all that money to buy Rolls-Royces while their citizens starve?"

"Jesus Christ, I forgot what a self-righteous prick you —"

"So do we have anything else to talk about?" Erin said, cutting him off.

"Come on, man. Quit breaking my balls. I've got a guy here who's supposed to be an expert, but he's not you, you know? Besides, since when did you become a nervous Nellie?"

"Why don't you —"

"I'll send a plane, okay? Hell, I'll send a jet with a vibrating bed, a hot stewardess, and some hundred-year-old scotch. Then we'll stick Uncle Sam for the entire bill, plus our fee. It'll be fun."

"No."

"Goddamnit, Erin! Quit being such a jackass. Do it for an old friend."

"I never liked you."

That wasn't really true. In his own obnoxious way, Rick was an okay guy. But there were so many reasons not to get involved in the oil business again that he'd need a calculator to count them. Those years didn't even seem real to him anymore. Just another one of the past lives he was collecting.

"My ass," Castelli said, and then his voice softened. "Hey, I know I should have called. I was real sorry when I heard about your girlfriend. What was her name?"

Erin felt a familiar tightness in his chest. It was hard to breathe for a few seconds, but only a few seconds. That was an improvement wasn't it?

"Jenna."

"Yeah, that's it. Jenna Kalin. I hear she was a nice girl. Kind of a tree hugger, though, wasn't she?"

Erin let out a breath that almost could have passed for a laugh. "I see you're still the picture of sensitivity."

"Jesus, Erin. That was what, two years ago?"

"A year and a half." Actually, nineteen months, four days, and an odd number of hours depending on how you treated the time zones. "It was just a few days after Christmas . . ."

"Well, nothing like a free trip to sunny Saudi Arabia to take your mind off it," Castelli interrupted, obviously not looking to dig too deeply into the subject. "And how 'bout I guarantee you'll get lucky with that stewardess —"

The phone went silent and Erin looked down at it. Dead battery. He stuffed it back into the cushions and reached for a framed photo propped on the table next to his feet.

It had been taken in better times. The beach he and Jenna were standing on was black from a tanker spill and she was holding an oil-soaked bird in her arms. The lines of her body were obscured by heavy overalls and a grimy, oversized sweater, leaving only her tan face and thick brown hair visible. Why had that always been his favorite photo of them? Was it the way she was looking at that stupid bird? Was it the memory of letting himself put his natural cynicism aside and get caught up in her moral certainty?

He remembered how the oil had caused her to break out and how she'd blamed each zit on a specific energy company, as though there was a massive corporate conspiracy focused on nothing but screwing up her complexion.

God, he wanted a beer. Even a warm one.

But he didn't drink anymore, and that was because of Jenna, too. She'd been the only person with the guts to correctly point out that he was a psychotic drunk. So now that she was dead, why hadn't he started again? Sure, booze brought out the worst in him, but sometimes the anger was easier to deal with than everything else.

Erin set the picture aside and sunk a little farther into the sofa, staring at the empty wall across from him. Everything had seemed so clear after he'd gotten his PhD. He was going to be a new kind of environmentalist. Instead of waving signs and trying to convince everyone that the sky was falling, he'd bring sanity to the debate by taking into account that no one was ever going to do anything for the earth unless there was something concrete in it for them. Preferably money.

On the surface, it had been a great idea — a revolution, he'd told himself. But there had been too many compromises. The truth was that the environment had become more of an emotional problem than a scientific one. No one wanted to look at his equations or listen to his carefully laid-out arguments. They just wanted to believe.

He'd laughed off the initial attacks, deconstructing his detractors' arguments and ramming them back down their throats. And he'd been thoroughly entertained by the occasional death threats, putting up a bulletin board shaped like a tombstone to hang them on. Things had become more difficult when his friends started walking away, but it was bearable. When Jenna had turned her back, though, he'd been completely lost.

Predictably, it hadn't taken long for his confusion and despair to turn to anger, which landed him with a job in the oil industry. He'd show them.

But what had he shown them? That he could become a fabulously wealthy and incredibly lonely thirty-seven-year-old, sitting around a dark house, surrounded by the ghost of a woman who had hated him before she died?

He wondered if that was what made it so hard. If they'd been on better terms when she'd . . .

"Then you'd probably be even more fucked up than you are now," he said aloud, forcing himself off the couch to sweep up the broken glass.

2

Mark Beamon slammed on the brakes too late, causing the subcompact he'd unwisely rented to fishtail along the dirt road before the front wheels dropped into a deep rut. He frowned as the dust caught up with him and billowed through the open windows, wondering if this time he was irretrievably stuck.

The idea of spending government money to replace the rain inundating Washington, D.C., with the blue skies of Tucson had been appealing in theory. A little sun, some Mexican food, maybe a quick round of golf. But this wasn't Tucson. It was a godforsaken desert in the middle of nowhere.

It was impossible not to wonder what would prompt a sane person to live in this cactus-strewn dust bowl. No pools, no manicured fairways. Hell, no shade.

He stuck his head out the window to make sure there were no buzzards circling before gunning the car out of the rut and continuing up the narrow scar that passed for a road.

When his phone rang five minutes later, he'd barely made it another mile. The nine holes he had planned for that afternoon were starting to look shaky.

"Hello?"

"Hey, Mark."

"It's about time."

"You said 4:00 p.m. It's exactly 4:00 p.m. Arizona time. In fact, the second hand is hitting the twelve. Now."

Beamon couldn't help smiling. Of all the people who worked for him, Terry Hirst was his favorite. Not only was he incredibly competent and annoyingly punctual, he simply couldn't be intimidated. A rare trait in the skittish, PC world of today's government.

"Fine, you win, Terry. What have you found out?"

"You received the email on his basics, right? Work history, education, and all that?"

"Yeah. Moving along . . ."

"Okay, first of all, the one thing everyone agrees on is that Erin Neal is a genius in the true sense of the word. He's *the* guy in the field of bioremediation."

"What the hell's bioremediation?"

"I asked the same thing. It's essentially the business of using bacteria to clean up toxic spills. So basically he breeds bacteria that eat all kinds of stuff. Mostly we're talking about oil, but he's also come up with bacteria that eat radioactive waste and ones that can work in really harsh environments, like in coal processing."

Beamon crested a hill, but still couldn't see any sign of human habitation. Did the guy live in a cave?

"Neal started a bioremediation firm that did work all over the world and made him a lot of money," Hirst continued. "Most of which he plowed back into research or used for environmental causes . . ."

"Christ," Beamon moaned.

"What?"

"He's a hippie, isn't he?"

"Not so much," Hirst said. "In fact, I think it would be fair to say that the hard-core environmentalists can't stand him. He wrote a pretty influential book called *Energy and Nature.* I ordered you a copy."

"Why don't you just give me the *Reader's Digest* version?"

"Essentially, it's about the future of energy and the environment, taking into account politics and human nature. He takes a dim view of people — that if it costs us abso-

31

lutely nothing, we might do something to protect the environment, but if it comes down to saving a tree or running our A/C, it's going to be no-contest. So he felt like the eco-movement needed to refocus itself on creating technologies and realistic strategies that would get people excited, regardless of any benefit to the earth. So, for instance, he'd say that building an electric car is pointless unless it's really sexy, four-wheel drive, and goes from zero to sixty in under six seconds."

"Let me guess," Beamon said. "He managed to piss off both sides."

"More or less. The environmentalists saw him as a sell-out and the business community wasn't really persuaded to cough up any money. Anyway, about a year after his book came out, he folded his company."

"His company went bankrupt?"

"No, he just shut it down. The guy was printing money as near as I can tell."

"You mean he sold it."

"I'm telling you, Mark, he handed his people big severance checks and closed the doors. Then he went to work consulting for the oil companies — Exxon, BP, and Saudi Aramco primarily. Then he dropped off the face of the earth."

"So he just walked away from that, too? I

gotta think the Saudis pay pretty well."

"No doubt. But other than his address and bank records, we've got nothing current on him. He doesn't have a job, he doesn't do research, and doesn't write anything that gets published."

"So he's some kind of hermit?" Beamon said.

"Seems like."

"You know what a hermit is?"

"No."

"A lonely hippie. Anything else?"

"I checked his criminal record —"

"Wait, let me guess. He chained himself to a tree in a logging camp."

"No —"

"They found marijuana plants growing in his VW bus?"

"Are you going to let me finish? He has two arrests for disturbing the peace and one assault. The charges were dropped in all cases. So maybe he's an angry, lonely hippie."

"I wouldn't —" A call beeped in and he checked the number. "Shit, Terry. I've got to take this. I'll talk to you later."

He picked up and hung his arm out the window, tapping a rhythm on the hot steel of the door. "Carrie? You there?"

"Mark, I just got your message — I was at the hospital late. What are you doing in

Arizona?"

"Vacationing on your tax dollar. Actually, we have someone we needed to talk to here and it's pretty important, so I had to come myself." He grimaced at his inelegant delivery of the obvious lie.

"Pretty important, huh?"

"As far as you know."

"Are you coming back tonight?"

"Not sure, yet. That's the plan, though."

"You know we're supposed to look at tuxedos."

In fact, he *was* aware of that. His secretary had not only put it on his calendar, she'd drawn a heart around it in pink highlighter. There was only so much he could take, though. As near as he could tell, wedding planning was a circle of hell Dante considered too terrifying to write about.

"I'm sorry, Carrie. It just couldn't be avoided."

"I'm ordering the baby-blue one with ruffles."

He snorted. "Let me save you the trouble. I've still got one in the attic from my prom. Just get the tailor to let it out."

Beamon wasn't sure what he was expecting, but this was pretty close. The white adobe house looked as if it had been inspired by

34

teepees and seashells in roughly equal parts, and there was no yard — just reddish dirt, looming saguaros, and various pieces of what looked like industrial junk. The gigantic solar panel was identifiable, as was the high-tech windmill, but the Honda hybrid parked next to a slightly crooked barn was so covered in unfathomable gadgets that Beamon recognized it only because one of his neighbors drove one. Most dominant, though, was a large above-ground pool surrounded by scaffolding. And standing on top of that scaffolding was a man dressed only in a pair of camouflage shorts, holding something that looked like a giant wooden spoon.

Beamon pulled the car up to a boulder and got out, shading his eyes and squinting at the man staring down at him through mirrored goggles. His shaggy hair was even blonder than in his photos, and his bare torso had a tan muscularity that suggested professional landscaper more than scientist.

"Are you Dr. Neal?"

"Who the hell are you?"

"My name's Mark Beamon. I work with Homeland Security."

An irritated smirk crossed Erin's face before he turned and went back to stirring his pool.

"I don't suppose you'd want to come down and talk?"

Erin just kept stirring, forcing Beamon to grab hold of the rickety two-by-four ladder that climbed the side of the scaffold.

By the time he got to the top, he had sweated through his thin golf shirt, but the rate of his breathing had hardly increased at all. As annoying as Carrie's vegetarianism and after-dinner power walks were, he had to admit that a few years ago, walking from his car to the Taco Bell had left him huffing. He was getting so used to feeling good, it was hard to remember his life before her.

Erin pretended to ignore him, continuing to swirl the green sludge that had taken over his pool.

"I'm no expert, but I'll bet a little chlorine would fix that right up."

Erin pulled his goggles up onto his head to appraise Beamon for a moment, obviously unimpressed. "It's an experiment."

"Bacteria, right? That's your business."

"Hobby," he corrected.

"Hobby. So what do these bacteria clean up?"

"Am I under arrest?"

"No."

"Then I don't have to answer your questions."

Beamon glanced up at the sky, futilely hoping the sun was about to dip behind a cloud. "You know . . ." he started, but didn't finish.

"What?"

"Nothing. Never mind."

"No," Erin said. "What were you going to say?"

"Just that if I was as rich and good-looking as you, I'd be less pissed off."

Erin spun in his direction and jabbed a finger violently in the air with his free hand. "Who the fuck do you think you are? You drive in here and start asking questions and judging me. You don't know the first thing about me. So why don't you just go tap someone's phone or something?"

Beamon nodded slowly but didn't move; instead, he examined the elaborate grid laid over the pool and tried to discern whether the goop varied from one compartment to another.

Erin moved around the scaffold with his spoon, but as the silence between them stretched out, he became visibly uncomfortable. "I'm experimenting with bio-solar. These bacteria generate electricity from the sun and other nutrients. It's sort of a cross between algae and an electric eel."

Beamon crouched and examined the

contents of the pool more closely, but it still just looked like sludge to him. "So I'll be able to throw some of this in a puddle outside my house and run my TV on it someday?"

"Nah. I don't think it'll ever work. Interesting, though."

"If you say so. You know, I'm burning up out here. Any chance we could go inside and talk for a few minutes?"

Erin eyed him suspiciously, but finally just shrugged, jumped off the scaffold, and stomped through the dust to his porch. Beamon considered the drop for a moment and then took the ladder.

Inside, the un-air-conditioned house was more seashell than teepee. Messy enough to be just on the border of saying something unflattering about Erin's psyche, with furniture that was half homemade and half mail order. Much more interesting was the artwork. As near as Beamon could tell, it consisted completely of photographs of the same woman. He walked up to one of her standing at the base of a cliff with a climbing harness on. Early thirties, pretty, with one of those smiles that made you sure you'd like her if you met her.

"Who's this?" Beamon asked. According to the information Terry Hirst had provided,

Erin had never been married and didn't have a sister.

"You can't search my house without a warrant. I know my rights."

"For Christ's sake, Erin. I'm not searching your goddamn house. I was just hot."

Erin frowned. The suspicion on his face was now marred by a hint of guilt at being the obvious bad guy so far in this relationship.

"Girlfriend," he said finally.

"Does she live around here?"

"She's dead."

Beamon kept his expression impassive, but he was imagining drowning Terry in a toilet bowl for missing that. "I'm sorry."

"She was an environmentalist. You know, one of those groups you people have been bugging and spying on because you think they're terrorists."

Here we go, Beamon thought.

"Her boat sunk with all hands a while back. I figure the government was probably behind it."

"You know, they don't give us torpedoes," Beamon said, and immediately regretted it. He'd tried to leverage the fact that his fiancée was a psychiatrist into some kind of improvement in his own bedside manner, but so far he'd accomplished zip.

"What do you want, Mark?"

"Actually, I want you to look at a sample of some sludge."

"What's in it for me?"

"You seem to like sludge."

"No."

"How about the warm fuzzy feeling of helping your fellow man?"

"You're getting colder."

Beamon sighed quietly. "Look, we've gotten wind of a problem at a Saudi oil field, and with all the turmoil over there, we're already kind of living on the edge where supply's concerned. Shit, the people I rented my car from said they're charging six bucks a gallon if I don't bring it back full. So we'd like you to take a look and see what you think. Tell us if it's something we need to worry about."

"Wait a minute," Erin said. "Did Rick Castelli put you up to this?"

Of course he had, but, because of Erin's tone, Beamon decided to remain silent on the subject.

"You government guys are so fucking melodramatic. Everything's a disaster to you unless it really is, and then you just ignore it. Well, I'll tell you what. I'm gonna ignore this."

Beamon looked around the house — at

the dirty dishes on the coffee table, the broken glass on the floor, the dead woman staring at him from all sides.

"So you can hang around here?"

"Fuck you. It's a free country. You can't make me go."

Beamon smiled. "Can't I?"

3

The helicopter finally began to descend, but that didn't bring the landscape into clearer focus. The sand seemed endless — a monochromatic blanket so devoid of features that it was almost disorienting.

Some people might have called it beautiful, and Erin Neal supposed it would have been if there weren't so many memories buried in those dunes. It wasn't far from here that the current chapter of his life had started. And now it just wouldn't end.

He glanced over at Mark Beamon dozing in the seat next to him, headphones propped crookedly across his ears. After a brief burst of energy on the jet from Tucson, during which he had plowed through an enormous tray of sandwiches and a few smuggled mini-bottles of bourbon, practically the only time he'd opened his eyes all day had been to transfer to the Saudi Aramco chopper they were now on. As near as Erin could tell, the guy was either some kind of Zen master, a great actor, or else completely disinterested in wherever it was they were going. Probably the last one.

As they got closer to the hot sand, the air got bumpy enough to cause Beamon to open his slightly puffy eyes and squint out the window. "Where are we?"

"How the hell should I know? You haven't told me anything."

Beamon stretched wildly and smoothed his thinning hair beneath the headphones. "I was supposed to be home trying on tuxedos, but you had to be a pain in the ass, so now I'm stuck babysitting. What the hell do I know about the Middle East? It's hot and sandy without the benefit of so much as a single burrito stand. So why don't you tell me where we are. You're the expert, right?"

There was a certain odd sincerity to Beamon's groggy protest, and Erin stuck his nose to the glass as they passed over a massive structure that seemed to be made up entirely of silver pipe. Beyond, the distant outlines of oil derricks were swaying in the heat distortion. "Northern Ghawar."

"That's an oil field, right?"

"It's not *a* field, it's *the* field. Most people think the world's oil supply comes more or less evenly out of thousands of individual fields, but it's not true. A few giants produce most of it, and of those Ghawar is by far the largest. It's responsible for ninety percent of Saudi Arabia's oil and almost seven percent of the world's."

When the skids touched down, Erin unfastened his harness and, before jumping out, waited for the tornado of sand the blades had kicked up to subside. They'd landed about two hundred meters from a small, lonely derrick that would have seemed almost laughably unimportant if it weren't for the gleaming trailers surrounding it and the soldiers moving toward them.

Although they were all running and had guns in their hands, Beamon strode forward confidently, holding his ID above his head. Erin hung back.

The royal family was in complete control the last time he'd visited Saudi Arabia, and he had been a highly valued employee of Saudi Aramco. It had been all smiles and bags of cash back then. Now, though, the atmosphere had changed.

"Hello! I'm Mark Beamon from U.S. Homeland Security. I think we're expected —"

One of the ten or so approaching guards aimed his rifle in their direction, prompting his companions to do the same. Someone started shouting in Arabic — too fast and complicated for Erin to follow, though the tone and the wall of gun barrels they were facing made things pretty clear.

To his credit, Beamon didn't seem bothered by the deteriorating situation, and he continued to make himself the center of attention; meanwhile, Erin slowly backed toward the helicopter. The whine of the motor gained pitch and he turned to run toward it, but he saw that the skids were already off the ground. He turned back to find that Beamon was now facedown on the ground, a rifle barrel pressed to the back of his head.

There were too many soldiers to search one person, though, and the ones who felt left out inevitably turned their attention Erin's way. A moment later, he was lying next to Beamon and being groped by men who smelled as though they hadn't showered in a month.

"Look, we're here to —" Erin started through the sand in his mouth, but then fell silent when he felt the jab of a gun barrel against his spine.

By the time they were through with him, Beamon had been rolled onto his back and was lying there squinting into the empty sky, his sunglasses already pocketed by one of the men patting him down.

"We had to twist a few arms to convince the Saudis to let us come here — they're kind of a secretive bunch and with all their political problems, I guess they're a little edgy."

"A little edgy?" Erin said as the guards retreated a few feet, guns still poised. He pushed himself to his feet and dusted off the sand as Beamon did the same. "As far as the royals are concerned, the U.S. isn't doing shit to help them keep their grip on the country, and letting a couple of Americans get killed would probably be a good illustration of their irritation."

"I've never been here," Beamon said, ignoring him. "Kind of stark, isn't it?" He actually used a finger to push aside one of the rifle barrels aimed at him and then strode off toward a white trailer, obviously attracted by the air conditioner humming on top of it. Erin slipped in behind him, careful not to make eye contact with the guards as he squeezed past.

The door to the trailer opened and a man waving energetically in their direction jogged down the steps. He wore thick glasses that glinted in the sun and a long black ponytail carefully concocted from what was left of the hair on his sunburned scalp.

"Dude!" he shouted, bounding toward them through the sand, only to stop short when Erin's angry expression became evident. He threw his hands out in a gesture of submission. "Not my doing, man. You've got Rick Castelli to thank for being here."

Erin's nod prompted the man to close the rest of the distance between them. He threw a bear hug around Erin that almost lifted him from the ground.

"How the hell are you, man? It's been way, way too long."

When Erin finally managed to pull away, he motioned to his right. "This is Mark Beamon. Mark, meet Steve Andropolous. He used to work for me."

"Yeah, we've talked on the phone," Andropolous said, thrusting out a hand. "How you doing, Mark?"

"I'm hot."

He laughed and turned back to Erin. "More important, how are *you*? That shit with Jenna? *So* fucked up."

Erin was surprised when he found himself fighting the smile threatening to cross his face — not his usual reaction to the sound of Jenna's name. For as long as he'd known Andropolous, the man's speech patterns had tracked the current high school fashion. Whatever the delivery, though, his words were heartfelt, and Andropolous was one of the few people who had always supported him. For a moment, Erin remembered what it was like to have friends.

"So what have you figured out?" Beamon said, looking back at the guards who seemed to have lost interest and were shouldering their rifles in search of shade.

"Weird shit," Andropolous answered. "You're gonna have to come and see for yourself to believe it."

The rig was only about a hundred feet high, and it seemed to be attached to the back of a truck. Erin circled, looking at something that resembled dried vomit splattered all over the rig's tower and the back of the truck used to transport it.

"What do you think?" Andropolous asked. "Look familiar?"

Erin tried to keep his interest from showing as he scraped some dried beige gunk from a pipe and rubbed it through his fingers. "Well, you've got a bacteria problem. But you didn't need me to tell you that."

"No, but you've dealt with this kind of thing before and I haven't."

Erin nodded. "Not far from here in the

Hawtaw Trend. But it wasn't like this. It wasn't all over the place. Did you try to punch through it?"

"Yeah, we went down another four hundred feet, but it just got worse."

"Four hundred feet? No shit?"

"And it's not easy drilling. Everything's gummed up, and it's corroding the crap out of the equipment. That's when the U.S. government started calling." He turned toward Beamon. "Guess you've got spies out here, huh? Or maybe those cool drone planes. Can you get me one of those things? How sweet would —"

Beamon interrupted. "Can it be fixed?"

They both looked at Erin, who was slowly shaking his head, seemingly lost in thought. "I don't really know."

"But you've fixed this kind of problem before, right? How did you do it?"

"Nothing all that creative. It was pretty easy to drill past, and then we pumped some toxic chemicals down the hole to see if we could kill it."

"That doesn't sound very environmental," Beamon commented.

Erin scratched the side of his face, making a show of extending his middle finger.

"Did it work?" Andropolous asked.

"I don't really know. We managed to get a

casing through it and that was the end of the problem. I wanted to go back and look to see what happened to the bacteria pocket, but the Saudis weren't interested. Their well was producing again and that's what they hired me for."

"It's not going to be so easy this time," Andropolous said, pulling a wad of damp papers from the pocket of his cargo shorts and holding them out. "You're gonna freak when you see this, bro. I looked over your data on the Hawtaw Trend bug and this stuff is *so* much more radical. Ridiculously corrosive, reproduces like nothing you've seen with basically zero oxygen, and, oh man, does it like to eat oil."

Erin took the sheets and slowly flipped through them. As he read Andropolous's initial analysis of the infestation, he shook his head. Finally, he handed the report back. "You've been smoking too much dope, Steve. There's no way those numbers can be right."

4

"All right, let's do it!" Erin shouted. He grabbed one side of a giant clamp suspended by chains while the other was handled by a man whose thick forearms were nearly black from years under the desert sun. They disconnected the drill pipe and were immediately covered in bacterial ooze as the back pressure blew it out with so much force that Erin was almost knocked off his feet. With a gloved hand, he scraped at the goo spattered on his goggles so that he could see well enough to connect another section of pipe. When it began spinning again, he walked over to a trough of water and splashed his face before the stuff dried and stuck to him.

He was drying off with a greasy rag when a familiar grinding sound drowned out everything else and the drill pipe came to a sudden halt. He didn't even bother to look up when a man leaning over the railing above shouted to him in Arabic. Another drill bit had twisted off.

He grabbed a piece of broken pipe and angrily threw it across the rig. It landed with an unsatisfying thud in the sand below just as the man he'd been working with started shouting and jabbing a finger in his direction.

Erin's Arabic was generally limited to a drilling vocabulary, so he had no idea what the guy was going on about, although he was pretty sure he heard Allah in there a few times. But then, he always thought he heard Allah when Arabs yelled at him.

"Fuck off," he said, even though the man was at least twice his size. He took off his dripping cowboy hat and held it out to shade his eyes. Five days in the Saudi desert and it just kept getting hotter — already 110 and it wasn't yet noon.

Of course, Mark Beamon wouldn't know anything about that. He spent his time in the air-conditioned trailer watching satellite TV until sunset; then he came out to drink the bourbon he'd had flown in and play backgammon with the guards, who, for some reason, thought the sun shined out of his ass.

Erin rubbed a raw, swollen hand over his dry lips and watched flakes of skin drift through the metal mesh that made up the floor of the rig. Everyone was just standing around waiting for him to decide what to do, but for the first time in his career, he wasn't sure.

It turned out that Steve's insane numbers were exactly right. Erin was now managing six rigs, trying everything he could think of to beat a bacterial infestation that seemed almost supernatural in its destructiveness. Going deeper was proving pointless, and might even be making things worse. He'd experimented with poisons to try to kill the stuff, but had met with surprisingly limited success. So now he was drilling at intervals around the infected wells to try to figure out the scope of the infestation and get some idea of the spread rate. So far, though, he couldn't find the edges of it.

And so what if he did? He was fresh out of ideas on how to contain it, which brought up the question of just what he was doing here. It was fucking indentured servitude. The government had kidnapped him, dropped him in the middle of the Saudi desert without so much as a dime for expenses, and said "Fix it!" Who the hell did they think they were?

Suddenly, a powerful hand clamped onto his shoulder and he was violently spun around to face the man he'd told to fuck off a few moments before. Apparently, the Arab didn't fully grasp the meaning of the phrase.

The man started shouting again, spit flying from his mouth and the wrench he was brandishing flashing in the sun. This time, there didn't seem to be any Allahs, but America was butchered in there a few times. Erin leaned to the side, glancing around the man's enormous torso, and saw that the rest of the workmen had paused to watch with glassy-eyed enthusiasm.

So there it was. Guys he'd treated with nothing but respect since he'd arrived were going to stand there and watch him get beaten to within an inch of his life because of where he was born. Or at least that's what they thought they were going to see.

"Look . . . Abbud, isn't it? You're about to do something you'll regret," Erin said, trying to hold back the blind rage that he'd been fighting all his life. He'd quit drinking for it, tried meditation — even sat through counseling. All to push it just barely below the surface.

The man shoved him, pointing with the wrench and starting another unintelligible diatribe.

"Blah, blah, blah," Erin said, talking over him. "You guys have it all figured out, don't you? You got a bunch of thieving princes doping you with religion so they can lounge around in palaces while you live in fucking huts in the desert. And now you finally figure that out and who do you get behind? A bunch of terrorists who won't be satisfied until they start an endless civil war that sets you back five thousand years."

The anger on the man's face faded into confusion at Erin's reaction. Guys his size were all the same. They expected everyone to shake in their boots and had no idea what to do when someone stood up to them.

"You think I want to be frying in this shit hole you call a country?" Erin continued, slamming his palms into the man's chest and knocking him back a few feet. "I couldn't give a rat's ass if your entire oil industry crashes and burns tomorrow. So let me give you the best piece of advice you've ever had: Step off and stop waving that wrench in my face before I shove it up your ass."

Of course, it wasn't likely that he was going to do as Erin suggested — or that he even understood. Erin was a little disappointed that his reputation in the oil fields had faded so quickly. No respect. No respect at all.

To his credit, the Arab was faster than he

looked, but Erin was still easily able to duck under the wrench aimed at his head and then drive a fist into the man's midsection hard enough to lift him off the ground.

He could feel the cuts on his hand spread open and the blood begin to flow, but the pain only heightened the familiar sense of release that he'd always hated himself for feeling. The ability to lose oneself in a violent frenzy, although occasionally useful for an environmentalist who worked with roughnecks, was, to quote Jenna, kind of a serious character flaw.

Abbud doubled over and Erin connected a knee with his face, sending him stumbling backwards, blood splattered across his thick beard. He was saved from falling by the railing that circled the rig, and Erin walked calmly toward him, grabbed his throat, and shoved him back so that his spine arched over the rail. The Arab didn't have enough strength to resist other than to raise his arms in a pathetic effort to ward off the blow that was about to slam into his mouth.

Erin hesitated for a moment and then lowered his fist. He crouched and grabbed Abbud's feet, lifting him up and sending him over the rail to the sand fifteen feet below. He landed hard, tried briefly to rise to his feet, and then just collapsed.

Erin was surprised that he felt no need at all to jump down on top of the guy. Maybe he was mellowing with age? Looming maturity? That couldn't be a bad thing.

The metallic ring of footsteps on the stairs behind him wasn't unexpected, and he turned to watch the soldiers flowing onto the platform.

The first one, running at him with the butt of his rifle raised, underestimated his own momentum and Erin sidestepped, clotheslining him hard enough that his feet flew up over his head. The glancing blow from the rifle butt of the next soldier was hard enough to send Erin to his knees, but not so hard that it kept him from kicking the man's feet out from under him and then slamming the back of his skull into the metal platform.

And then they were on him. Five, maybe six, he couldn't be certain. He rolled into a ball and tried to protect his head with his arms as they hit him with rifles, fists, boots. He managed to topple one of them, but in the process opened up long enough to take a hard shot to the forehead. The relentless blue sky above him started to look more like the ocean, flowing gently before turning dark.

■ ■ ■ ■

At first Erin thought the thudding sound was just the throbbing in his skull, but after a few seconds he realized that it was faster and heavier than anything biology could dream up. He opened his eyes slowly, the light stabbing into them.

"What happened?" he croaked when he finally managed to focus on Mark Beamon strapped into a seat above him.

"You're one lucky son of a bitch," he shouted over the helicopter blades. "If I hadn't happened to walk out of that trailer to take a leak at the exact moment I did, you'd probably be dead or in a wheelchair right now."

Erin tried to push himself up off the floor, but then thought better of it. "What do you want me to say? Thank you? If it weren't for you, I'd be sitting on my sofa right now."

"Doing what?" Beamon said. "Staring at a picture of a woman who's been dead for two years?"

Erin lunged forward, but he was still weak enough that Beamon was able to stop him by sticking a foot against his chest.

"Son, have you ever considered seeking therapy for that temper of yours?"

5

"Don't see why I need to be here," Erin whispered loudly as he and Beamon were led down one of the many corridors at the Department of Energy. "Stevie's the guy on the ground doing the work."

Mark Beamon reached out to give him a reassuring pat on the back, but then realized that there probably wasn't a hand-sized spot anywhere on Erin's body that wasn't bruised or cut. "Look, I've been unfortunate enough to work for the government most of my life, and the trick is to just recognize when things are out of your control and go with it."

"But I don't work for the government."

"Uh huh."

The woman escorting them took a hard left, and they followed silently.

"So that's what you do?" Erin said finally. "You just go along?"

Beamon let out a snort that seemed to

have real humor in it. "Do as I say. Not as I do."

Their guide veered left again, and Erin started to follow, but Beamon pulled him through a set of open double doors. He nodded absently at the woman sitting behind an elaborate workstation, but didn't stop. "Hey, Ruth. Is he here?"

"Go on in, Mark."

Erin entered the next room hesitantly, immediately recognizing the man standing in the middle of it as Jack Reynolds, the energy secretary. A few years back, Erin had blown up a photo of him to use as a dartboard.

"Jack, this is the guy I've been telling you ab—"

"What the hell is going on?" Reynolds said. He stared directly at Erin, but seemed not to notice his swollen face. "I just got a call from the Saudis saying that you assaulted an oil worker — who is now in the hospital with a separated shoulder — and that you were both deported."

"What are they whining about?" Erin shot back. "That guy landed in the sand. I got the shit beat out of me with rifle butts."

"Come on, Jack," Beamon said before the exchange could escalate. "The Saudis wanted us out of there from day one. They were looking for an excuse."

"And you didn't miss any opportunity to give them one, did you? Were you really drinking and gambling with the guards? It's a goddamn Muslim country, Mark!"

"Screw the Saudis," Beamon said, falling into a chair uninvited.

"No, screw *you*, Mark. We need them, and as long as that's true, you'll treat them with respect."

Beamon's nod was noncommittal.

For a moment, Reynolds looked as if he had more to say, but then appeared to conclude that there was no point. He let out a long, frustrated breath and pointed to the empty chair next to Beamon. Erin sat carefully. He'd originally thought his head was the worst of it, but now he'd swear those assholes had managed to crack his tailbone. Completely worth it, though. There was always a nice long calm after one of those storms, and even better, it might have the unintended benefit of making him useless to the government.

"All right," Reynolds said. "Tell me what's happening over there."

"You should ask Steve Andropolous," Erin replied.

"I have. And he told me that *you're* the expert. I think his exact words were that you've forgotten more about these things than anyone else knows."

He'd remember to kick Stevie in the nuts for that one.

"Fine. Whatever. How much do you know about this kind of problem?"

"Why don't you assume nothing."

Erin turned to Beamon. "Mark, you're the head of Homeland Security's energy branch, right? You must have some idea of how these things work."

He shook his head. "Got this job entirely through nepotism."

"Christ. Okay. Oil is a hydrocarbon and hydrocarbons are part of nature. And if something exists in nature, it's a pretty good bet that there's something out there that's evolved to use it in some way."

"Like these bacteria," Reynolds said.

"Exactly. If there's an oil spill in Mexico for example, I'd go there, find an indigenous oil-eating bacteria in the soil, and then figure out how to grow a whole lot of it. Then I'd throw it on the spill and let it do its work. That's an oversimplification, but it gets the point across."

"So you're saying these types of life forms are fairly common?"

"They're all around us. And they're in pretty wide use commercially. I mean, you can buy them by the pound to clean up the floor of your garage if you want."

"Then why haven't we run into this problem before?"

"Actually, oil companies deal with this kind of thing all the time, but in a much smaller way. Generally, these bacteria need a fair amount of oxygen to survive and replicate. That keeps them from destroying oil reservoirs —"

"But this one is different."

"Yeah, it can spread with virtually no oxygen at all, and it's really voracious. Also, the chemicals you'd normally use to kill it don't seem to faze it all that much."

"And why is that?" Reynolds asked. "It seems odd to me that these bacteria would be resistant to chemicals that don't exist in nature. Or destructive to something like drilling equipment that isn't exactly part of the ecosystem either."

"It's not as strange as it seems," Erin said. "For instance, if they evolved where a lot of metal ore was in the ground, the corrosive ones would be more successful and evolve toward being destructive to drilling gear. As far as resistance to chemicals goes, it's probably just an adaptation to an environmental challenge that was somehow similar. Did you know that a percentage of European descendants are immune to HIV? Not because they specifically evolved a resistance to the disease, but because the same mutation made their ancestors resistant to the plague."

"So you aren't surprised that these bacteria exist."

He shook his head. "Why would I be?"

"Can it spread?"

"Through a reservoir? Absolutely, depending on permeability of the rock. The bad news is that it can live without oxygen in water and oil. The good news is that, based on Stevie's research, this strain doesn't do so well out in the open elements. It dies almost immediately. So it's not like you could get it on your shoes and track it to Kuwait."

"Where did it come from, Erin?"

"Not a clue. Could just be Mother Nature defending herself."

The smile that spread across Reynolds's face had more than a hint of condescension. "Ah, yes. We all have to sell our cars and take up organic farming or we're going to die, right? Isn't that what you people believe?"

"You people?" Erin said. "Who's 'you people'? In the past few years we've had to face SARS, AIDS, Lyme disease, and bird flu. As far as I'm concerned, the environment is doing a pretty good job defending itself on its own."

Reynolds folded his arms across his chest and stared at Erin for a full thirty seconds. "I just can't get a read on you, Erin." He pointed to Beamon. "Mark here doesn't trust you, but then he's suspicious of his own mother. So I'll ask you point-blank: Whose side are you on? Are you willing to help us with this problem?"

"Doesn't really matter anymore," Erin said, smiling painfully. "The Saudis deported me. I'm out of the game."

Reynolds ended another long silence by shaking his head in resignation. "My back is against the wall here. I've spoken with our people at the CDC, the army's bioweapons people, and just about everyone else I could think of. It's hard to believe, but the only thing everyone agrees on is that you're the expert."

"I'm sure you'll find someone," Erin said. "Now if you guys wouldn't mind, I'd like to get home. If someone could just call me a cab to the airport, I'll even buy my own ticket."

Neither Reynolds nor Beamon responded.

"No problem. I'll call my own cab. May I use your phone?"

"What would you say," Reynolds started

slowly, "if I told you — in strictest confidence — that two more wells are showing a similar infestation?"

Erin shrugged. "It wouldn't surprise me. Ghawar is really permeable. Or maybe it was introduced to those wells by contaminated equipment or something else they're putting in the ground."

Reynolds nodded. "Well, then, how about this: Would you be surprised if I told you that the affected wells are in the Alaska National Wildlife Refuge?"

Erin had started to rise from his chair, but now stopped. "What?"

"Was I not clear?"

"You're telling me that the exact same bacteria have shown up thousands of miles from Saudi Arabia?"

"That's my understanding."

"I think your people have made a mistake."

"My thought exactly. If you were to go up there, you could probably straighten the whole thing out in a few days."

"You want me to go to Alaska? What is it you guys don't understand about me being retired? Besides, I never thought you had any business drilling in ANWR anyway. Remember a few years back when someone sprayed 'save the caribou' on your Audi?"

Reynolds' brow furrowed a bit. "It was a brand-new car."

"Well, I pitched in for the paint. So at the risk of sounding rude, I want to be completely clear that I don't really give a shit about your problems."

"You should, Dr. Neal. Because I'm making them *your* problems."

6

"There," Mark Beamon said, pointing weakly through the Cessna's windscreen. "Thank God. You can see lights."

Erin pushed the yoke forward, causing the plane's nose to dip violently. Beamon grabbed the instrument panel, but once again managed not to throw up. He was a hell of a lot tougher than he looked. The combination of the snow beating against the glass, the profound darkness extending out in every direction, and Erin's artfully simulated turbulence would have broken most people.

Erin swung the plane wide and circled, looking down at the well-lit drilling rig centered in a meticulously scraped snow-field. As they continued to lose altitude, he could make out a tangle of trailers, snow cats, and weathered machinery, but no people.

"Where is everybody?"

Beamon started to take a deep breath in preparation for answering but then seemed to conclude that it made him feel even worse. "All the normal personnel were re-assigned when the bacteria was discovered. There are people who think the price of gas could go up as much as twenty percent overnight if this got out — and that's something politicians don't like telling the people who vote for them."

That explained why Beamon had been so pleased when he'd discovered that Erin was a pilot — one less chance of a leak. Of course, it was a decision that Erin was taking great pleasure in making him regret.

He eased back on the throttle and the plane started to dive — too fast and angled improperly into the wind, of course. It was a shame the flight wasn't longer. Another hour or so and he was sure he could have Beamon burning through air-sickness bags like a newborn went through diapers.

On the other hand, he had to admit that he, too, was feeling a little queasy — but not for the same reason. Just being back in Alaska was enough — the strangely unique feel of the cold, the empty scent of the air. This was where he and Jenna had spent some of their happiest times, but now those memories mocked him with the absolute certainty that they'd never be repeated. Even worse, it looked as if he was about to replay his brief and incredibly self-destructive stint with the energy companies. Outstanding.

The plane's skis touched down and he glanced over at Beamon. His eyes were tightly closed, but he wasn't actually praying — at least not out loud. Erin shut down the engine and Beamon immediately threw open the door and dove out.

"You made it!" Steve Andropolous shouted as Erin dropped to the snow and retrieved his duffle from the back. "I wasn't sure you'd come."

He thumbed at Beamon, who was teetering around as though he'd never felt solid ground before, but was still holding down that stubborn lunch. "Didn't have a hell of a lot of choice."

"But did they tell you? It's the same bacteria." He grabbed Erin's arm, dragging him along. "My mind's officially blown, man. I mean seriously, do you have any ideas on this? It's freakin' me out."

"Have you checked their data, Steve? This doesn't make a lot of sense to me."

"No mistakes, dude. You wouldn't believe the shit you can get done when the oil companies and the government are with you instead of against you. We've already done a full genetic profile of both the Saudi and Alaskan bacteria. They're exactly the same."

"So what's the verdict, then?" Beamon said, his breath coming out a thick fog as he caught up to them.

Andropolous shot the man a nervous glance, but didn't answer. It was a trait Erin had found infuriating when they'd worked together — Stevie hated delivering bad news and, if given the choice, would just remain silent.

"Spit it out," Erin said.

"Uh, yeah. This well's offline — basically it's a rerun of one you worked on in Ghawar."

"What about the other wells you tested?" Beamon said. "What did those samples show?"

"You're not going to believe it, man. More than seventy percent of them are showing at least trace infestation."

"Jesus Christ," Beamon said, putting a gloved hand to his face and wiping at the sweat that was already starting to freeze. "Why the hell am I just hearing this now?"

"The satellite's out! There's no way I could contact anyone. And with all this secrecy shit . . ."

Erin threw an arm around Andropolous's

shoulders. "Relax, Steve. What would a bunch of politicians and FBI guys do with that information other than go out and short a bunch of oil stock in their IRAs?"

Beamon ignored the insult. "Look, you've been clear on how you feel about drilling here, and I'm sure you're enjoying the hell out of all this, but for your own good I suggest you start taking the situation a little more seriously."

"Are you threatening me, Mark? Because if so —"

"I'm not fucking threatening you. What I'm saying is that if you just forget about the hundreds of millions of dollars invested here, the incredible political costs of getting drilling in the wilderness approved in the first place, and the billions the energy companies expected to make here, it's still one of the country's biggest oil reserves. And that's a national security issue — something a lot of very powerful people don't have much of a sense of humor about."

"The bacterial loads aren't high enough to bring down production in most of the other wells," Andropolous interjected hopefully, then looked at his boots. "Yet."

"Yet?" Beamon said, working to keep his voice even. "Could you define yet, please?"

Andropolous pushed through the door of a trailer and Erin followed, peeling off his jacket and feeling the warmth soak painfully into his bruised, sunburned, and now half-frozen skin.

The trailer was a typical wreck, just like he remembered from the old days: card tables covered in papers, an old sofa with the stuffing coming out of it, carpet covered with dirty footprints. Andropolous grabbed a damp notebook off the floor and tossed it to him. "This is everything we've got."

The first few pages consisted of maps of the ANWR fields with well positions superimposed and individual bacterial loads noted. Erin fell onto the couch and stared down at the diagrams, trying to make out a pattern.

"Well?" Beamon said.

He didn't answer, instead picking up a pencil and shading the different wells. The higher the bacterial load, the darker the shading. Then he connected them, gradually darkening and lightening the shading to smoothly join all the wells and give him a picture of how the bacteria might be traveling.

"Erin?" Beamon prompted again.

He ripped the page from the notebook and held it out. "Look at the different levels,

Mark. This didn't start in one place and radiate out. And it wasn't already there or you'd have more random variation in the loads."

"So?"

"So in my opinion, you had a number of wells contaminated all around the same time, and now it's spreading from those individual wells."

"What are you saying?"

"If I had to guess — and it's only a guess — I'd say that some of the drilling chemicals were contaminated, and when they got pumped down the holes, the bacteria took hold and started to spread. I'd look at suppliers the Alaska drilling companies have in common with the Saudis."

"Okay, let's say you're right. What can you do about it?"

Erin thought about it for a moment. "Nothing."

"That's not going to go over real big, Erin. You're going to have to do better."

"What the fuck do you want me to use on this stuff, Mark? Harsh language? I just spent an entire week in Saudi Arabia and got exactly nowhere."

Beamon's face, which had lost the green pallor it had taken on in the plane, now looked pale. "So you're saying more wells are going to go down?"

"Yeah."

"How many?"

"Eventually, all of them, I guess."

"All of them. That's just great. How long?"

Erin shrugged and looked over to Andropolous, who was trying to disappear into a corner. "Did you look at the spread rate?"

"We don't have any history, Erin. And we don't really know much about this reservoir. So, it's impos—"

"For God's sake, Steve!" Beamon said. "I'm not here to shoot messengers. Just give me your best guess! A year? Two?"

Andropolous chewed his lip for a moment. "Oh, no, definitely not years. At this point, we're talking about months."

The two other men were sound asleep — Beamon on the couch and Andropolous sitting in a chair with his chin tucked into his chest. Erin was on the floor, squinting blankly at the loose papers surrounding him. Another one of his many failings was his uncanny ability to obsess. Any problem that he couldn't solve, no matter how complicated, or even how trivial, could consume him. He'd once lost three days of sleep over why the door on his truck wouldn't close properly.

But this wasn't a truck door. How had the bacteria traveled between Saudi Arabia and Alaska? His initial idea that it had been carried by drilling chemicals didn't bear hard scrutiny. But every other idea he had was even worse. At this point, he was down to imaginary host animals that liked to swim across oceans specifically to crawl down drill holes.

Jet lag was catching up with him and it was obvious that he wasn't going to figure it out tonight, but he also knew that his mind wasn't going to let go easily. He needed something to shut his brain off, something mind-numbingly dull. He glanced around him, and finally settled on Andropolous's genetic profile of the bacteria.

In the dim light from a distant desk lamp, he leafed disinterestedly through the initial pages, but then stopped and flipped back to the beginning of the report. Even to his sleep-deprived brain, something here was familiar. The DNA structure of the bacteria had similarities to concepts he'd played around with years ago — before Jenna had finally convinced him to abandon his genetic engineering ambitions because the world wasn't ready for a Frankenstein bioremediation bacteria. Now it looked as if nature had beat him to it.

He flipped forward and again stopped short, blinking hard as he tried to focus on a description of a specific and unusual adaptation displayed by the bacteria. This one wasn't just recognizable, it was an exact duplicate of an alteration he'd hypothesized could be achieved by inserting genetic material from a bacteria common in the Amazon Basin into a hydrocarbon-consuming bacteria he'd found in Nigeria.

Erin dropped the report and looked up to see if the sound had woken the other two. Beamon rolled onto his back and began snoring. Andropolous just looked dead.

He rose silently, finding it hard to balance himself as his tired mind grasped for an explanation of the contents of that report. He went out into the cold night, gently pushing the door closed behind him, and began walking across the brightly lit carpet of snow beneath the rig.

He continued past the equipment and through a break in the snow bank that surrounded the area, finally finding himself back out in the silent tundra. There had to be an explanation. If he'd found that adaptation potentially useful, maybe nature had too? Yeah, right. Nature had adapted an African bacteria to survive in Alaska and then combined it with one that wasn't found anywhere near either place.

He was staring at his feet as he moved forward, the cold penetrating his sweater. When he finally stopped and looked up, the plane was only about twenty yards away. He headed toward it and climbed in, taking one last look at the rig before starting the engine and opening the throttle.

7

It was only the middle of September, but the wind was already carrying the season's first snowflakes. Jenna turned her face upward and closed her eyes; she felt the cold sting against her skin and tried to push away thoughts of that storm in Alaska. Most of the time it seemed as if it had all happened to someone else, and then something would trigger the memories and they would consume her. She wondered if that would ever change.

Her modest house sat on an exposed knoll about an hour from Bozeman, Montana, surrounded by nothing — no neighbors, no paved roads, no far-off glow of town at night, not even a distant glimpse of the dense forests that covered so much of the state. She increasingly found emptiness and bad weather comforting. Maybe it was just her penance. When the sun shone and she found herself seized by an unexpected moment of real happiness, it would inevitably bring back the image of Erin's expression when she'd told him she didn't love him anymore. More well-deserved punishment, she supposed.

Jenna grabbed the grocery bags from the back of her Subaru and began teetering up the driveway, using considerable athleticism to unlock the door and push through it with her back. Frozen pizza in front of the television again tonight. Or maybe Kraft Macaroni & Cheese. In her previous life, she'd liked to set out the good dishes and slave over some elaborate, experimental meal. But now cooking just amplified her loneliness and brought back more of those damn memories.

"Jenna Kalin."

She spun toward the voice, dropping her bags on the slate floor.

"No. It's Baker now, isn't it? I'm sorry, Jenna. I didn't mean to frighten you."

The adrenaline coursing through her made it hard to think coherently, but still she knew it was a lie. Frightening her had been exactly his intention.

Michael Teague was sitting in the living room, partially obscured by the semidarkness provided by the worsening storm outside. He waved her forward and she took a few hesitant steps but stopped again when she saw two more figures backlit by the window that dominated the room. Although she couldn't see their faces, there was no mistaking Udo and Jonas Metzger.

"What . . ." She discovered that her mouth was so dry it was hard to speak. "What are you doing here, Michael?"

"It's been a long time," he said. "Aren't you happy to see me?"

"It's not that . . ." she said, and then fell silent, realizing that she had no idea how to complete the lie.

When the four of them had scuttled their boat and run for opposite corners of the earth, she'd been surprised at the powerful sensation of weight being lifted from her. Despite having spent a great deal of time working together and for a while having similar goals, she'd never been comfortable with Teague. And now, with the benefit of hindsight, she realized that she was a little afraid of him.

"It is good to see you after so many years," Udo said, seeming to want to move toward her, but then deciding that he was close enough. His German accent had become more subtle since they'd last spoken, and he'd abandoned his comb-over for a much hipper buzz cut. His clothes were more

81

expensive and carefully chosen, too, with the effect of transforming the forty-five-year-old biologist into something closer to a forty-five-year-old Cadillac salesman.

In truth, during all the time Udo had worked for her, he'd never been anything but pleasant. And yet, there was something about him — the way his polite smile always lingered a little too long, the way his eyes fixed a little too blankly — that made her think everything she saw was just a carefully crafted façade.

He jabbed his brother gently in the ribs. "Say hello, Jonas."

Unlike his brother, Jonas hadn't changed at all. He was still spectacularly handsome, with smooth, almost feminine skin and dark eyes that always seemed to be looking at something horrible. Jenna knew very little about him and, frankly, preferred it that way. In her estimation, he had been born a true believer — one of those rare people who craved a cause to lose themselves in and to justify following the voices in their heads. If he'd been Muslim, he'd be a member of al Qaeda. If he was African, he'd be leading a genocidal campaign against a neighboring tribe. But he wasn't. He was an environmentalist — a path he'd undoubtedly chosen for no other reason than his brother's involvement.

"You told me we'd never see or speak to each other again," she said. "That it was too dangerous. What's changed?"

"How have you been adapting?" Teague responded, his tone reminding her that he didn't like to be questioned. "You have a lot of time. What do you do with it?"

"I stay busy."

He smiled and pointed behind him at a nine-foot-tall artificial climbing wall bolted to the side of her fireplace. "Going up and down on that like a rat in a cage?"

"Sometimes," she said, though it was just another lie. Climbing had been one of her great passions, but now she couldn't remember the last time she'd so much as touched that wall.

Faking their deaths by sinking that boat had been the only solution to the fact that the FBI was using terrorist paranoia to intensify its scrutiny of environmentalist groups. Teague had been overly vocal in his beliefs about global warming, and there was little question that he and his associates were being watched.

Of course, he had planned their "deaths" with his normal efficiency, and it had gone flawlessly, allowing them to work without the fear of being exposed. But then she'd discovered one small detail that she hadn't considered: pretending to be dead wasn't all that different from actually being dead.

Teague stood and wandered around the living room, looking at things she knew he had no interest in. His hair was still long and thick, with just a little gray to hint that he was nearing fifty. Pale skin suggested that he rarely ventured into the environment he was so concerned about, and his clothes still appeared to be chosen for no other reason than to highlight the enormous personal fortune he'd amassed.

"We're getting reports that a number of rigs have been shut down in the Alaska wilderness," he said, finally.

Her legs suddenly went weak and she reached out to a small table for support. When she regained her balance and pulled her hand away, it left a palm-shaped sweat stain.

"It worked," Udo said as Teague silently appraised her. "Your bacteria, your delivery system. It all worked just like you designed."

Teague nodded, being careful to maintain eye contact. "Ten billion barrels of oil that won't destroy the land it's extracted from, Jenna. Ten billion barrels of oil that won't fill the air with its poisons or kill the animals that make their homes over it."

The emphasis seemed to be on the destruction of oil — not the rest of it. Teague was a power addict in the truest sense. While most people were only interested in the outward trappings of power — what it could get them or how it impressed other people — he could feed on it directly.

"Humanity is leading itself off a cliff," he continued. "We deny global warming despite overwhelming evidence. When storms wipe out our coastlines and our refining capacity is damaged, does the government create environmental policy to stop that kind of disaster from happening again? No, they lift environmental restriction on energy production and move the refineries farther from the ocean. It's insanity. The oil is running out. They can deny it all they want, but it's a finite, nonrenewable resource. One day, we *will* live in an oil-free society. The question is how much destruction do we inflict on the earth before that happens?" Teague paused and once again proved his uncanny ability to read her expression. "You still like to wallow in self-doubt, I see."

"And you still like to make speeches."

There was a brief silence before he laughed and Udo followed suit with a broad grin. Jonas just stared at her as if she were a ripening corpse.

"Fear can protect you, Jenna. Love can make you happy. Even hate has its purpose. But regret? Guilt? Neither of those emotions have ever produced anything useful."

"I did what I did because I thought the benefits outweighed the drawbacks, Michael. But I don't have your iron grip on certainty. I never have."

"So you're arguing that what I just said isn't true?"

She didn't want to be there. She didn't want to be talking about this. She just wanted to sit in her dark, lonely house and eat food from a box for the rest of her life.

"Whether or not it's true isn't really the issue."

"No? What is, then?"

She knew that she was just prolonging his time there, but couldn't help herself. "Whether or not the four people in this room had the right to make this kind of decision for the rest of the world."

"Someone had to."

"I've spent a lot of time trying to define the word 'terrorist,' " she started.

"You believe we're terrorists?" Udo blurted out.

"Don't all terrorists believe what they're doing is right? Aren't they all *certain*?"

"Jesus Christ," Teague said, his voice rising. "This isn't about someone's interpretation of God or some insane conspiracy theory. We acted on a goddamn mountain of scientific evidence that has proven beyond a shadow of a doubt that we're destroying everything we count on to keep us alive. We're trying to *save* people, not harm them! And at what expense? The Alaska wilderness accounts for less than one tenth of one percent of the world's oil production capacity. It's not exactly bombing the World Trade Center, is it? We took on a great responsibility, Jenna. Made great personal sacrifices. But look what we've achieved. We shouldn't be doubting ourselves now. We should be proud."

When she finally met his gaze again, he didn't look proud. He looked intoxicated.

"I'll ask you again, Michael. What do you want?"

He shrugged — a mannerism that seemed incongruous with everything she knew about him. "To see you again. I'd actually hoped to celebrate. Maybe I was being naïve in thinking that you'd be happy something you'd worked so hard to accomplish actually worked."

She didn't respond.

"Then if not to celebrate, to talk about the future."

"Future?" she said. "You made sure we didn't have a future, Michael. We don't even have pasts."

"There's a lot more to do, Jenna. A billion people in China all want SUVs. The world continues to warm, species continue to go extinct, forests continue to be destroyed —"

"And there's not a thing we can do about it," she said.

"Because we're in hiding?"

"No, not just because we're hiding. How can we stop the Chinese from getting cars? I have one. You probably have five. So who are we to say they can't? And even if I wanted to, who would I lobby? The government? The U.S. government doesn't have any power over the Chinese. In the end, it's the people. If everyone demanded environmental consciousness, the politicians and corporations would be falling all over themselves to give it to them. How can I convince billions of people to give up things they think are essential for some vague benefit ten or twenty years down the road?"

Teague's expression darkened visibly at her last statement. It was purposely a nearly verbatim quote from Erin's book. And of all the people in the world Michael Teague hated, Erin Neal was hovering near the top of the list.

"Then the world's on its own, is that it, Jenna? You're washing your hands of it?"

She thought about his question, about the goals she'd once had, about the joy and pride she'd once felt about her work. "I've done my part, Michael. Now it's time for the world to protect itself."

8

"How do you do this, Mark? Seriously . . ."

The ANWR story had broken while Beamon was stranded in Alaska, prompting Jack Reynolds to leave no less than fourteen hysterical and as yet unanswered messages on his cell.

"This is not some diabolical plot on my part," Beamon protested. "This Alaska thing just kind of came up."

"The scary thing is that I actually believe you," Carrie Johnstone said, turning in the passenger seat so that she could look directly at him. "To be completely honest, the first year we were together I thought you were sneaking out of the house looking for trouble, but I couldn't figure out how you were managing to squeeze your stomach through the window."

"Oh, now that's just cold . . ."

"Then around the second year, I decided that it must be some kind of strange subconscious affliction. But you've finally broken me. I now believe with all my heart that if you got a job as a security guard at a 7-Eleven, al Qaeda would break in and take hostages."

The traffic on the Washington Beltway had come to a halt, but he let the car drift slowly forward as an excuse not to look at her. They were less than a mile from the hospital where Carrie worked, and she was already in full psychiatrist mode. Her normally flowing hair was pulled back tight, and a vaguely stern set of glasses had replaced the subversive round ones she wore at home.

"Did you hear that, Emory?" Beamon said, glancing in the rearview mirror at Carrie's nine-year-old daughter. "It took almost a third of your life, but I finally won an argument."

She glanced up from whatever strange electronic device was currently fascinating kids. "Won't last."

"Am I being ganged up on?" Carrie said.

Emory grinned at the opportunity to use her favorite new word. "Don't be so paranoid, Mom."

Carrie rolled her eyes and settled back into her seat. "It's bacteria, Mark. What do they expect you to do? Make a billion microscopic handcuffs and arrest them?"

"You have the right to remain silent," Emory said in a deadpan voice.

Beamon laughed. While the thought of having a stepdaughter was deeply disturbing to him, Emory Johnstone couldn't have been a better choice. The child had a bizarre and advanced sense of humor, and although it worried Carrie more than a little, he loved it. Kid-speak wasn't his thing, and Emory didn't require it.

"Honestly, I think my involvement's going to pretty much fade away in the next few weeks. Like you say, this is a job for a biologist — not a broken-down former FBI agent."

"You're not *that* broken down," she said, giving him a quick peck on the cheek and then jamming herself between the seats to kiss her struggling daughter as he eased the car into the hospital parking lot.

As Beamon watched her disappear through the glass double doors, Emory climbed gracelessly into the front seat.

Who would have thought that after forty-odd years he would finally get a life? And that he would like it?

"Let's blow off work and school today, Mark. Let's do something fun."

He stepped on the accelerator, shaking his head. "I'm still in the doghouse for the last time. Let's give things a few months to settle. Then I've got something big planned."

"Is it cool?"

"Let's just say it involves automatic weapons and leave it at that."

"Somebody talked!" Jack Reynolds shouted, holding up a stack of newspapers as thick as a phone book. For a moment, Beamon thought he was going to throw them across the room, but they proved too heavy and he just dropped them back on his desk.

"Jack, I —"

"Don't talk, Mark. Do yourself a favor and just don't talk. Do you realize that the price of oil is already up more than two dollars a barrel? That's billions of dollars to the world's economy. Billions of dollars! What I want to know is where the hell you were during all this?"

"Can I speak now?"

"Don't push me, Mark. I'm warning you."

"Well, I spent almost two days stranded in the middle of a frozen tundra with only a crazy hippie biologist to talk to. Then, just when his leg was starting to look like chicken, we came up overdue and someone finally rescued us. After that, I went home and got some sleep."

"Went home? You went home?"

Beamon had known the energy secretary for years, and as politicians went he was less sleazy than most. But his habit of repeating himself when he got mad could be really grating.

"Jack, there are thousands of people involved in Alaska's oil production. I had all the nonessential personnel pulled from the affected rigs, I controlled their communications as much as I could legally, and I sent a bunch of our people up there to keep an eye on things. But I can't throw a small city's worth of oil company employees down a dark hole. We talked about this. It was going to get out sooner or later."

"I want to know who leaked this and I want their asses. Do you understand me?"

"That horse has bolted," Beamon said. "There's no point in slamming the gate now."

"I don't give a shit. That was an order."

"I'm not going to follow it, Jack. It's a waste of time."

Reynolds reached for the stack of papers again, thought better of it, and fell into the chair behind his desk. "Fuck. Where are we now?"

"There are nine wells down as of this morning. Apparently, Erin Neal thinks that within a few months we won't be getting any oil worth mentioning out of ANWR."

"And what's he doing to fix that?"

"My understanding is nothing."

"Nothing? Nothing? Why the hell not?"

"Two reasons," Beamon said calmly. "First, because he says it's impossible —"

"Jesus Christ! Isn't he supposed to be some kind of genius? Look, that guy's a closet tree hugger and you know how tree huggers feel about the Alaska wilderness. Is he really trying or is he just pretending to try?"

"I can't answer that question with a hundred percent certainty, Jack, but we've bounced what he's saying off people in the field and they don't disagree."

"You said there were two reasons he isn't fixing it. What's the second?"

Beamon took a deep breath and let it out slowly. "Well . . . he's not actually there."

"Excuse me?"

"If you want to be technical about it, he stole a plane and flew away."

"That's a joke, right? You're joking."

"Not really, no."

"You just let him fly out of there?"

"Well I didn't exac—"

Reynolds was standing again, leaning over his desk, supported by two fists jammed into his blotter. "When did this happen?"

"A couple days ago. That's how —"

"A couple days? A couple *days?*"

"The communications were down and —"

"What are you doing about this, Mark? He hijacked a plane for Christ's sake!"

"Actually, I think the plane has to be in transit when you steal it for it to be hijacking."

"Shut up! Just shut up! What the hell's going on with you, Mark? This was a simple operation and now I've got every newspaper in the country running it on the front page and the one scientist everyone agrees we need has disappeared. Is there anything you *haven't* fucked up?"

Though it was barely nine o'clock in the morning, Beamon gazed longingly at the poorly stocked bar in the corner of the office. What the hell was he doing there? Carrie made good money and he was old enough to take early retirement.

"Come on, Jack. I sacrificed everything for the FBI, and when I left there it was because I was done. I only took the job running energy security because you begged me and because you promised it would be easy. What the hell *is* energy security anyway? I run the place and even I don't know."

"Do you have a point?"

"Yeah. If you don't think I'm getting the job done, you should replace me."

"Oh, right. You're getting married soon, aren't you? So it's Mark Beamon the family man now? I'm not buying it."

"Buy it, Jack."

"So let me get this straight. The legendary Mark Beamon has been outmaneuvered by some greenie because you were what? Distracted by napkin holders?"

Beamon crossed his legs and bounced his foot in the air. He wished he could say yes. But he hadn't evolved quite that much.

"Not exactly."

"Well why don't you tell me what happened *exactly*."

"Don't you find any of this at all strange?" Beamon said. "That at roughly the same time some incredibly destructive bacteria has hit both the largest oil reserves in the world and one of the most controversial?"

"What do you mean?"

"Well, like you said, environmentalists — who tend to be biologists — weren't fans of the drilling in ANWR. And suddenly we're heading toward a total shut-down."

"You're saying someone purposely engineered these bacteria?"

"Why not?"

"Jesus Christ, Mark. You've read the

background. These kinds of bacteria exist all over nature and we've seen similar problems a hundred times in the past."

"Not on anywhere near this scale."

"Erin Neal didn't seem to think it was all that far-fetched, and everyone says he's the go-to guy on this."

Beamon's foot stopped bouncing.

"What?" Reynolds said.

"Is it possible that we have the fox watching the hen house, here? I mean, if anyone in the world has both the ability and motivation to pull something like this, it would be Erin Neal."

Reynolds sat back down again with an exasperated shake of his head. "If you ask an accountant what's wrong with a company, he'll say it's something financial. Ask a marketing guy, he'll tell you it's marketing."

"What's that supposed to mean?"

"You're a criminal investigator, Mark. I send you out to look at a natural phenomenon and what do you see? An elaborate environmentalist conspiracy."

"What I see is an environmentalist with the expertise in biology to develop these bacteria and the expertise in oil drilling to deliver it."

"Have you ever read his book, Mark?"

"No."

Reynolds walked over to his bookshelf and pulled one of the volumes from it. "I have. It's probably the best thing ever written on the environment and the future of energy. There's no denying he's passionate and sometimes misguided, but he's not a nut. More of a realist, really. If it was politically feasible, I'd probably do three-quarters of what he recommends in here."

"If he's the realist you say he is, maybe he realizes what you just said — that none of his ideas are politically feasible. Maybe he decided to take things into his own hands."

"Oh, for God's sake, Mark —"

"Okay, it's probably not him. But it could be somebody. I want to look into it."

"No," Reynolds said forcefully. "No way. If the markets were to get wind that we're investigating this as a terrorist act —"

"I know, I know. But what if it's just me? What if I just do a little background myself with no one else involved?"

"Oh, well, that puts my mind at ease," Reynolds said sarcastically. "You've done such a great job keeping things quiet so far. Listen to me very carefully, Mark. You will not do any digging into this. Am I understood?"

Beamon shrugged.

"That requires an answer. Am I understood?" he repeated.

"Yes. Fine. I won't dig."

Reynolds circled around his desk and sat again, staring down at Beamon for a few seconds before speaking. "How many people know that Erin Neal thinks the whole field is going down?"

"You, me, and Steve Andropolous. That's it."

"We need time, Mark. The Saudis say that their bacteria problem is isolated to one area and that they still have plenty of excess capacity. The president's working out a deal with them to increase production. The full extent of the Alaska problem can't come out until there's ink on that agreement."

9

Jenna Kalin's Subaru scraped bottom for the fifth time as she wound cautiously up the steep dirt track thirty miles north of her house. Teague's directions hadn't mentioned the condition of the road, and she drifted to a stop in front of yet another rock ledge. Her battered car had been over worse, but the more distance she covered, the more difficult it seemed to be to propel it forward. Why the hell had she agreed to this? Everything they had to say to each other had been said at her house. Probably more.

She rolled down her window and let the cool air flow across her as she watched the gentle sway of the trees in her headlights. The sense that her life wasn't her own — that everything was beyond her control — was something she'd been struggling with since all this had begun. And just when she'd started to achieve some hint of balance, Michael Teague appeared. Why? His explanation of a celebration was so obviously ridiculous, it was hard to keep a straight face just thinking about it.

She coaxed her car over the ledge and kept going, finally coming around a corner that revealed an imposing log mansion. She drifted to a stop again, staring disapprovingly at the garish reminder that if you tried hard enough you could cut down an entire forest of trees just to house a couple of rich white people.

Lights burned through the large windows, casting a glow over the circular gravel driveway that Michael Teague was striding across. She found herself wondering if he owned the house — if he'd built it just for this rendezvous, spending a tiny fraction of the personal fortune that he constantly insisted had been completely drained by his quest to "bring his organizational and business acumen to the wallowing environmental movement."

How many times had she heard him utter some version of that phrase — to play the martyr from the soft leather seats of a new sports car or from the grand entry of a custom-built home. When he talked about people — "people have to understand" or "humanity can't survive their own selfishness and shortsightedness" — it was always strangely clear that he wasn't including himself. And honestly, she didn't think it was even a conscious thing. It was as though it had never occurred to him that he was just another person.

Teague waved from the driveway as she sat there asking herself once again what this could possibly accomplish. She wanted to be gone. She wanted to put a backpack on and head out into the wilderness — as far from televisions and newspapers and people as she could get. To sit out what was coming in the lonely silence she'd become accustomed to.

Teague froze when she bounced the car over the edge of the road in a wide U-turn and started back down the way she'd come. By the time she turned the corner, he was running toward a Ford Expedition parked in front of the garage.

The temptation to just stomp on the accelerator and speed down the dark road ahead of him was as powerful as it was pointless and cowardly. The time had come to face Teague and get everything out on the table. She just wanted to be left alone. The part of her life that included him was over.

His headlights reflected in her rearview mirror as she eased onto a relatively flat pullout by the side of the road and stepped out into pine-scented air.

"What the hell are you doing?" he said, throwing his door open and jumping down into the dirt.

"Michael —"

"I thought we agreed that we were going to talk," he said as he approached. "To make sure we're on the same page with everything that's happening."

"I think we both understand what we did and where we stand, Michael."

"I used to think so. But now you seem confused."

He stopped less than a foot away, close enough to make her have to fight the urge to step back, but he wasn't completely focused on her. Part of his mind seemed to be somewhere else.

"Do I? I don't feel confused. In fact, everything seems very clear to me right now."

"Then why —"

This time it was her turn to interrupt. He wasn't going to control this conversation the way he did everything else. "You want to make sure that I'm not going to do anything that might expose you. That I'm not going to get hit by a sudden wave of guilt when gas prices go up a few cents and turn myself in. I'm not ashamed of what we did, Michael. I'm not sure we had the right, but that's not the same thing. So, don't worry. I would never dream of doing anything that would destroy the lifestyle you've become so accustomed to."

She expected a counterattack, but instead he just stood there, looking right through her. Was he having an honest-to-God moment of introspection? Had he actually listened to another human being?

"I just want to disappear," she continued, her voice losing some of its force as Teague shot a glance toward the dark forest at the edge of the road. "All I —"

There was a quiet rustle to her left and a moment later Jonas burst into the circle of illumination created by Teague's headlights. Jenna didn't move, her mind temporally unable to interpret what was happening. In the end, it wasn't the speed at which the German was coming toward her that broke her from her stupor, it was Teague's hand clamping over her wrist.

She jerked back, but he held fast.

"Let go!"

Instead, he used his free hand to reach out for her hair, and it was at that moment she realized that if he succeeded, she'd never leave that place.

Erin had taught her a few of his exhaustively tested self-defense techniques years ago, and she reacted with the most straightforward of them: she brought Teague's hand to her mouth and bit down hard on one of his knuckles.

He jerked away and then lunged for her, missing by a few feet as she took off in an unexpected direction. Her vehicle was turned off, but Teague's was still idling. She had just passed the SUV's front fender when Jonas dove onto the hood, sliding across it with hands outstretched.

His fingers grazed her back as she pivoted around the open door and threw herself into the driver's seat. The SUV's bulk was enough to keep it going forward when she rammed her Subaru's rear quarter panel, but the impact diminished her momentum just enough to allow Jonas time to roll to his feet and get hold of the still-open door.

The force of her acceleration and the swinging of the door forced him to focus entirely on not being pulled beneath the wheels, but it only took him a few seconds to get his feet planted on the running board and grab the steering wheel.

Since it required all of Jenna's strength and concentration to keep the car on the road, she didn't notice the gun until it was coming even with her temple.

Without thinking, she threw herself sideways across the seats, shielding her head with her arms. The sudden release of the steering wheel caused it to spin left and the shot shattered the glove box instead of her skull as the car swerved off the road.

A tree branch hit Jonas in the side, knocking his feet from the running board and leaving him dangling from the steering wheel while his legs dragged the ground.

Jenna pulled herself upright again, grabbing one of the fingers Jonas had wrapped around the wheel and bending it back violently. The satisfying snap that Erin had promised didn't materialize but the German released the wheel and landed hard in the dirt, rolling uncontrollably until he was stopped by the trunk of a tree.

The vehicle still had enough momentum to jump back onto the road, and Jenna twisted around to look behind her as she slammed the door shut. The headlights of her car were still on, but it wasn't moving. She patted her jeans and discovered the keys safely in her pocket.

Another shot rang out, creating a spider web pattern in the rear window before exploding into the back of the passenger seat. She ducked down as far as she could, watching the tree tops to keep herself in the middle of the road and listening to bullets slamming into the Expedition's hatch. Then, silence.

She didn't sit fully upright again until she'd gone around a sharp corner, but when she did there was nothing but darkness behind her.

"You had a gun three inches from her head and you missed!" Teague shouted, the throbbing of his injured hand amplifying his rage and frustration. Blood in the pattern of Jenna Kalin's teeth was beginning to seep through the handkerchief wrapped around his finger.

"My brother was holding onto the side of a moving car," Udo said, using a kitchen knife to pull a sizeable chunk of wood from Jonas's shoulder. "Be reasonable, Michael."

"Be reasonable? Exactly what skills does your brother bring to this organization? I financed it, I planned every detail, provided everything you asked for. I'm the one keeping us from being exposed." He indicated with his bleeding hand around the opulent living room. "I arranged it so Jenna would come here. All he had to do was deal with one unarmed woman."

Jonas showed no interest in defending

himself, or even that he'd heard; instead, he just sat there staring blankly as his brother continued to dig into his shoulder.

"She was to come into the house, Michael. Jonas wasn't prepared to run through a dark forest chasing a car."

"A car that I stopped!"

"This should have been finished years ago," Jonas said, finally. "She should have never left the boat. I told you this."

"Except that Udo couldn't guarantee he would be able to finish this thing without her help. So we had to keep her around, didn't we? And I was stupid enough not to worry about it because it never occurred to me that you couldn't be counted on to take care of —"

"Michael!" Udo said, jerking around and pointing with the bloody knife. "What can be gained from this? We need to find her before she discovers what we've done. You know her best. What will she do? Will she go to the police?"

Teague turned away, starting for the hallway but then pausing at the threshold. In the end, it wasn't a difficult question to answer. "No. Not yet. First, she'll try to find Erin Neal."

10

At two in the morning, the temperature was still above a hundred in the loft of Erin Neal's barn. It had taken almost an hour to find the boxes he wanted amidst the useless junk he'd collected over the years, and now they surrounded him, torn open and empty.

He let the stack of papers fall from his hand and leaned back against the wall, staring at the yellowing notebooks and loose pages piled next to him. He hadn't thought he'd ever have a reason to look at all this old stuff again, but like everything else in his past lives, he'd never found the strength to just throw it away.

There was little question anymore that the bacteria had been engineered and that the design was based on work he'd abandoned years ago. *His* goal, though, had been to create a versatile, durable, and effective creature that could be deployed to clean up oil spills.

Because of the sensitivity of the environmental movement toward genetic engineering, he hadn't talked to many people about his ideas, and the only person who had ever looked at his research was Jenna. Ironically, it was on a trip to her beloved Alaska wilderness that she'd convinced him to give up on the project.

"Jesus Christ, Jenna," he whispered to himself as he slid an as-yet-unopened box toward him. It was essentially her tomb — or at least the best facsimile he'd been able to come up with. Her body had sunk in thousands of feet of dark, freezing cold water, as had most of her possessions. With the exception of the pictures he had hanging in his house, this single box contained everything that was left of her.

He tore open the top and pulled out some clothing she'd forgotten when she left, a few photo albums, and a stack of stale-smelling letters. At the bottom he found what he was looking for — the clippings about her death.

Her ship — actually Michael Teague's ship — had gone down with more than just her. Teague had died, as had Udo and Jonas Metzger.

He'd known Teague pretty well, though he still couldn't think of anything positive to say about him even now that he was dead. His ego had eclipsed everything, creating its own constantly shifting reality with no regard to fact or for the opinions of others. He'd been the ultimate scare monger, never missing an opportunity to absolutely guarantee that exhausting the planet's oil supply would leave the earth a lifeless wasteland. A tortured leap of logic that Erin had gleefully shredded in a number of papers and articles.

The German brothers he didn't know as well. Udo was a biologist of moderate gifts, and Jonas was . . . what? A creepy thug as near as he could tell.

Erin leaned back again, the relative cool of the adobe wall seeping through his sweat-soaked shirt. It had always perplexed him that Teague had suddenly shrunk down the large environmental organization he'd started, and that had provided him so much notoriety, to a core group that consisted only of Jenna and the Metzgers. Now it was crystal clear.

Jenna had dumped him and more or less immediately disappeared with Teague, leading Erin to partially convince himself that she'd developed a romantic attachment to the man. But even in his darkest moments he'd never really been able to believe that. Now it seemed fairly certain that she'd had other things on her mind — namely, developing the bacteria he'd theorized and modifying it to destroy oil reserves in the ground.

After another hour of riffling through boxes, the answers he thought he'd found began to turn into questions. Why had she left him? Was it really because she didn't love him anymore, or was it because she didn't want to involve him in what she was going to do? When she went under for the last time in that cold water, did she —

He shook his head violently. No, this went against everything he thought he knew about Jenna. Sure, he could see ANWR. She could be a little nuts sometimes, and when drilling had been approved there, she'd reacted as though someone had authorized bizarre medical experiments on her dog. Besides, ANWR was nothing more than a government publicity stunt that produced a completely insignificant amount of oil, most of which was sold to the Chinese.

Ghawar, though? That wasn't a little nuts, it was bat-shit insane. You were talking about virtually shutting down Saudi Arabia's already shaky economy and sending economic ripples — tidal waves, actually — throughout the world. One way or another, if Ghawar went down, people were going to die — maybe in a civil war in the Middle East, maybe from the United States falling back on military power to replace the lost oil, maybe from poorer countries being cut off by higher bidders. The bottom line was that this went way beyond a little overly passionate environmentalism.

So he had to ask himself again: could these bacteria have evolved naturally?

And again he had to answer that it was one in a billion. Could someone else have come up with it without having seen his notes? The chances were better, but still only one in a million.

No matter how the facts were twisted and turned, Jenna remained at the center.

He began flipping through a photo album full of pictures of her as a child, stopping at one depicting her sitting in an open field when she was about three. The color was faded, but her eyes were still bright and full of the wonder that hadn't dimmed in adulthood. What would she have thought if she'd lived to see her bacteria succeed?

The sound of an approaching engine wasn't exactly unexpected, and he hastily began refilling the boxes and slapping tape across the tops.

"Dr. Neal!"

With the last box sealed, he descended the ladder and paused in a deep shadow at the entrance to the barn. There were four men in all, one standing by a stereotypically black Suburban, two disappearing into his house, and one coming his way.

Erin held his hands up and stepped out of the shadow. "Peace, guys. I'm sorry about the plane, okay? Just a little joke, you know?"

They didn't handcuff him, which he figured was a good sign, but they weren't gentle when they shoved him into the back of the SUV. He found himself crammed between two sizeable men in dark suits, and the driver stared at him in the rearview mirror as though he thought Erin was going to jump through one of the closed windows.

The man in the passenger seat was silently dialing a cell phone, but instead of putting it to his ear, he held it back over the seat.

Erin took it. "Uh, hello?"

"Quite a stunt," Mark Beamon said. "You'll notice I'm not laughing, though."

"We need to go back to Saudi Arabia," Erin replied.

It obviously wasn't the response Beamon had been expecting. "What?"

"Get us a plane. We need to go to Saudi Arabia right now."

"Why?"

"I'll explain later."

"Getting in there would be kind of complicated. You got us deported, remember?"

"I'll deal with the Saudis. You deal with the plane."

There was a long silence. Finally, "Okay."

The line went dead and Erin dialed a number into the phone from distant memory. The connection failed, but on his third try it rang.

The greeting was in Arabic and it cut out a few times, but it was still intelligible. "Mohammed! It's Erin Neal."

"Erin!" came the lightly accented reply. "It is wonderful to hear your voice. I'm sorry that I could not see you when you were here. And about the problems you had."

"Then you'll be happy to hear I'm coming back." He had to shout to be heard.

"That could be difficult," came the hesitant reply. "The approvals would be —"

"I also need unlimited access to your imaging computers."

"Erin, you know full well that no one gets —"

"I'm not bullshitting here, Mo. I'm going to be there in a few hours. You know me, and I'm telling you that this is important."

116

There was a long silence and then a resigned sigh that was difficult to differentiate from static. "Let me know when you're landing. I'll send a car."

The headlights of the Suburban turning onto the road made the night-vision scope on his rifle useless and Jonas put it down in the dirt next to him. The vehicle's windows were opaque, making it impossible to see whether Erin Neal was inside. His instincts said he was.

Jonas slid forward on his stomach, enjoying the sensation of the jagged rocks beneath him, and focused his binoculars on the vehicle's license plate before it sped out of sight.

He'd parked behind a low ridge a few hundred meters from the entrance to the dirt road leading to Erin Neal's house, and he expected to be there for the foreseeable future. So far, there was no sign of Jenna, but while Michael Teague had many limitations, he was usually right about these kinds of things. Jenna would come. And when she did, she would be dealt with the way she should have been long ago.

He went back to his vehicle and slid into the driver's seat, gunning it over a small rise and pointing it toward Neal's house. There was no telling how long he'd be gone, and Jonas knew this might be his only opportunity to gain a better surveillance position. He dialed Teague's number and listened to it ring in his ear piece as he bounced up the road.

"Did you find her?" Teague said in the way of a greeting.

"No," Jonas answered, concentrating on making his English understandable over the phone. "She hasn't come. But there was a car here. A government car. It's gone now."

"A government car? Did Neal leave with them?"

"It is impossible to be certain yet, but I believe so."

"How long was it at his house?"

"About fifteen minutes."

"There's no reason to drive out there for fifteen minutes other than to pick him up," Teague said, more to himself than to Jonas. "He's gone with them."

"Yes," Jonas agreed. "This has just started and already Neal is working for them. He knows a great deal."

"Do you have a point, Jonas?"

"I can take care of him when Jenna comes."

"That wouldn't be suspicious, would it? A scientist investigating a bacterial infestation that people still believe is natural turns up murdered. How does that help our cause exactly?"

Jonas didn't answer. Teague was right when he said that he was the one who had made this possible. But as far as Jonas could see, it was simply because he easily could. He'd sacrificed little and was, in his soul, a weak man enslaved by his own cravings — for superiority, for power. Jonas would not stand by and allow those failings to jeopardize what they were so close to accomplishing.

"He is dangerous, Michael."

"Don't think, Jonas. Do you hear me? Just take care of Jenna like you should have in Montana."

11

"It's good to see you, Mo," Erin said, shaking hands with the balding Arab over a set of concrete barricades intended to separate suicide bombers from the towering glass building behind. He was tall — probably six foot six — and the stoop he used to compensate seemed more pronounced than Erin remembered.

"Mark, this is Dr. Mohammad Asli. He is Saudi Aramco's chief geologist."

Beamon climbed out of the limousine and thrust out a hand, which Asli took with reluctance. "Your reputation precedes you, Mr. Beamon."

Asli didn't elaborate, but Erin noticed that he seemed to hold the government agent's hand a little too long — a brief battle of wills that Beamon obviously didn't want to fight.

"Please come with me inside where it's cool."

Erin had taken a sleeping pill on the flight over to shut off his head and, amazingly, it had worked. He'd slept almost the entire way and now was able to put together a few coherent thoughts as they crossed the lobby to an elevator. Interestingly, Beamon hadn't tried to wake him or press him with questions. For now, at least, he appeared satisfied to sit back and watch.

It was a little unnerving, really. Although he didn't look all that bright, Erin was starting to think his demeanor was calculated — that the man understood more than he let on.

Asli inserted his ID card into a slot and they began dropping beneath the Aramco building to the chambers that held a computer system that Erin had never actually laid eyes on, but supposedly it rivaled the one used by America's National Security Agency.

"Now that you're here, perhaps it's time you tell me what is so important?" Asli said.

"How many more rigs have gone down since I left, Mo?"

"What makes you think we've had more problems? It was an isolated incident and we've closed the affected area." His tone suggested that he was reading from an unseen cue card.

"I imagine it wasn't easy for you to get me in here after your government was so anxious to get me out. Why would they change their minds?"

"Because, like me, they were intrigued," Asli said, leaning against the back of the elevator and focusing on Beamon. "You and I have a relationship based on trust, Erin. Is that not right? But — and I don't mean to offend — Mr. Beamon here is a well-known former FBI official with undeniable connections to the Central Intelligence Agency and rumored connections to Eastern European organized crime."

"No way," Erin said, genuinely surprised.

Beamon just smiled and pulled a pack of cigarettes from his pocket. He took one for himself and held the pack out. Erin shook his head, but Asli accepted and let Beamon light it for him.

"And now," the Arab continued, letting the smoke billow from his mouth as he spoke, "he's the head of a Homeland Security division that we know very little about beyond the fact that it is concerned with securing America's energy supply. At any cost, I assume. Would you care to comment, Mr. Beamon?"

The elevator stopped and the doors opened, but Asli didn't move.

"A lot of the stories about me have been exaggerated," Beamon said. "And the reason you don't know anything about the organization I work for is because it doesn't actually do anything. Not that unusual for Homeland Security, really."

"So I'm to understand that they inserted a man with your background and reputation to head an organization that, as you say, does nothing?"

"It's the God's honest truth, Mohammed. I'm getting married and inheriting a kid pretty soon. I go to the zoo. I play golf."

It was clear from Asli's face that he wasn't buying any of it. "So, you vouch for this man, Erin?"

He wasn't sure what to say. Beamon had been a bit of an enigma since they'd met, and now he was starting to sound like a dangerous enigma. "I barely know him, Mo. You make your own decision."

The door began to close again and Asli stuck a hand out at the last moment, reversing it. "Since you left, three more wells have failed."

"And are you seeing any indication of problems at other wells?"

He glanced at Beamon again before starting down the empty corridor. "At four more."

Erin let out a long breath and watched Asli punch a code into a pad next to a heavy steel door. The room beyond wasn't as impressive as Erin had imagined — just a few computer terminals and some chairs scattered about.

"Okay, we're going to run a simulation," Erin said, rolling a leather chair up to one of the terminals and inviting Asli to sit. The Arab did, but obviously he wasn't happy about it.

"We're going to assume that the bacteria came in through water injectors, Mo."

"No," Asli said. "Our water is treated to prevent this. In fact, the treatment process is based on your design."

"Humor me."

Beamon wandered around behind them looking for an ashtray. "What's a water injector?"

"Don't you know anything about oil drilling, Mark?"

"Not really. Why would I?"

"Because you run . . . oh, never mind. Think of a reservoir as just a big cave full of oil that's under pressure. You drill a hole and the oil shoots out, right? But after you take a bunch out, the reservoir loses pressure and that means you have to pump in a corresponding amount of water to keep the

124

pressure up. It's about a thousand times more complicated than that, but you get the point." He turned to Asli. "Do you have water-injection history on the problem area, Mo?"

"Of course."

"Okay. Then here are the assumptions. Let's say it got into the water supply through all the treatment facilities in the span of a week."

"That's simply not possible," Asli protested. "The water for the different treatment plants doesn't even come from the same places. Some is aquifer water, some is seawater —"

"You're humoring me, remember?"

He shrugged.

"With how much bacteria?" Asli asked.

It was a good question. Probably no more than a person could reasonably carry. "Call it three liters per injector."

"Okay. When?"

"Let's start with three years ago and see where that gets us."

"How fast does it spread?"

Erin pulled the keyboard toward him and typed in the numbers that Andropolous had come up with.

A detailed map of the reserve appeared on the screen and they watched a purple stain begin spreading out from the water injectors.

After about twenty seconds, Asli paused the simulation. "It doesn't work. The wells are going down in the wrong order. In fact, three years ago, there *was* no injection program in the area of one of those wells, so your scenario is impossible."

Erin jammed his hands into the pockets of his shorts. The problem was that Asli and everyone else was assuming this was a natural event and not someone purposely pumping bacteria into the system. Now the question became how far in that direction did he want to lead them, in light of the fact that it was his genetic design.

"Erin?" Asli prompted.

"I'm thinking."

He turned and paced back and forth across the room, feeling a chill that he told himself was caused by the air conditioning.

This wasn't Alaska. It was Ghawar — the largest oil field in the world. He glanced up at the ceiling, but wasn't sure what he was looking for. Ghosts? A whisper from Jenna about what the hell was going on?

The bottom line was that he could have ignored what was happening in Alaska, but he couldn't ignore this. If he was right, this could affect the entire world. And worse, it might just be the beginning.

He finally walked back and leaned over Asli's shoulder. "Okay, we know which wells have gone down and when, the permeability of the reserve, and the spread rate of the bacteria. We're going to assume that about three liters of bacteria came in through the water injectors over the span of a week. With that information, can you solve for the date it was introduced?"

Asli caressed the computer's space bar for a few seconds. "Yes, it can be done, but it's beyond the software's built-in capabilities. It's going to take some specific programming."

Erin patted him on the back. "Do it."

"I actually used two variables," Asli said, jerking Erin awake and nearly causing him to fall off the chairs he'd fashioned into a makeshift bed. "The date and the amount of bacteria introduced — which you didn't seem certain about. It made for an incredible number of permutations, which is why it has taken the computer so long to calculate."

"You got an answer?" Erin said, grabbing his cold coffee from the floor and walking up behind the man. Beamon leaned against the back wall, his expression approximating resignation.

"I got a nearly exact match." Asli tapped the screen. "It was actually two liters of bacteria, thirteen months ago."

Erin frowned and watched the simulation on the screen take down the wells in the correct order and timeframe. But thirteen months couldn't be right. That was *after* Jenna and the others had died. "I think you made a mistake, Mo."

"Why?" he heard Beamon say. "That date and amount seems as good as any to me."

"It's hard to explain in simple terms," Erin fumbled. "It, uh, doesn't seem like it could spread that fast."

He could feel Beamon's eyes drilling into his back, but tried to ignore it. "Could it have been earlier, Mo? Maybe there was less bacteria to start."

Asli shook his head. "Maybe a month earlier. Two at the most. But one of those injection wells is only fifteen months old, so that brackets it."

A hot sweat broke across Erin's forehead.

"Are you alright?" Asli asked.

"Could you excuse me for a second?"

He concentrated on walking as naturally as he could past Beamon and through a door that led to a tiny bathroom. Locking the door behind him, he slowly slid down onto the floor.

No bodies were ever found.

There was the distress call saying they were taking on water, but the seas had been calm. An hour later, a plane had flown overhead, but there was no sign of Teague's ship. No debris, no people in the water, no oil slick. Nothing.

Erin pulled his knees close to his chest and wrapped his arms around them. As self-described radical environmentalists, Teague and his people would have been on a list somewhere in the government — not exactly an ideal situation for creating a bacteria to destroy oil reserves. Now that he actually gave it some thought, it made complete sense.

"Oh, my God," he said quietly, burying his head in his knees. Jenna hadn't drowned. None of them had.

The banging on the door broke him from his trance and he jumped to his feet, taking deep, controlled breaths.

"Erin?" came the muffled voice. "Are you okay?"

He pulled the door open and yanked Beamon inside, slamming it behind them and then just staring stupidly at him.

To his credit, Beamon didn't press, instead filling the silence by lighting another cigarette. "So how bad is it, Erin?"

"Bad. Mark —"

"Yes?"

"I . . . I think it's time for us to go talk to the president."

Beamon took a long drag on his cigarette and blew the smoke at the ceiling. "We're already on his schedule. Ten tomorrow morning."

12

"Excuse me. Sir?"

Jenna Kalin watched through her open window as the gas station attendant approached a man pulling what seemed to be an endless series of gas cans from the back of his pickup.

"You can't fill those," the attendant said, pointing to a large handwritten sign saying just that. "Tanks only. There are a lot of people waiting and we don't have another supply truck coming in for a few days."

"Who's going to stop me?" the man responded without looking up from what he was doing. His confidence was undoubtedly the product of outweighing the attendant by a good hundred pounds, most of which appeared to be fat.

Jenna refused to look in her rearview mirror as the sound of car doors opening became audible. Just one minivan was gassing up in front of her, then she could fill her tank and get the hell out of there. Living with what she'd done was hard enough without being trapped right in the middle of the consequences.

"You too stupid to read?" someone shouted. "No fucking gas cans!"

More car doors opened, and she rolled up her window in a futile effort to block everything out.

All the economists had said the same thing: ANWR just didn't produce enough fuel to affect the U.S. economy. There would be an initial panic and the ensuing run on gas stations would create a temporary shortage that would last no more than a few days. But it wasn't getting better, it was getting worse.

When the minivan in front of her pulled away, she idled forward and jumped out to unscrew the gas cap on Teague's now-battered Expedition, trying to ignore the two men shouting at each other behind the pump. The attendant had retreated in favor of the more appropriately sized owner of a Bronco four cars back in line. The rhythm of the horns around her suggested that the people were out for blood.

Jenna had barely pushed the nozzle into her tank when one of the gas cans in question skittered across the ground and slid beneath her rear wheels. When the two men started shoving each other and the horns increased in intensity, she almost jumped back into her car and took off. But she'd been in line for over an hour and needed to go farther than two gallons could get her. Really, she needed to go farther than a thousand gallons would get her.

When a distant siren became audible, she yanked the nozzle out and sped away, running over the gas can as she accelerated toward the exit.

Instead of turning back toward the highway, she went in the opposite direction and followed the winding street until the traffic disappeared. Her breath was coming in short, uncontrolled gasps as she pulled onto the shoulder.

The phone resting on a stack of newspapers in the seat next to her began ringing for the twentieth time that day, but she refused to look at it, instead concentrating on slowing her breathing. There was little question about who was calling.

By the time the phone fell silent, she'd managed to quell her rising panic.

"What now?" she said to the empty car.

Her life alone on that windy knoll in Montana hadn't been much, but it had been something. Now all she had was a damaged

SUV rented to someone else, the clothes on her back, a credit card that Michael Teague could probably track, and a few investment accounts that he probably had access to.

The phone started ringing again and this time she picked up.

"Jenna, we have to talk."

"You tried to kill me, Michael."

"It's not true. You're being hysterical. I wanted to control you, Jenna. Not hurt you."

"Control me?" she said quietly. "Jonas —"

"You did what you did, Jenna. We both know it was necessary and turning yourself and us in won't change anything. I wanted to keep an eye on you until all this dies down. In a month, no one will even remember ANWR or a few insignificant delays at the gas station. You know that."

What she knew was that she'd been a complete idiot. To Teague, everything was a selfish act — even friendship. He surrounded himself with people who admired him, or could help him, or entertained him. But he valued you only to the degree that you did one or more of those things. How could she let herself become so blinded that she would get involved with someone like him?

"Let's meet," he said. "We'll just talk. You

pick the place — anywhere you're comfortable."

"I don't think we have anything to talk about."

"How about your life, Jenna? You mentioned terrorism, and in a way you're right. That's exactly the way the government would view this. Do you know what they do to terrorists now? Where they'll put you?"

"Don't try to handle me, Michael. You know as well as I do that you don't give a crap about me. You're just worried about yourself."

"That's nonsense, Jenna. I have unlimited funds and the ability to live as well as I want far from the eyes of the U.S. government. Do I want to spend the rest of my life looking over my shoulder? No. But it will be a hell of a lot better than what you're thinking about dooming yourself to."

"Fuck you."

She shut off the phone and leaned her head against the steering wheel, turning it to look at Erin's photo on the front page of the *Washington Post*. She wasn't sure where it was taken, but he looked vaguely pissed off — as though he was judging her. Again.

He'd been so angry when she joined Teague's organization. He'd seen Teague as an arrogant radical who embodied everything that was wrong with the environmental movement. She still wasn't sure why she'd originally signed on with Teague. Fear, maybe. She'd never experienced feelings like those she had for Erin, and maybe the loss of control scared her. Maybe joining forces with Teague was a last pathetic attempt to hold onto the independence she was so happily allowing to slip away.

Not long after, Erin's book was published to a great deal of fanfare and even more controversy, but it was typically brilliant. It drained the idealism out of the environmental lobby and exposed the sloppy research, hypocrisy, and lack of credibility that he saw as plaguing the movement.

Predictably, everything in the book was exactly right — exhaustively and methodically proven beyond a shadow of a doubt. But, in the end, it was like someone trying to convince you that there was no God. Even if they were right, was ripping the passion and mysticism from the world really a step in the right direction?

Of course, Teague's feelings on the subject had been much stronger. He'd seen Erin's book as an attack on him personally, and he was probably right. His reaction was predictable and incredibly stupid — he set out to destroy Erin.

It soon became apparent to everyone but Teague that he was intellectually outclassed and that his attacks were just further publicizing Erin's theories. And as *Energy and Nature* rose up the bestseller list, Teague settled into what would have undoubtedly turned into a long, bloody, and ultimately pointless battle.

That is, until Jenna shifted the balance of power.

By the time Erin's book had been fully digested by a reluctant scientific community, she'd already agreed to help Teague with his ANWR plan. The escalating feud between the two men was the opportunity she'd needed to leave Erin, a break that had to be made if she was to go down the path she'd chosen.

And so she'd sided with Teague, attacking both Erin's book and his beliefs, trying to set fire to that famous temper of his. It had been the most painful thing she'd ever done, but she knew that if she could turn Erin's love to hate, it would be so much easier for him when he learned of her "death."

Of course, it had all gone horribly wrong. Instead of lashing back, Erin just stood there, unable to fully understand what was happening. She could still remember driving away for the last time, her belongings jammed into the back of her car, while he ran after her, trying to get her to tell him why she was doing it. She'd cried almost nonstop for two days. A lifetime's worth it seemed, because she hadn't been able to shed so much as a tear since.

But it turned out that wasn't enough. Now she was back from the dead to wreak even more havoc on a man who had been nothing but good to her. Just how would she do it this time? She could turn herself in and have him learn that she was alive from a television image of her shuffling along in chains. Or maybe she could just run for cover and leave him to his own devices. There was little doubt that Teague read the papers and would be extremely concerned with Erin's involvement in the government's investigation. Would he send Jonas? Would he figure out a way to heap any suspicion that might arise onto Erin's shoulders?

Would she ultimately be responsible for destroying the life of the only man she'd ever loved, not once, but twice?

13

It could have been worse, Erin Neal told himself. At least he wasn't standing in the middle of the Oval Office.

Neither he nor Beamon had been invited to sit, so they just stood near the wall, watching the seats around the conference table fill with men in suits and military uniforms. Erin shifted nervously from foot to foot as the men leaned into one another, talking in low tones, occasionally glancing in his direction.

He'd never been to the White House, and at that moment he couldn't think of anywhere he'd rather be less. On the long, sleepless flight back from Saudi Arabia, he'd tried to absorb himself with work, but had spent most of the time thinking about Jenna.

Jack Reynolds entered and was the first to make eye contact. He strode across the dense carpet and gripped Erin's sweaty palm. His smile was polite, but the intensity of his stare and the tone of his voice belied it. "Whatever you have, it better be good."

He started to pull away, but Erin clamped down harder on his hand. "Thanks, that helped a lot." And then he mentally added *"Prick."*

As the energy secretary retreated to his seat, Beamon leaned into Erin's ear. "Relax. They're just people and half of them are dumber than a box of hammers."

Erin snorted quietly, but then fell silent when President Dunn walked in and took a seat. He was shorter than he looked on television, but it didn't matter. He was still the President of the United States. The Leader of the Free World. The Guy With His Hand on the Button. The —

"Okay," the president said. "I don't have much time. Can we get started?"

"Yes, sir." Jack Reynolds indicated behind him. "This is Erin Neal. He's been working on the bacterial infestation problems at ANWR and just got back from Saudi Arabia, where, as you're aware, they've found a similar problem. Dr. Neal?"

He didn't move, forcing Beamon to give him a not-so-gentle nudge.

"Uh, yes. Thank you," he said, approaching the end of the table where he'd set up the laptop Mohammed Asli had given him.

"In fact, the infestation in Saudi Arabia isn't similar to the one in Alaska. It's exactly the same. The same bacteria."

"You're certain," Reynolds said.

"Yes."

"That seems like a long distance for it to travel. How did it get into those reservoirs?"

Erin took a deep breath. "Differently than in Alaska. In ANWR I suspect that it was introduced to the wells individually through the chemicals pumped into the ground during production. In the case of Ghawar, it appears to have gotten in through the water injection system about a year and a half ago."

"My understanding," Reynolds said, "is that the water is specifically treated to prevent this kind of contamination."

"That's right," Erin said, grateful for Reynolds's prompting, even though it was almost certainly self-serving. "And the treatment is pretty effective. But it assumes a naturally occurring bacteria and not one that was introduced on purpose."

Dead silence. It lasted for a good ten seconds before the president spoke. "You're saying this is a terrorist act?"

The image of Jenna in full Arab garb, complete with a belt made of dynamite, flashed across his mind. "I'm saying . . . I'm

141

saying that it was deliberate."

"Now hold on," Reynolds said, suddenly finding himself in the uncomfortable position of not knowing the answers to the questions he was asking. "Just a few days ago, you told me in no uncertain terms that this was a natural phenomenon."

"Yeah, it never occurred to me that someone would do something like this, so I was biased toward a natural explanation. But I know now that I was trying to fit a square peg into a round hole."

"How sure are you?" the president asked.

"Pretty sure. Ninety-nine percent."

Dunn turned toward Jack Reynolds. "And is there any way to corroborate this?"

Reynolds tapped the table nervously. "We can have our people look over the data, but I think everyone agrees that Dr. Neal here is the world expert by a fairly wide margin."

"Jesus Christ, Jack. We first heard about the Saudi problem, what? Over a month ago? And we're just finding out about this now?"

"Sir, I —"

The president held up his hand and turned back toward Erin. "What kind of damage are we talking about?"

"I've made some assumptions and created a simulation," Erin said, pulling a stack of folded 3-D glasses from his back pocket and sliding them to the center of the table. "Put these on please."

He tapped a few commands into the laptop and a three-dimensional map of the Ghawar reservoir came up on a screen behind him. The lights dimmed automatically and that, combined with the cardboard glasses now perched on the faces of his audience, created a scene eerily reminiscent of *Dr. Strangelove.*

"The purple stain you see spreading through the reservoir represents the bacteria. You'll notice that the date counter at the top started about thirteen months ago, which is when we determined the bacteria was introduced."

He paused the simulation on the current date. "So here we are now. You can see the wells that have gone down and get an idea of which are next." A tap on the ENTER button started the stain moving again until it covered the entire field.

They all just sat there staring until a pale man with slicked-back hair finally broke the silence. "Are you telling us that the rest of the Ghawar field will go down within the next four months?"

"Four months-ish," Erin said. "I don't know if it will be completely down by then, but I'm absolutely certain that there won't be a significant amount of oil being produced there."

"And just how much oil *is* produced at Ghawar?"

"It's by far the largest field ever discovered. It accounts for about six percent of the world's supply and ninety percent of Saudi Arabia's production."

"Let me get this straight," the president interjected. "You're telling us that in a few months, we're going to have a six percent drop in oil availability?"

"Worldwide, yes. But keep in mind that Ghawar actually accounts for more like thirteen percent of U.S. imports."

Another long silence.

"If this is true," the president started, "can we get the Saudis to ramp up production at their other fields to cover the shortfall? They've already agreed to make up for the reduction in Alaska."

Erin wasn't sure that the question was aimed at him, but no one else seemed particularly anxious to answer. "Unfortunately, Ghawar accounts for most of their useful excess production capacity. So, in a word, no."

"Then it's your opinion that we're going to see a sudden thirteen percent drop in our oil imports," the president said, clearly having a hard time getting his mind fully around the ramifications of what he was saying. "And that there's nothing we can do about it?"

Erin didn't answer.

"Dr. Neal?" Reynolds prompted when the silence became uncomfortable.

"That may be . . . well, it may be optimistic," Erin said. "As I said, this appears to have been done quite a while ago. Now, if *I'd* gone through all this trouble — to create a highly sophisticated bacteria and to get it into reservoirs, I wouldn't have only hit Alaska and Ghawar. I'd . . . well, I'd have hit them all."

He punched a few commands into the laptop and a color-coded list replaced the map on-screen.

"Because there are thousands of oil-producing fields in the world, most people think we're pretty diversified. But actually, twenty percent of the world's oil comes from just four giant fields. Another thirty percent comes from a hundred more fields, and the last fifty percent comes from about four thousand small fields. The list you're looking at shows fields in the logical order someone would target them based on size and how easy it would be. So, as you can see, you'd start with Ghawar in Saudi Arabia, then move on to Burgan in Kuwait, then Kirkuk in Iraq, and so on. Keep in mind that all the water-injection systems that I'm aware of are unprotected — meaning the security on them is limited. No one really anticipated this threat."

"How much oil is represented by that list?" Reynolds asked.

"About a third of the world's production and reserves."

Everyone began talking at once. The general tone hovered between skepticism and outrage, all aimed directly at Erin.

The president raised his hand again and everyone fell silent. "Who stands to gain from this?"

"What?"

"I notice Iran isn't on your list. Why not?"

Erin was suddenly aware that what he said here had the potential to ripple through the world in ways he'd never considered. If he gave the wrong answer, could he wake up to news of the bombing of Tehran and all the innocent people who lived there? "Sir, I'm a biologist. That's not really my area."

"Then make it your goddamn area," the president said. "Why isn't Iran on that list?"

"Because they don't use water injection. They keep their reservoir pressure up with natural gas."

"Then they wouldn't be affected by the problems we're talking about."

"No, but —"

"And would you say that it's likely the shortage you're describing will cause a massive increase in the price of oil, which could potentially make them one of the wealthiest countries in the world?"

"I don't know if I'd jump to that conclusion," Erin said, finally gaining his footing again. "You know who the real beneficiaries of this would be? The Canadians. Not only do they not use a lot of water injection, but they have the second largest reserve in the world — the vast majority of which is in the form of oil-impregnated sand that isn't at risk. These bacteria can't survive out in the elements."

He was met by silent, suspicious expressions and he began to think that in his zeal to save Tehran he'd doomed Toronto.

"Look, I don't think we should be focusing on blaming someone, I think we should be focusing on trying to limit the damage. Whoever's doing this started a while ago, but it wouldn't be quick or easy work. Maybe all the fields on my list haven't been hit yet. Protecting water injectors, once you figure out you need to, isn't going to be all that hard —"

"So your thirty percent number is a worst-case scenario?" Jack Reynolds interrupted.

Erin chewed his lower lip for a moment. In truth, thirteen months was more than enough time to hit all the reserves listed and then some, but it seemed like a good idea to get them thinking about something more productive than revenge. "That's right. Definitely worst-case." He paused, then added, "But if it did happen, I think you can expect all that production to go off-line over the next two years. You should probably try to be ready for that."

"Ready for that?" the president said, his face looking a little red in the glow of the screen. "And how the hell would you suggest we 'get ready for that,' Dr. Neal? We're talking about an entire world economy that revolves around the availability of oil — an economy that amplifies the slightest constriction in supply or increase in price. Your scenario simply isn't acceptable. What can we do to stop it?"

"If you mean in the sense of reversing the effects to date, nothing. Whatever the bacteria have eaten is gone. And we have no capacity to stop the spread — it's too large a problem."

"I don't accept that," the president said.

"There's always a solution."

"You're talking about finding something that kills this bug, delivering millions of gallons of it into these wells, and then figuring out how to get it to spread through the infestation in a way that would completely eradicate it. And again, that wouldn't reverse the effects to date, it would just keep it from getting worse. But I have no idea how you would do that and, in all modesty, if I don't know, no one does. So if I were you, I'd think about securing the water injectors on the remaining wells. But mostly, I'd start preparing the world for a new energy reality."

Silence. This time, it just went on and on.

"Everything I know is on this computer," Erin said finally. "You should probably get in touch with the Society of Petroleum Engineers — I did a lot of this from memory and they can help you fill in the blanks."

The president seemed lost in his own thoughts and no one was eager to disturb him.

"Okay, then. I'll leave you to it," Erin said. "Good luck and give me a call if you have any questions."

He was surprised when no one tried to stop him from leaving. Even Beamon just watched him with that enigmatic expression he always seemed to wear.

Erin made it almost fifty feet down the hallway and nearly to freedom when two men in dark suits pulled up alongside him.

"If you could just come with us, please, Dr. Neal."

14

Ignoring as best he could the unintelligible roar from the conference table, Mark Beamon looked longingly at the door Erin Neal had just disappeared through. When the president stood up and the room went quiet, Beamon began inching toward the exit.

"How could this have happened?" President Dunn demanded, staring directly at the director of Homeland Security — theoretically Beamon's boss, but a man who had always made a Herculean effort to pretend he didn't exist.

"Sir . . ." he began slowly, giving the excuses time to form in his mind. "The fields we're talking about are under either foreign or private control. We have focused — successfully — on attacks targeting refinery capacity and interruptions in transportation. Like Dr. Neal said, no one ever considered a bioterrorist attack."

"No one," the president repeated, the volume of his voice rising. "Why is it we're always fighting the last war? We spend billions on intelligence and every time some semiliterate Arab fanatic comes up with a half-baked plan to blow something up, I have to hear that we never thought of it."

He looked around the table as everyone pressed themselves back into their chairs, trying to move as far from the table as possible without being obvious. Except Jack Reynolds. He leaned forward.

"Mr. President, when ANWR started having problems, I asked Mark Beamon to look into the possibility that it wasn't a natural occurrence."

Beamon's eyes widened as the president looked directly at him. *That backstabbing son of a bitch. He'd given specific orders not to pursue the terrorism angle.*

"Why wasn't I told about this?" the president asked.

"Because it seemed almost laughably farfetched," Reynolds replied smoothly. "We consulted the top people in the world and there wasn't so much as a suggestion that this was a purposeful act. But it seemed to make sense to have Mark do some general legwork. Just in case."

There was a quiet rustle as everyone in

the room turned toward him.

"Well?" the president said.

"Iran seems unlikely to me," Beamon said slowly, trying to give himself time to come up with something coherent to say. "They probably do have access to people with this kind of know-how, but there would be a lot of blowback. It has the potential to collapse the entire Middle East politically."

"What about al Qaeda?"

"I honestly doubt they have anyone who could pull it off. Besides, it seems like an overly complicated solution to a simple problem. Much more likely they'd create something easy like anthrax and then walk it over the border."

"So who?" the president said.

"If I had to put my money somewhere, I'd put it on an environmentalist group. Probably an American one. Notice how ANWR doesn't fit Erin's pattern? It's not that significant in capacity and it doesn't have a water-injection system. I'd be willing to bet those were the first wells hit and then, when it worked, the people involved decided to go after bigger fish. The FBI has a fair amount of data on the most radical groups, but I haven't dug into any of them specifically yet." He looked directly at Reynolds. "Jack was concerned about publicity and didn't want me to do anything that could cause a potential leak and upset the markets."

"I want everyone the FBI thinks might be responsible for this picked up and interrogated," the president said. "And I want it done today."

Beamon stared at the carpet.

"Is there a problem?"

Hell yes, there was a problem. Sure, this had the potential to be an incredible case — something that he would have killed to be involved in when he was younger and less wise. But now he had other things in his life, and he knew himself well enough to recognize how easy it would be to backslide. Before Carrie, his career had taken everything and given virtually nothing in return. Erin was right. This wasn't their problem.

"Sir, I really don't think I'm qualified to lead an investigation like this. I wouldn't know a bacteria from a hole in the ground, and I've been pretty much sitting behind a desk doing nothing for the past few years. There are some people at the FBI I could recom—"

"I think most of us here are familiar with your reputation, Mark. That, and the fact that we don't exactly have a lot of time to bring someone else up to speed leaves you at the top of the list, doesn't it? No one here has even considered the ramifications of something like this, but I don't think I'm exaggerating when I say we could be talking about a massive worldwide depression. I don't mean to be melodramatic, but it seems your country needs you."

"Again," Beamon said quietly.

"Excuse me?"

"I said 'again.' Your country needs you *again*."

"Mark . . ." Reynolds cautioned.

Beamon ignored him. "With all due respect, sir, you don't need an investigator, you need a cruise director. On something like this, I'd spend ninety percent of my time fielding pointless questions and stupid suggestions from politicians with backgrounds in tax law and acting. And because I wouldn't have any time to do my job, I'd probably fail and Congress would set up a commission to crucify me."

Jack Reynolds's head sunk into his hands.

"Am I to understand that you're offering your resignation?" the president said.

Yes, Beamon thought. *Hell, yes.* Things were going so well for him right now. Better than they ever had. He'd have to be a complete moron to screw that up.

So why was he just standing there? Was it

because he believed deep down that he really was the man for the job? Because he understood what was at stake? Or maybe it was just that he missed the feeling of doing something he was good at.

Despite having political instincts sufficient to get him into the White House, the president mistook Beamon's silence for resolve. "Personally, I'm having a hard time believing Dr. Neal's analysis, but if it is true, I don't think anyone would want to do anything to stand in the way of the progress of your investigation. So I'm going to tell everyone involved that all inquiries go through Jack Reynolds's office and that Jack, you have the responsibility of filtering and responding to those inquiries. Does that satisfy, Mr. Beamon?"

Beamon remained silent.

"I'll take that as a yes."

15

Michael Teague stepped out of the van and shielded his eyes against the glare coming off the metal warehouse in front of him. In the distance, he could see ancient oil derricks jutting from the open land. They dated back to the early days of Texas oil exploration and their presence created a historical symmetry that he found eminently satisfying.

With the price of gas approaching five dollars a gallon, the ANWR infestation was the focus of virtually every news program in the country. But they could do little more than speculate stupidly about why gas lines continued to lengthen while trying to top their competitors' increasingly theatrical displays of outrage.

The Arabs had always kept their export numbers confidential, and that constriction on the flow of information had tightened as the region continued to destabilize. According to Saudi Aramco and the others, the output from their reserves was on the upswing as they compensated for the destruction of the Alaska fields. An obvious and desperate lie. Teague had little doubt that the shortages in the United States and around the world were the direct result of his attacks on Ghawar and the other major Middle Eastern fields.

Soon, the problem would grow to a point that it could no longer be kept from the public. When the supergiant fields finally collapsed, the economic impact would be beyond anything that had ever occurred in recorded history. It would be the first necessary step toward the end of human civilization as the world had come to know it.

He glanced at his phone — something he did more and more often these days — but there was no message from Jonas. He was still in the desert waiting for Jenna, perhaps futilely. Erin Neal was still gone, once again showing his true colors by working for the very men whose zeal for giving their constituents more and more unnecessary things had created this situation.

A smile spread slowly across Teague's face at the thought of the desert shack where Neal had spent the last year and a half in hiding. Wallowing in his loneliness and dreaming of his beloved Jenna.

It hadn't been that difficult to ostracize and isolate Erin Neal after the publication of his book, which attempted to destroy everything the environmental movement had achieved. With a little prompting, even his closest friends and colleagues had turned against him. But Teague considered his greatest triumph to be stripping Jenna from him. Not in the way he'd hoped, perhaps — she saw something in the disgraced scientist that Teague couldn't understand — but the end result was the same. Erin Neal was a broken man.

Jonas's idea of killing him was admittedly tempting, and might eventually become necessary, but for now seemed so unsatisfying. He had to survive to see what was coming and fail to stop it. He had to understand that he and people like him were ultimately responsible. And finally, he had to succumb, just like everyone else.

Teague grabbed the supplies he'd purchased from the van and pushed through the door to the utilitarian warehouse, weaving through the microscopes, incubators, and a host of other equipment he didn't really understand.

It was a far cry from the environmental protection organization he'd built with the millions he'd made selling his computer company to Google. At its apex, he'd employed more than fifty full-time operatives — biologists, lobbyists, marketing people, protest organizers — and had occupied three floors of a skyscraper in Seattle. But it had quickly become apparent that being more efficient at doing what had failed so many times before was a dead end. How ironic that, with only two people, he would finally win a war that had been lost by so many.

"Michael!"

Udo's face was twisted into a rare display of emotion as he ran across the room and grabbed Teague's arm.

"Udo, what —"

"Michael, come! There is something you must see."

A jolt of adrenaline caused sweat to break across Teague's back as the German pulled him through the building's crowded interior.

It was true that the bacteria Jenna had developed performed beyond their expectations, but its very design resulted in significant limitations. Udo had spent nearly two years working to correct those limitations — to create something beyond anything Jenna or anyone else had ever imagined.

His work had started well enough and he

was able to make the bacteria more broadly destructive and prolific with little difficulty. Then the delays and excuses had begun. Although insanely committed, Udo simply wasn't as talented as Jenna, who had gone to great lengths to ensure that her creation would never get out of control. Reversing the safeguards she'd built into the bacteria's genetic structure had proved more difficult than anyone expected.

The large Plexiglas tube that they stopped in front of was one of the few pieces of equipment in the lab that Teague was intimately familiar with. More than twenty feet long and a foot in diameter, it was surrounded with sunlamps and connected to various cooling hoses. It expanded at both ends into a bulb the size of a beach ball, each filled halfway with oil.

Udo pointed to the right side of the tube. "There. Look at it, Michael."

Teague took a hesitant step forward and reached out, brushing the cold glass with his fingertips.

He'd seen this experiment fail so many times before. At first, when Udo contaminated the oil on the left side of the tube with bacteria, it would almost immediately die from solar radiation, ambient temperatures, and overabundant oxygen — just as

Jenna had designed it to do. Eventually, the German managed to improve it to the point that it could survive long enough to destroy the oil it was in contact with, but it died the moment it lost its food supply.

Now, though, just inches beyond his fingers, Teague could see the telltale reddish slick on top of the oil — twenty feet from the initial contamination.

"It survived," he said quietly. "It spread."

Udo reached for one of the cooling hoses and then withdrew his hand, leaving a well-defined print in the frost. "It's below freezing in there, with extremely low humidity and UV more powerful than it would ever encounter in nature. And despite all that, it crossed a sterile seven-meter gap."

"Is this it, then? It's ready?"

"I need to perform a few more tests, but I'm hopeful. With luck, we'll be able to start breeding it within a week."

Teague turned and walked unsteadily back out into the hot Texas sun. He had begun to wonder whether this day would ever come — whether Udo would be able to deliver what he had promised.

But now everything had changed. They were standing on the precipice of a completely new world. With a sufficient initial release, this new strain had the ability to spread through the air without the involvement of human hands. While the governments of the world panicked over the reserves that were already infected, a new kind of bacteria would silently infiltrate petroleum in all its forms, no matter where it was hidden. The brief aberration that was industrialized society, made possible by abundant energy, would collapse.

That collapse, though, was inevitable whether he acted or not. No matter how carefully people blinded themselves to the reality that the oil was running out, it was a geological fact that would eventually devastate the world in ways few had even imagined.

At first, people would compensate by stripping the earth of what few resources it had left, abandoning any pretense and environmentalism in a futile attempt to maintain the unsustainable living standard of billions of people. Then, as the dense, readily available energy dwindled, the wars to control what was left would begin. Eventually, though, governments and militaries would disintegrate and chaos would descend as neighbor turned on neighbor in a desperate bid to stay warm and keep their bellies full. Animals worldwide would be hunted to extinction as the forests were burned and the air filled with greenhouse gases. Finally, when everything was destroyed, the light would go out on the miracle of life.

His plan, though almost certain to cause a die-off of at least two-thirds of the world's human population, would ensure a future for his species and the other wondrous forms of life that had spread across the earth. Brutality and chaos would still flare, but it would be mercifully brief. There would be no time for sophisticated war machines to go on genocidal rampages, no time for humanity to burn or irradiate the surface of the earth, no time to cause the global climate to spin out of control and turn his home into just another lifeless rock circling the sun.

He would return the world to a sustainable balance. Plant and animal species would once again thrive, the climate would stabilize, and humans would return to being nothing more than another widely scattered cog in the wheel of life.

16

"That was great, Mark. Just fucking great," Jack Reynolds said as he burst through the door. "Ever think that maybe telling the president of the United States to screw off isn't the smartest thing to do?"

Erin leapt from the chair he'd been sulking in as Beamon slammed the door.

"I'm always the one who gets stepped on in the end, Jack. And maybe I'm stupid and desperate enough to live with that, but I sure as shit don't have to take it with a smile."

"Hey!" Erin shouted. Both men looked at him as though they'd just realized he was there. "Who the hell do you think you are, having your thugs lock me in here? I told you everything I know. You don't have any right to hold me."

"I have the right to do whatever I god-damn well want," Reynolds said.

Erin watched Beamon slide a chair up

next to him, unable to ignore the change in the man. The skin seemed to hang a little looser from his face, creating a tired worldliness that hadn't been there before. Suddenly, it was possible to see the man Mohammed Asli had described.

"What Jack means," Beamon said, "is that you dropped kind of a bomb in there and you're the only person who might know how to defuse it. Constitutional rights get a little gray when the scale gets this large."

There was a hint of anger in Beamon's expression, but it didn't seem to project anywhere — as though he was angry at only himself.

"I already told you that there's nothing I can do," Erin protested.

Reynolds fell into the chair behind his desk. "Let's forget stopping the bacteria for a minute. Let's assume you're right and it's going to run rampant. What happens then?"

"How should I know?"

"Because you wrote a fucking book about it."

"Hold on, now. I wrote a book about oil slowly becoming scarce. Not about the spigot suddenly being turned off on a third of the world's supply."

"Guess."

"I'm not an economist. I —"

"Jesus Christ, Erin! Here's your shot. How many people like you do you think have ever sat in this office? Now's your chance to do what you've always dreamed of — directly affect government policy. If what you're telling me is true, we have to prepare, right? Do you want to be part of that preparation? Or do you want to leave it to the government hacks you people always complain about?"

Erin eased back into his chair. Reynolds was right. He'd spent a lot of time thinking, though not about this particular problem but one very similar. And there was no doubt that the U.S. government had the potential to react with incredibly destructive stupidity. It almost always did.

"It's hard to predict," Erin said finally. "Oil is so cheap and plentiful it's almost impossible to follow the economic chain. I mean, everyone thinks it's great to buy a hybrid car, but no one thinks about how much energy it took to build it. In the end, would it have been more environmentally friendly just to keep your old SUV? The world is full of examples like that."

"You're not helping me," Reynolds said.

"Well, then, why don't you call a goddamn Republican think tank. I'm sure —"

"Erin!" Beamon cut in. "Calm down.

We're all on edge. Go on. Jack's just going to sit there and listen. Right, Jack?"

Reynolds frowned deeply. "A lot of books out there say the loss of oil is going to be a disaster for the world. That everybody's going to freeze or starve —"

"Yeah," Erin said. "The peak oil Chicken Littles. In my mind, oil prices were set to rise slowly and we would change our behavior and find power substitutes as they became economically attractive. This is different. There's no time to build solar panels or nuclear power plants, no time to beef up public transportation — let alone to completely redesign the way our economy works. Take food for example. The average distance food travels from farm to plate in the U.S. is thirteen hundred miles. It might take a hundred calories of energy to produce and deliver one calorie of broccoli."

His mouth was becoming increasingly dry as he thought through the ramifications of what was happening. Of what Jenna had started.

"Our entire economy is based on people spending hours a day in the car — going to the store, to work, whatever. Heat, medicine, and clothing all take huge amounts of energy to produce. And then you have the shipping costs of imports. Did you know that no shoes are made in the U.S. anymore? So if we suddenly can't fuel the ships to get shoes here, everyone goes barefoot. It sounds kind of stupid, but think about what it would take to create a shoe industry that had the capacity to cover the feet of more than a quarter of a billion people."

"You assumed that virtually *all* the oil will run out in the next fifty years," Reynolds said. "We're going to lose it faster, but not as much. Thirty percent, right?"

"Right. But it's impossible to predict exactly how it will affect us because nothing like this has ever happened before. I mean, we're not just talking about some minor supply fluctuations that cause an increase in prices or a few gas lines. We're talking about an actual long-term shortage. The oil just won't be there, no matter how much you're willing to pay. Figure ninety-seven percent of petroleum in the U.S. is used for transportation. If it's just Ghawar, then the market can probably deal with that. Gas prices would go up to six dollars a gallon or so and people would react by driving more efficient cars fewer miles, and forgoing luxury products that have huge transportation costs attached to them. Painful, and probably pretty devastating to the economy in the short term, but not really a disaster."

"But you don't think it's just Ghawar."

"No. And that leaves you in a gray area. You're talking about a complete reorganization of the world economy in an environment that will make it hard to reorganize because creating energy-efficient systems takes energy. Depending on how you calculate the numbers, it might take a hundred gallons of oil to make one solar panel."

"So, at some point between a ten percent reduction and a thirty percent reduction, the government is going to have to institute some kind of rationing," Reynolds said. "Isn't that right? Agriculture, for example."

"Yeah, I suppose. Below ten percent, you'd probably do a little pandering with the strategic reserve and run up the deficit a little more with tax rebates, but in the end the market would take care of things through pricing. Eventually, though, you cross the first line, where oil becomes so valuable to the public good that it has to be centrally controlled to some degree. You don't want ambulances to run out of gas because some rich guy wants to drive his Hummer around."

"So where is that break point?" Reynolds asked. "The point where the government has to take control of the market?"

"I wouldn't worry about that so much.

It's the next line that you should be think-ing about."

"The next line?"

"Where the reduction in energy avail-ability creates a cascade effect. The eco-nomic cascade is obvious: If people can't get to the mall, the people at the mall lose their jobs. Then they don't have the money to go out to dinner, so the restaurant people lose their jobs, and so on. But the energy cascade is way more dangerous. To get energy, you have to input energy. An obvi-ous example is the big diesel engines that drive coal extraction. If you can't get fuel to run the mines, then we lose most of our electricity. If you lose your electricity, what happens to all the industries that count on it? Lights? Heat? Communications? The In-ternet? And if we lose those —"

Reynolds held up his hand. "I get the point. We'd go back two hundred years."

"Yeah, but with a complete loss of survival skills. How many people even cook their own food anymore, let alone grow and butcher it? And our population isn't a hundred thousand, it's three hundred mil-lion — all of whom would start fighting for what few resources were left. Who's going to keep the peace? The army? No way. Even when it's not fighting, the U.S. military still

171

uses more energy than the entire country of Austria."

Reynolds turned and looked out the window behind his desk, following the cars crowding the street below. Washington D.C.'s rush hour had expanded over the years, and now the city seemed to be constantly flooded with the bumper-to-bumper traffic that kept the country — and the world — moving forward.

"Okay," Beamon said. "Maybe you could talk about what we can do to make sure none of that happens."

Erin didn't answer. He just wanted to get the hell out of there. To figure out how Jenna did or didn't fit into this. To find out if she was alive or if this was just another desperate fantasy he'd conjured up.

One thing he was sure of, though, was that she didn't have anything to do with Ghawar. Or was he? What was it people always said about the serial killer who lived next door? "He was a nice, quiet guy — used to lend me his lawn mower." Did anyone really have any idea what another person was capable of?

No. He did know her. She wouldn't have anything to do with this. If his predictions were right, even the best-case scenario was a disaster. The industrialized world would do everything in its power to shore up its supply, leaving countries without economic and military power out in the cold. What would happen to all those people who already lived on the edge? To the people who relied on foreign aid? There was no way she would be involved in something like that. Would she?

"Dr. Neal?" Reynolds prompted.

"I don't know how to kill it. Don't you think I'd tell you if I did?"

Beamon nodded thoughtfully. "Then it seems to me the person to ask about how this stuff can be killed is the person who created it. Right?"

"I don't think they'd have an answer."

"But they might."

"Yeah, I guess."

Erin thought of Michael Teague — an arrogant prick who thought because he had a lot of money he was the world expert on everything. He was almost certainly capable of something like this. But where did that leave Jenna? Dead? Her plan would have ended with ANWR, and then she would be a liability.

He sagged in his seat, suddenly drained of energy. Although he'd never come to terms with Jenna's death, at least she'd been dead. There had been certainty to that. Permanence. Now, it was all chaos again.

"So who did this?" Beamon said.

Erin looked over at him. "What?"

"You heard me."

"How the hell would I know?"

"Who would care about Alaska's wildlife refuge?" Beamon asked.

Erin tried to keep his expression blank, but wondered if the perspiration starting at his hairline was visible. "People like you think all environmentalists are crazy. A few people care enough to speak out about what we're going to leave our kids, and you bug their houses because, of course, the next step is blowing up a logging operation."

"Or creating a bacteria that could destroy a third of the world's oil supply."

"It could have been Arab terrorists — they have access to Ghawar. It could have been some country that hates us. It's not too hard to find one of those."

"Maybe," Beamon said. "But what if it wasn't? Are you going to deny that there are environmental radicals out there who are off their rockers? My understanding is that you've been one of their favorite targets over the years. Come on, Erin. There can't be more than a dozen people who have both the motivation and the expertise to do something like this. Including you."

174

"Me?" He looked over at Reynolds, who seemed satisfied just to sit and watch. "What the fuck are you talking about?"

"It is your area, right? I mean, everybody says you're the go-to guy on the subject."

"I'm also the guy who told you it was engineered."

"Sure, but Steve Andropolous would have figured that out pretty soon anyway, wouldn't he? So it would make sense for you to blow the whistle yourself and deflect suspicion."

"Why would I? Why would I do something like this?"

"I don't know. To save the African mud-sucker snail? Why do you people do anything?"

"We *people* do things because the world is being destroyed for no reason," Erin shouted. He knew that Beamon was baiting him, but as usual, he couldn't just let it go. "Are people happier now that they have a four-mile-to-the-gallon truck to drive on dead smooth pavement? Or are they just trying to keep up with the Joneses? Today a family of three buys a six-thousand-square-foot house with four rooms they don't use, but still have to heat and cool. Tomorrow, their neighbor gets a bigger one, so they have to move to a house with eight rooms they don't use just to stay even. Are they better off?" He pointed through the window at the stopped traffic outside. "Are you happy spending half your life sitting in that?"

Beamon followed his finger and pondered the traffic for a moment. "So it would make perfect sense for you to use that pool of yours to cook up a bacteria that eats oil. You're not trying to hurt anyone. You're trying to help us. To help the earth. I can see the argument."

"Screw you."

Beamon shrugged. "Okay. If you didn't do it, who did?"

"If you think I'm going to start naming names so you can put the thumbscrews to a bunch of innocent people, you're nuts. Create your own witch trial."

"But if this is as bad as you say it could be, shouldn't you be doing what you can to help?"

Erin ignored the question. "Am I under arrest?"

Beamon didn't answer immediately, instead folding his hands over a middle that looked slightly larger than the first time they'd met. "So far, there's only one thing I'm certain about: you know more than you're saying."

Erin just sat there, struggling to keep his stare indignant in the face of an accusation that was completely true. Was he the one in the wrong here? Should he talk? Was he making a looming disaster even worse, all for a woman who was probably dead, and even if she was alive, clearly didn't give a shit about him?

No. What difference would a few days make? If Jenna was out there, he needed to find her and talk to her. To figure out what to do. If Beamon tracked her down first, there was no way he'd believe she'd just been after ANWR. He'd treat her like a terrorist, and everyone had seen the pictures of what happened to terrorists these days.

"You didn't answer my question," Erin said. "Am I under arrest?"

Beamon shook his head disappointedly. "Lucky for you, what I know and what I can prove are two different things."

17

Mark Beamon paused at a fork in the hallway, dialing his cell phone and regretting refusing an escort. Did they say right or left?

Carrie's voice mail picked up and he decided to go with something more involved than the ineffective "call me" message he'd left the last eight times.

"Okay, I know you're mad at me for not showing up to the caterer thing," he said, arbitrarily deciding to turn left. "But I have a good excuse. I was out of the country and then I had to meet with the president. So it's not like I blew you off to go to a ball game or something." He winced. The ball game comment would come off as glib and he was shooting for something more along the lines of groveling. On the slightly brighter side, his instincts had been right and he was now standing in front of the door he'd been trying to find.

"It turns out that this job is going downhill even faster than we thought. I've gotten caught up with some stuff that —"

The door was suddenly jerked open and he found himself face-to-face with a man whose well-tailored suit filled nearly the entire jamb. "Can I help you?"

Beamon made a cutting motion across his throat, and then pointed to the phone, trying to stay on script. "Anyway, I'm kind of caught up in —"

"Sir, I'm going to have to ask you to move on if you don't have business here. This is a secure area."

Beamon jammed his free hand into his jacket and pulled out his ID. The man leaned down to read it, immediately recognizing the name of his new boss and retreating back inside.

"Christ. Where was I? Look, I can't really talk about particulars, but you're going to find out soon enough and then you're going to understand. Anyway, could you please call me?"

He shoved the phone back into his pocket, but didn't reach for the door.

He should just turn around right now and pick up some solar panels on the way home. Maybe plant a garden.

When he finally pushed through the door,

the twenty or so people inside fell silent. He recognized about a third of them — staff from his until recently backwater division. The others had been assigned from other areas of Homeland Security for their expertise, and probably their willingness to spy for their respective agencies and political sponsors. Computers were abundant, but still lined up on the floor waiting for furniture.

"Hello," he said, detecting a slight echo in the cavernous room. "For those of you who don't know me, I'm Mark Beamon. It looks like I'm going to be running this investigation. At least for the time being. Could someone tell me where we stand?"

A woman he'd never met raised her hand hesitantly.

"Yes. You. Go ahead."

"We've collected all the FBI's files on environmental radicals and have people trying to put threat levels between one and ten on each person and organization."

"How many have we gotten through so far?"

"About seventy-five."

"Seventy-five? Jesus. How many are there?"

"Two hundred or so."

"Okay. I want to pick up all the sevens

and above. Physical and electronic surveillance on everyone who rated four through six, and electronic surveillance only on all the others."

"We're already working on the warrants."

"Don't worry about warrants. Just do it," Beamon said, hoping his voice didn't betray his reluctance. He'd never been comfortable with the government's ability to do whatever it wanted as long as it said "terrorism" three times fast. If history taught anything, it was that absolute power corrupted absolutely. He told himself that he had it under control, but isn't that what everyone said?

"Who's looking at equipment dealers?"

Another hand went up. Surprisingly, it was the well-toned appendage of the man who had challenged him at the door. "We've made a list of the items you'd need to create a bacteria like this and we've already got the sales records from all the domestic suppliers of that kind of equipment. We're going through it now."

"And I assume you're cross-referencing it with the threat list?"

"Absolutely."

"If anyone finds they have a manpower issue, let me know right away. I'm told we're going to get whatever we need, but my preference is to keep things as small as possible.

"Do we know who's dealing with securing the oil fields themselves?"

"The state department," someone said. "They're warning other countries and the oil companies about possible attacks on water injectors — though they're being vague about what kind of attack. The White House has been pretty restrictive about what we can say."

"Okay," Beamon said. "Let's get in touch with State and figure out a way to set a trap. Maybe we can catch someone in the act."

"I'll give them a call this afternoon and try to coordinate. Also, we've found a guy who can probably help us figure out any weaknesses in the security. His name's Erin —"

Beamon held up a hand, silencing the man. "No one talks to Erin Neal unless it goes through me, understood?"

"You know him?"

"Unfortunately, yes."

"Unfortunately?" the woman coordinating the research into environmentalist groups said. "Are you saying you think he could be involved? Should we be looking at him?"

It was a good question. At this point Beamon had a slightly queasy feeling about the guy. Not full-on nausea — more like a mild hangover. But it was getting worse by the minute.

"Is he on our list anywhere?" Beamon asked.

She shook her head. "I don't think anyone considers him particularly radical, or even interested anymore."

"Put him on. I want to know everything there is to know about him."

"What about surveillance?"

"Full electronic. And we might as well put someone out there to follow him if he goes anywhere. It shouldn't take much manpower — there's only one way in and out of his property as near as I can tell." He looked around and no one seemed to have anything else to say. "Okay. Any problems, come directly to me. At least for now, I seem to have the power to cut red tape. Any ideas — even stupid ones — I'm always ready to listen."

His phone started ringing and he looked down at the screen. Carrie. "I've got to take this. I'll be in my office . . . does anyone know where it is?"

Everyone pointed toward the back and he started off in that direction, putting the phone to his ear.

"Thanks for returning my call," he said quietly.

"I was kind of irritated, Mark."

Other than a desk, the room he was to inhabit was empty. He pushed the door closed and sat on his blotter. "Are you in a better mood now?"

"I chose all food you hate for the reception. That helped."

"I can see how it would."

"I saw the president's speech today."

Beamon had managed to miss it. "What did he say?"

"That there's evidence terrorists are going to be targeting the world's oil supplies."

Beamon nodded into the phone. The main idea behind the announcement was to get the world thinking in terms of energy insecurity, just in case Erin Neal was right. It seemed kind of pointless as far as he was concerned. Way too little, way too late.

"I take it that's why you're going to be eating lutefisk at your wedding?" Carrie said.

"More or less."

"It's interesting . . ."

"What?"

"That you went to Saudi Arabia and then you went up to Alaska to look at that bacterial contamination. You know, there are naturally occurring bacteria that eat oil. I wonder if there's a connection? If it would be possible to engineer —"

"Stop."

"What?"

"We're on an open line, Carrie. No speculating, okay?"

"What about at dinner tonight?"

He stared at the empty wall to his right and imagined the chaos just beyond it. "I'll do my best, okay?"

18

Erin Neal leaned his chair back against the wall and questioned his sanity for the fifth time that night. The more he thought about the scenario he'd dreamed up, the more far-fetched it seemed — nothing more than an elaborate fantasy that brought Jenna back to life, made her innocent, and heaped the blame on someone he'd always hated. A neat little package without so much as a single loose end. How convenient.

Michael Teague was a hypocritical, arrogant prick who cared only about himself, but even Erin had to admit that he wasn't a *complete* idiot. What could he hope to accomplish by all this?

It seemed nearly impossible that these bacteria had been designed independent of the work Erin had abandoned years ago, and that still pointed to Jenna. But maybe her involvement was less direct? Maybe she'd talked to someone about his theories.

Or maybe she'd written something down and someone had gotten hold of it, then sunk the ship she was on to cover his tracks.

Maybe, maybe, maybe.

He reached for the legal pad on the table in front of him, but then stopped, staring blankly at it by the dim glow of his laptop screen.

The list wasn't even close to being complete, despite the time and money he'd spent creating it. If Jenna really was alive, was her new name and address on it?

She didn't have any family she was close to, so that was a dead end. And he knew she wouldn't be stupid enough to contact old friends. So that left him trying to narrow things down by answering less pointed questions. Would she hide in plain sight or in a remote area? Probably remote — she'd never been one for cities or crowds.

In the U.S. or in a foreign country? That was a harder question, but he was assuming the U.S. because she'd stand out more in a foreign country.

Obviously, she couldn't work as an environmentalist or biologist — it was too small a world — and she'd never mentioned another interest that might lead to a career. Every path that might lead to her became an obvious dead end after even minimal thought. All except one.

He'd never shared Jenna's passion for rock climbing, but he was certain she wouldn't be able to give it up. The problem was that the world of climbing wasn't much bigger than that of biology or environmentalism — making it impossible to go out to the cliffs without running the risk of being recognized. And she couldn't use climbing gyms for the same reason.

So her only choice would be to build a home wall like the one she'd built in her apartment in Salt Lake. And to do that, she'd have to buy handholds — an unusual specialty item manufactured by only a few companies in the world.

He'd purchased the mailing lists of nearly all the businesses selling holds over the Internet and was in the process of creating a prioritized spreadsheet. She was a woman, she would have purchased them all over a short period within the last eighteen months, and she probably wouldn't live in an urban area. Although general, those parameters narrowed things down by almost ninety percent.

Erin ran his finger down the pad in front of him and dialed another number into his phone.

"Hello?"

He sat upright at the sound of the woman's voice, but then sagged back down in his chair when he was forced to admit to himself that it wasn't Jenna.

"Is Sara there?"

"This is Sara."

"Hi. I work for Nicros. I'm just following up to see how you like the climbing holds you purchased from us."

"Well, they were a gift for my boyfriend and he isn't here. But I think he likes them."

"Great," Erin said, already looking for the next phone number on his list. "Remind him that if he has any problems, we're here."

"I will. Thanks."

He started dialing again, but then stopped and walked off his porch into the darkness. He'd called more than a hundred numbers and every time Jenna didn't answer, he felt another piece of his soul being chipped away. How much was left?

He cocked his arm back to throw the phone, but managed to regain control before he doomed himself, once again, to hours of wading through cactuses with a flashlight.

"Self-control? Who would have ever thought?"

He spun toward the voice, losing his footing and falling backward into the dust. She

189

was just a vague, colorless form in the starlight, but it didn't matter. The shape of her, the way she stood, the pace of her speech — it was all indelibly burned into his mind.

Jenna Kalin resisted the urge to run to him, to pull him to his feet, to wrap her arms around him. The dark helped, though not as much as she'd hoped. At least his expression was softened by shadow. After everything that had happened, she didn't think she had enough strength to take the full brunt of his reaction.

She'd been rehearsing this moment for the last five hours — the time it had taken her to hike there through the desert, avoiding roads and open areas where she suspected Jonas was waiting. And despite that silent practice, all she could do was stand there, not breathing.

After so much time, how could her feelings for him not have diminished? If anything, they had become starker against the loneliness she'd created for herself in Montana.

"Are you all right?" she finally managed to say. "You . . ." Her voice trailed when she realized there was nothing she could say. The elaborate apologies and lengthy explanations that had sounded so reasonable alone in the dark suddenly seemed meaningless.

He put his hands behind him, but didn't try to stand. He just scooted back a few feet before seeming to lose all strength. He pulled his knees up and his forehead sank to them. In the dim glow of a single light inside his house, she could see the raggedness of his breathing.

"I'm so sorry, Erin."

His body convulsed in a bitter laugh before he raised his head. His face was briefly illuminated and she looked down at the ground, but not before seeing too much.

"About what, Jenna? Turning your back on me when I needed you? Or do you mean making me think you'd drowned in the middle of a freezing cold ocean? Or using one of my ideas to build a biological weapon?"

She didn't look up. "All three?"

He finally found the strength to stand and walked past her to his house. She considered just walking back out into the desert, and for a moment even thought about going out to the road to let Jonas finish what he'd started. In the end, though, she followed him inside.

He was in the kitchen, sweeping the

contents of a high shelf onto the floor, finally coming up with a grimy six-pack of beer. He twisted the top off one of the bottles and took a long pull before turning around.

She forced herself to look directly at him, a task made easier because he wouldn't do the same. The blood had mostly drained from his face, but otherwise he hadn't changed at all. The same soft eyes, the same barely controlled blonde hair. When she looked deeper, though, she saw a sadness so intricately woven into his expression that someone meeting him for the first time would assume he'd been born that way. She knew better.

"I was the first person the government called," he said.

"I know. There was an article about you in the paper."

When he finally met her gaze his eyes were a little glassy and, for a moment, she thought a tear was going to break loose and run down his cheek. In all their time, she'd never seen him cry. God. What had she done to him?

"I've been looking for you," he said.

"What do you mean?"

"I ran back the time on Ghawar. It happened *after* your boat went down."

"I don't understand. What does Ghawar have to do with anything?"

The intensity of his gaze increased, as though he was searching for something, but it quickly faded into something she'd never seen in him: hopelessness.

"I used to think I could tell when you were lying," he said. "Kind of funny after everything that's happened."

"I never wanted to hurt you, Erin. I know how empty that sounds right now, but you have to understand what I was doing. What I was trying to save. You've seen firsthand what they're doing in Alaska. I know you think Mother Nature is going to wake up one morning and kill us all, and maybe you're right. But what if it's too late? There's no reason to drill in Alaska —"

"And how does Saudi Arabia fit into all that?"

"What are you talking about, Erin? What does Saudi Arabia have to do —"

He let out a frustrated breath and stalked past her, throwing the swinging door to the kitchen open hard enough to crack the wood around its hinges. After a few moments, she followed, finding him in his small living room staring out a window that the darkness had turned into a mirror.

"How could you be so stupid, Jenna. How

could you let Michael Teague manipulate you like this?"

"Don't try to twist this around and make it about Michael. It wasn't."

"You really don't know what you've done, do you?"

"I'm not stupid, Erin. And I don't do things without thinking. This wasn't something I just suddenly —"

He slammed his empty beer down on a table and then charged past her again, this time on his way back to the kitchen. A moment later, he reappeared with a fresh bottle.

She caught him by the arm as he passed, the act of touching him sending a jolt of adrenaline through her that she tried to hide. "I think one's enough, Erin."

"Don't even fucking start," he said.

She released him and let him return to his position in front of the window. He was right. She'd abandoned him in the worst way imaginable and now, when she found herself alone and in trouble, she showed up on his doorstep and started telling him what to do.

"Ghawar has the same bacterial infestation, Jenna."

She didn't answer immediately, thinking for a moment she'd misunderstood. "That's not possible. It can't spread. It —"

"Wake up, for Christ's sake! It didn't spread. Somebody dumped it into the water injectors."

"That doesn't make sense, Erin. We —"

"And not just Ghawar," he said, finally turning away from the window. "If I'm right, they hit all the major water-injected fields."

"No. It can't . . ." she said, her voice faltering.

"Come on, Jenna. Did you really think Michael Teague was going to be satisfied with Alaska? Or did you just tell yourself that so you could go out there and save your stupid caribou?"

19

"You don't have anything at all to say?"

Mark Beamon remained silent, staring down at the wilted food perched on plates in front of him. As promised, it was all there — lutefisk, vegetables wrapped in wheat tortillas. Even a bran muffin topped with a tiny statue of a bride and groom.

"Jesus, Mark. Are you okay? This was supposed to be a joke." Carrie abandoned the pots she was washing and sat down next to him. "It's not really what we're having at our reception. I'm just winding you up."

He nodded absently.

"So I take it this is a disaster in the making."

"What?"

"This oil thing you've gotten yourself involved in."

"No, I'm just a little tired. It's fine."

"How long have we been together, Mark? I know the signs. That hangdog expression means problems at work. That expression with the smell of cigarettes means big problems at work. That expression with the smell of cigarettes and Twinkie crumbs on your shirt means a disaster in the making."

Beamon jammed the muffin into his mouth to avoid answering. On one hand, he hated being so easy to read, but on the other he was glad that someone cared enough to bother.

"Would it be fair for me to assume that the bacteria in question isn't just in Alaska?" Carrie asked, leaning back in her chair and smoothing the oversized Buffalo Springfield T-shirt she wore as an apron. "I read that we import more oil from Saudi Arabia — your new favorite travel destination — than any other country but Canada."

"Really?" he said through a mouthful of muffin. "I didn't know that."

Carrie grinned. "Not going to talk, huh. Then tell me how you feel about suddenly being in the middle of whatever it is you're in the middle of."

"I'm not happy about it."

"Really?"

"You're psychoanalyzing."

"I'm not! We're having a conversation. I mean, you went from pretty high-powered to basically no-powered. I recognize you did it for us, but sometimes I wonder if it was too much. Maybe a happy medium would have been better."

"Mediums are never happy for me. You know that."

She pointed to the beer on the table in front of him. "You managed to moderate your drinking. You didn't just give it up. I've said it before, Mark. I'm not trying to get you to live a healthy lifestyle — physically or spiritually. All I'm asking is that you don't go out of your way to kill yourself."

He smiled and shook his head.

"What?"

"I'm marrying a woman who uses the word 'spiritually.' "

The doorbell rang and she stood, making sure he saw the deep frown on her face before she padded down the hall.

Beamon heard the door open and then Jack Reynolds's voice, but he didn't get up from the table. Instead, he drained his beer in a vain attempt to dislodge what was left of the muffin from his dental work.

Carrie leaned into his ear as she came back into the kitchen. "That expression, the smell of cigarettes, the Twinkie crumbs, and the energy secretary at my door. I don't even have a category for that."

■ ■ ■ ■

The study at the back of the house wasn't that different from the one he had downtown. His furniture hadn't been delivered yet, leaving it empty of anything but stacks of boxes and a few framed pictures leaning against the wall.

"We've got problems," Reynolds said, closing the door behind him.

Beamon tested a particularly sturdy-looking box and sat down on it. "What kind of problems?"

"The Saudis have completely clammed up, but our spy satellites are telling us that the fields are shutting down just like Erin Neal said they would. That's why the gas lines keep getting longer."

Beamon nodded but didn't say anything.

"And that's not the worst of it. We have Steve Andropolous testing other reserves across the Middle East and, according to him, a lot of the fields are coming up positive for the bacteria."

"You came all the way out here to tell me that?"

"This has now officially risen to the very top of the president's agenda. He's talking to some of our allies about what we know, but we have to be careful. Everyone's jumpy as hell and we have to make sure we're protecting our interests first."

Reynolds backed away and leaned against the wall as though he needed it for support. "Jesus, Mark. Neal might actually be right. We could see a thirty-five percent drop in oil availability over the course of a year. I've got ten economists working on the problem and the only thing they agree on is the word 'catastrophe.' We're talking about the entire world's economy tanking. And you know who's going to lead the way? We are. We use more energy than anyone else by far and we're heavily reliant on water-injected wells. We're trying to figure out how to mitigate the effects and to let the problem go public as slowly and evenly as we can, but I'm not sure any of it's going to make any difference."

Beamon just sat there and let Reynolds's words sink in. He could almost feel the autonomy and filters he'd been promised disintegrating. Imploding might be a better word.

"Where are you on finding these psychopaths, Mark?"

"Nowhere Jack. I just started, remember?"

"What the fuck's that supposed to mean? You had no evidence at all. I couldn't agree to a politically suicidal investigation based on a goddamn hunch!"

Beamon put his finger to his lips. Emory was asleep in her room above them. "That wasn't an accusation, Jack. I'm just saying don't come to me expecting miracles. You'll be disappointed."

"Don't fuck this up," Reynolds said loudly enough to suggest he didn't care that it was a school night. "You've had a lot of political problems in the past, but if you get this wrapped up quick and neat, I'm guessing they're all going to be forgotten."

Beamon smiled and shook his head. "Then what? The government doesn't give bonuses. And I don't want to be a congressman. No, I think this is all downside for me, Jack. No matter when I catch these guys, someone's gonna say I should have done it faster. Someone's going to have to pay for the economic disaster everyone keeps talking about. And I'm guessing it's not going to be the president."

"I want hourly reports," Reynolds said, clearly unconcerned about Beamon's problems.

"I'm not doing hourly reports, Jack. I probably won't even do daily ones."

"Have you been paying attention to what's going on, Mark? It's possible — likely —

that in a few months, Iran will be all that's left of the Middle East producers. And we don't deal with them. We can't take a hit like this. Do your job and stop it before it gets out of control."

Beamon nodded noncommittally, noticing that his job had suddenly gone from catching the people responsible to ensuring that Iran didn't end up OPEC's last man standing.

The muffled sound of a doorbell drifted in and they sat in silence until there was a quiet knock on the office door.

"What?" Beamon said, glancing at his watch and confirming that it was indeed after eleven.

The door partially opened and Terry Hirst's worried face appeared in the crack. "Can I talk to you for a second?"

"Why the hell not? Everyone else is."

Hirst was the model for Beamon's stereotype of the Jewish New York lawyer — which is exactly what he'd been before joining the FBI. He was barely five seven, and not fat so much as slightly swollen looking. He'd been on the fast track at the bureau until he started having heart problems and needed to slow down. Beamon had hired him less for his considerable talent than to give him a job so easy that it would be virtually impossible to cause even the mildest cardiac episode. At least that had been the plan.

Hirst nodded nervously toward Reynolds as he closed the door quietly behind him. "Okay . . . I don't want you guys to freak out. I've already got people on this."

"On what?" Beamon said.

"Well, we were going through Ronald Denizen's email —"

"Who?"

"He's a biologist on our list. He's a ways down, though. Number fifty-six. I think."

"You're saying you found something?" Beamon asked. Normally, he preferred bad news to come in the morning and not when it would cause him to lay awake all night turning it over and over in his mind, but in this case he was willing to make an exception.

"Yeah. An email speculating on how to create a bacteria that would eat through oil faster. Our people tell me that it's essentially an exact description of the structure of the bacteria found in Saudi Arabia and Alaska."

"Jesus Christ!" Reynolds said. "Tell me we have this guy."

Hirst nodded. "We're holding him with the other scientists we picked up. The thing is, though, the email wasn't *from* him, it was *to* him."

"To him?" Beamon said. "Who wrote it?"

Hirst put his hands out in a gesture for calm. "I don't want —"

"Tell me who wrote it, Terry!"

He winced slightly as he spoke. "Erin Neal."

20

Erin Neal ascended the spiral staircase in bare feet, hardly noticing the normally pleasant sensation of cold stone against his skin. When he topped out in his tiny living room, he found Jenna lying motionless on his sofa, breathing in the soft, steady rhythm that he remembered so well. Stress had always made her retreat into sleep just as it kept him awake.

The moon had cleared the mountains and its light streamed through the windows, making her look like the ghost she'd been to him for so long. He stopped and stared down at her, feeling the breath constrict in his chest. Of all the emotions he could have predicted he'd feel at a moment like this, he would never have guessed the overriding one would be disorientation. Maybe that was how the mind dealt with being barraged simultaneously with anger, relief, sadness, fear. And, of course, love.

She stirred, as though she knew he was looking down at her, and the sheet began to slip slowly from her leg. He turned and walked into the kitchen before it slid too far.

The burst of light from the refrigerator blinded him as he fished out a beer and popped it open. The darkness descended again when he nudged the door shut — a more appropriate setting to contemplate the gigantic blank that now represented his future. Of course, it was easy to superimpose Jenna's image on it and pretend she belonged there, but for some reason, everything else seemed to be swallowed by the emptiness of that canvas.

He heard movement in the living room and looked over at the closed kitchen door. Maybe she'd changed and couldn't sleep either. Maybe she'd want to talk — or to throw herself into his arms and pretend for a few hours that none of this had ever happened.

He pushed the door partially open and saw her dim outline standing next to the sofa. Before he could say anything, though, she turned and her silhouette bulged unnaturally.

There was someone behind her.

"Erin! Come out! I have Jenna."

He pulled back, letting the door slowly close until there was only a thin crack to see through.

"Erin! Come out *now!*"

To him, Jonas Metzger had never been anything but another object Michael Teague used to adorn his inflated opinion of himself. What would all the expensive cars, private jets, and tailored clothing be without a creepy bodyguard? They'd stared each other down a few times, but unfortunately, nothing had ever come of it. And now he was here to finish what they had never quite had the opportunity to start.

Jonas pulled back and the moonlight once again fell on Jenna's face. She was trying to speak, but the son of a bitch was choking her. Erin's jaw tightened and he reached out to throw the door open, but then withdrew when he saw the gun pressed against the side of her head.

"Come out!" Jonas shouted at the empty loft above him. When there was no response, he started edging toward the hallway that led to the bathroom. His path took him within a few feet of the kitchen door, but with his chest pressed against Jenna's back and the barrel of the gun still against her temple, there was nothing Erin could do.

Jenna grabbed the German's arm and managed to loosen his grip on her neck enough to speak. "He's gone, Jonas."

The strangled quality of her voice caused Erin's stomach to clench. A few years ago, he would have lunged through the door, completely blinded by rage. But he'd learned to control that part of him. To a point.

"He went to the police," she continued. "Don't get yourself in more trouble than you're already in. We —"

He tightened his arm around her throat again, silencing her as he moved cautiously down the hall. When they faded into shadow, Erin looked behind him. There was a block of knives on the counter, but that wasn't terribly comforting when faced with a gun. His gaze wandered to the refrigerator, the microwave, and finally stopped on the stove. It was a long shot but nothing else was coming to mind.

He turned on all the burners without lighting them, holding his breath as the gas began to fill the room. Selecting the most deadly looking knife from the block, he shoved the rest in a drawer and went back to the kitchen door to peek out. Jonas had been forced to turn a light on in the hallway and was most of the way down it, still using

Jenna as a shield. Erin waited until Jonas sprang through the bathroom door before moving silently across the living room and hiding behind the couch.

"Erin!" Jonas shouted. "Don't you care? Don't you care what I can do to her?"

There was a dull crack and a shout from Jenna. Erin jumped from his crouched position, the knife clenched in his hand.

No. If he let his temper take over, they were both dead. Jonas knew that and was using it.

"I think she's hurt," the German said. "She's bleeding very bad, Erin. You better come and help her."

When they appeared again a few moments later, Jonas's arm was still around Jenna's throat, but instead of silencing her, it was supporting the weight that her wobbly legs no longer could. Erin remained completely motionless when Jonas kicked open the door to the kitchen and then paused when he smelled the gas.

"Are you in here?" he said, starting forward again with the gun partially obscured in Jenna's hair. "Are you wanting to blow up your woman?"

The door swung shut behind them and Erin ran across the room, ending up with his back pressed against the wall next to the jamb. A few deep breaths and he slipped inside.

The gun was now aimed at Erin, but he ignored it and concentrated instead on the blood that had flowed across Jenna's face and down the T-shirt he'd given her to sleep in. In the moonlight streaming through the window, the stains looked black.

She appeared not to realize that he was standing in front of her as she struggled to regain her equilibrium, pulling weakly at Jonas's forearm.

"I knew you would come," the German said. "She was taken from you for so long. How can you lose her again?"

Still holding his breath, Erin pointed at the gun and then indicated around them at the gas-filled room.

Jonas's teeth glowed white as a smile spread across his face. "Of course you are very smart. The great Erin Neal, yes? The great environmentalist who tells the world to do whatever they want. To destroy whatever they want."

He released Jenna and she sank to the ground, pausing briefly on all fours before she collapsed onto her stomach. Jonas stuffed his gun in the back of his pants and slid a switchblade from his pocket. His smile broadened as he charged.

Erin feinted left, then went right, slamming against the counter and narrowly avoiding a slash that wasn't as well-timed as Jonas had expected. His reflexes and balance were just a bit off from the gas.

Erin let the German's momentum carry him and instead of launching forward like he normally would, backed away. It wasn't his kind of fighting — the strategy of taking a few shots and going for the knockout wasn't as effective when the shots were coming from a knife.

The aching in his lungs finally forced him to take in some of the gas-laden air as Jonas turned and ran at him again, knife outstretched. The kitchen was too small for any real maneuvering and the German wasn't going to fall for the same feint twice. Erin thrust his own knife out in front of him, realizing there was no way to avoid Jonas's attack this time. All he could hope to do at this point was take the son of a bitch with him.

He tensed, hoping there would be enough adrenaline flowing through him to mask the pain caused by a knife penetrating his chest and allow him to concentrate entirely on the pleasure of jamming his in Jonas's neck. Instead, the German jerked unexpectedly to the right, his blade slicing through Erin's side instead of delivering the fatal blow he'd been expecting.

His own knife missed completely, and in a desperate bid to keep the German from slashing again, Erin grabbed the front of his shirt and lifted him as they toppled.

He'd built the entire house with his own hands and knew every inch of it, including the exact position of the concrete counter-top behind him. He continued lifting as he fell backward, tucking his head forward and narrowly missing the edge of the counter. Jonas wasn't so lucky. The crack of his forehead slamming into the hard surface filled the room just before Erin's back slammed into the floor.

He twisted out from beneath the German, trying to get away from the knife, but then realized he was the only one moving.

After sliding the switchblade across the floor to a safer distance, he fell back against the cabinets, finally realizing why he was still alive. From her position on the floor, Jenna was looking up at him, her hand still holding the leg of Jonas's pants.

Jenna used her sleeve to wipe away the blood running from the gash near her temple and concentrated on bending the needle in her hand to a satisfactory curve.

"You've done this before, right?"

She didn't answer, instead, plunging it into one side of the gash in Erin's ribs.

"Jesus! What are you using? A knitting needle?"

"Hold still. If you squirm, it's going to take longer."

He stared directly forward, jaw clenched as she continued to stitch the wound left by Jonas's knife. It was hard not to dwell on the fact that she was once again causing him horrible suffering, so she focused on the throbbing in her own head. Unfortunately, it wasn't all that bad. As always, she had screwed up and he had taken the hit. It had been a mistake to come there — a selfish mistake. He could have died.

"Thanks, by the way," he said, his voice constricted from the pain.

"What?"

"If you hadn't tripped him, he would have gotten me with that knife. You saved my life."

She tied off the last stitch and backed away, stepping over Jonas's still-unconscious body on the floor behind her.

"Jesus, Erin. Don't thank me, okay? Just don't."

He looked down at his side and then began the difficult process of putting his shirt back on. "Are you married?"

"What? No, of course not."

He nodded slowly, his brow slightly furrowed. It was a mannerism she remembered well. He had something to say, but was having a hard time finding the right words.

"Why did you do it, Jenna?"

"You know why."

"No, I don't mean Alaska. I don't care about that. I guess what I want to know is, was it easy for you to walk away and make me think you died?"

"Easy? It was the hardest thing I ever did. I . . ." She fell silent for a moment. "At the time, I thought what I was doing was more important than me or you or anything."

"You don't have to lie to make me feel better, Jen. I know you didn't like what I had to say in my book. I mean, our relationship was built on things we had in common — just like everybody else's. Maybe I changed and you didn't. I can understand why you could have stopped loving me."

"Is that what you think?"

"I don't know."

She stared down at the duct tape securing Jonas's hands, but didn't really see it. What was the right thing to do? She wanted to tell him the truth — that there hadn't been a day since she'd left that she hadn't thought

214

about him. But would that just make things worse?

"We need to call someone," she said, silently praying that he would let this go. At least for now.

He turned and walked out of the house without a word.

What had she expected? A joyous, easygoing reunion with no baggage or expectation?

When she found him, he was standing at the edge of his driveway, looking out into the dark desert. Her footsteps made no sound at all in the soft ground, but he seemed to sense her coming up behind him.

"Erin. We've got to call someone."

He didn't answer and Jenna took a few steps closer, but stayed behind him.

"If you're right and Michael is targeting the rest of the water-injected wells, we've got to try to stop him."

"It's too late, Jenna."

"It's not too late! It can't be. What's going to happen if he succeeds? We're not talking about a minor irritation anymore, Erin. We're talking about people starving. Starving because of *my* bacteria. Because of something *I* did."

"Yeah. Because of something you did."

"Thanks, Erin. That's just what I needed to hear."

"What *you* needed to hear?" he said suddenly turning toward her. "I'm sorry, have I said something indelicate? Are you feeling a little put out that you trashed my life and fucked the world over?"

They hadn't fought much when they'd been together but when they did, it had always been at the very edge of control. They were both so passionate about so many things, and those things didn't always mesh.

"You're always right, aren't you, Erin? You'd never do anything that isn't calculated to the fifteenth goddamn decimal point, would you? But who was it that used to come and get you when you'd been drinking? Or get between you and some motorcycle gang you picked a fight with?"

"You're equating a little drunk roughhousing with destroying the planet's energy supply?"

"I'm acknowledging that I fucked up. And that I did it in a really big way. But you of all people should have some inkling of *why* I did it."

They both fell silent, staring at each other through the darkness, neither wanting to be the first to speak.

As usual, he broke down before she did. "The government's looking for someone to blame, Jenna, and if we call them, it'll be you. They aren't going to care that you had nothing to do with it."

"I had everything to do with it."

"You know what I mean," he said. "You should run. Go to Eastern Europe or South America or Africa or something. If you need money, I've got enough for you to live on for the rest of your life."

"I have money."

"The money Teague gave you?"

"We don't have time for this, Erin."

"I'm not going to do something that ends with you in Guantanamo. How is that going to help anyone?"

"So your plan is to do nothing?"

He shrugged.

"And what about Jonas? He's taped to your living room floor."

"You disappear and give me your word you'll stay that way. In a couple of days, when I know you're safe, I'll call the guy in charge of the investigation and hand Jonas over."

"A couple of days?" she said. "A couple of days is too late."

"Teague's been at this forever. What's two more days going to matter?"

"Think, Erin. It's what you're good at,

right? How did Jonas get here from Montana?"

Erin folded his arms defiantly across his chest. "I don't know."

"Yes you do."

"He probably flew, I guess. He used to pilot Teague's plane."

She nodded. "So it seems kind of likely that his plane is at an airport somewhere around here. Probably with a flight plan that will take the FBI right to Michael's door."

"Fuck the FBI. They'll just have to get to his door a few days from now."

"Come on, Erin! How long until Michael realizes that he can't get in touch with Jonas? And the minute that happens, he'll be gone."

21

Mark Beamon entered the oval office quietly, pausing for a moment to scan the faces of the men and women sitting in a semicircle around the president's desk. Jack Reynolds was there, as was the chief of staff. The rest of the people were only vaguely familiar. What was it Carrie was so fond of saying? "Sometimes it's hard to tell all you rich, white government guys apart."

Everyone was focused on the president, so no one paid any attention as Beamon took a chair at the far left of the group. Not far enough, though. He hated the White House. Almost by definition, if a guy like him was there, it meant something had gone horribly wrong.

"So we think there's a connection between the attacks and the Al Jazeera story?" the president said.

The man directly to Beamon's right responded. "Obviously, the Saudis were having problems before, but we're talking about three hastily organized bombings in one day. It's probably that the growing insurgency there sees this as something they can exploit to bring down the monarchy."

"And then we end up with a bunch of fanatics running Saudi Arabia," the president said. "How much does Al Jazeera know?"

"Not that much. The story started running last night. They know there's a bacterial contamination at Ghawar and that there have been some shut downs. They've made speculative comparisons to Alaska, and they're being fairly alarmist about how widespread the contamination is, but, ironically, their worst-case scenario is still a lot better than our predictions. You can count on the U.S. networks picking the story up by this afternoon and for Al Jazeera to keep expanding their coverage. I think you can expect the American press to connect the Saudi problems and the fact that the gas shortages we're having can't be explained by the shut downs in Alaska. It's the puzzle piece they've been looking for."

Beamon glanced at his watch. This thing was just about to blow up all over television and here he was — indefinitely bogged down in a political strategy meeting that had nothing to do with him.

"The Saudi government is requesting help," the man continued.

"What's in it for us?" the president asked. "I'm told that ninety percent of Saudi Arabia's oil comes from the Ghawar field and, as far as anyone can tell, that field is on its way out over the next year. If Saudi Arabia collapses, how are we affected?"

"It could destabilize the region even more, and that could amplify the effects of the damage to the reservoirs. If the Middle East descends into chaos, you could easily see another forty percent drop in exports."

"Bullshit," the president said. "A seventy-five percent drop in exports from the Middle East is *unacceptable.* This country can't run with that kind of an energy reduction. What about military options? Can we take control of the production and distribution facilities that are still viable?"

There was a brief silence before one of the military men spoke up. "No, sir. They're simply too spread out to defend. And the amount of fuel we would need even to attempt an operation like that would be more than we'd get back."

"Jesus Christ," the president said, running a hand nervously through his hair. Even at a distance, Beamon could see that he was actually sweating.

"Sir, the Saudis —"

"I don't give a fuck about the Saudis!" the president shouted. "I've got both GM and Ford getting ready to announce more layoffs. I've got every airline in the country drawing up bankruptcy papers and canceling flights because of a lack of fuel availability. And all I can get from you is that there isn't anything we can do?"

"Mr. President," his chief of staff started, making a valiant attempt at a soothing tone. "In the end, the media picking this up has a silver lining for us. It'll go a long way to explaining the administration's reaction, and it's going to help us get through whatever regulations we need to. Also, the windfall profit tax on the oil companies is almost ready to go to Congress."

"Any resistance?" the president asked.

"It'll pass almost unanimously. The oil companies aren't fighting it because they know it'll be largely symbolic. Their profits from increased prices will be offset by writing off the losses resulting from the damaged fields."

Beamon shifted impatiently in his chair. Accounting? Now he was going to have to sit through a goddamn accounting discussion?

"What about Canada?"

"A couple of people were injured at a protest in front of their embassy yesterday."

Beamon sighed quietly. As one of the world's larger oil producers, and with a population of less than thirty-five million, the Canadians were actually benefiting from all this. Their fuel prices had barely budged, and they were seen as gouging by the average American waiting in line to pay one hundred and thirty dollars to fill up his tank. Of course, the truth was much more complicated — an incomprehensible web of international agreements, oil company contracts, and free market pricing — but the media didn't like to be bogged down with facts when there was blood in the water.

"The Canadian government is understandably angry, and they're demanding we do something about the bad publicity they're getting."

"What the hell do they want me to do?" the president asked. "I don't control the goddamn press, and I've got my own problems. What about Iran? They're benefiting a hell of a lot more than the Canadians. Can we plant some stories to deflect attention?"

"We're trying, sir, but it's not as good a story. We don't import from them, and their standard of living is still a lot lower than ours. We're finalizing the deal to jointly ramp-up production in the Canadian tar sands. When it's signed, it'll be the largest deal of its kind in history. Hopefully, we can spin that in a way that'll quiet things down, but it's hard to predict. You could also look at it as pumping a huge amount of tax dollars into an increasingly wealthy country for something that won't have any immediate effect."

"I'm holding you personally responsible to make sure it goddamn well doesn't get spun that way," the president said.

"Yes, sir. We're already planting stories about Canada's tar sands being as large a reserve as Saudi Arabia's. The pictures have a lot of impact — overhead shots of thousands of miles of oil-impregnated sand right there for the taking. Obviously, it's more complicated than that. The retrieval of that oil is technologically and environmentally much more difficult than drilling, but we're downplaying the negatives as well as the time it will take to scale-up production to a point where it can compensate for the Saudi decline."

The president had obviously had enough of that subject, and he turned to Beamon. "Where does the investigation stand? Do you have any substantial leads?"

Beamon nodded. "Yes, sir. We found an old email from Erin Neal to a colleague describing the steps for manufacturing a bacteria almost identical to this one."

"Erin Neal? I don't understand. Isn't he the consultant we're using?"

"Yes, sir."

"How does he explain the email?"

Beamon fidgeted in his chair, for a moment lost in a fantasy that he'd done the smart thing and run hard and fast from this investigation. "We're not sure, sir. We haven't actually been able to find him."

When the president's expression went from confused to enraged, Reynolds's instinct for self-preservation kicked in. "Jesus Christ, Mark. We knew he was a potential problem — we talked about this. You told me you were watching him."

"He was low priority and we were having problems coordinating manpower," Beamon said. "So we only had one guy on him. It seemed reasonable since there's only one way in and out of his house."

"Then why the hell don't we have him?"

He really wasn't looking forward to saying this.

"Mark?" Reynolds prompted.

"Because the guy who was watching him

ran out of gas."

"What?"

"Apparently he forgot his government ID and he didn't have time to wait in line at the gas station before he started his shift. Neal drove out around three in the morning and our guy . . . well, he ran out of gas following him."

"So you're telling me that we now have a solid suspect," the president said. "The guy you were relying on as the expert on these bacteria — and you have no idea where he is?"

When he put it like that it sounded really bad.

"We have a nationwide APB on him and we're going through his phone records to see if we can figure out where he went. Hopefully —"

"Hopefully? Are you goddamn joking with me? Hopefully?"

Beamon could feel the sweat starting to fill his shoes. Normally, the thought of being screamed at by the president of the United States would illicit nothing more than mild annoyance in him. But in this case it was well deserved. He'd fucked up and fucked up in a big way. There was so much to keep track of, he'd never considered that an inexperienced first-year agent might be assigned to watch Erin Neal and that he'd neglect to fill his tank. How could he have forgotten his most cherished principle? What can go wrong, will go wrong.

22

Not surprisingly, the Tucson traffic was light, with an unusual number of bicycles weaving in and out of the cars — some a bit unsteadily. At first, Beamon thought their erratic trajectories were caused by the heat, but more likely some of these people hadn't ridden since they were children. According to National Public Radio, virtually every bike shop in America was sold out, and used bicycles were going for more than they had new.

He slumped down in the back seat of the car and looked out the window at a hitchhiker standing on the edge of the highway. He was a clean-cut kid holding an artistically rendered sign offering five dollars for a ride to the university.

Beamon had watched the president's latest address the night before and found that the message had evolved a bit since the planning session he'd attended. The contamination data coming in continued to agree with Erin Neal's now somewhat suspicious projections, forcing the government to take a tougher stance than had at first been considered.

The basic thrust was that the world would be facing a substantial and most likely permanent drop in oil availability. The president kept the tone upbeat, talking about the adaptability of the American people, technologies that were right around the corner, and the spirit of working together. But the tone was clear — things were going to change and there was nothing anyone could do about it.

A fuel-rationing program was being instituted, though no one was sure how it was going to work. The government was also introducing a fairly radical incentive program for conservation, along with a significant loosening of environmental regulations regarding the generation of energy. So far, there wasn't much reaction from the environmentalists on that last one. Some were still being held, despite Beamon's efforts to get them released, and the general public was in no mood to do without heat and transportation because it might get the wildlife sooty.

Of course, the president hadn't been

completely honest. He'd suggested a fifteen percent drop instead of the thirty-five percent that was more likely. Even with that questionable bit of soft-pedaling, the market was down more than seven hundred points. Ultra-conservatives in the government were beginning to wonder aloud why the military wasn't being sent to secure supply from countries that had been proven "unreliable."

Beamon tipped sideways, lying down on his side in the spacious back seat and closing his eyes. He remembered the good old days when he could go for weeks on little more than excitement and caffeine. God, he hated getting old.

"Mr. Beamon? Sir?"

Beamon stirred and finally pushed himself upright in the seat. His driver, whose name he'd already forgotten, was leaning in through the open back door. "We're here."

Erin Neal's house was pretty much as he remembered it, except for the conservatively dressed and profusely sweating men and women swarming all over it.

"It's cooler inside," his driver said. "The house is generating enough power to run the air conditioner for a few minutes every hour."

Beamon frowned deeply, looking around him at the greenhouse, the solar array, the windmill. If there had been a little stream to run a hydroelectric dam, Neal would have had the power to actually put up a neon sign announcing "I did it!"

A self-sustaining environmentalist with a PhD in biology who'd become a hermit after the death of the woman he loved. Yeah, no one would ever have called that one.

He held the door open for a woman carrying a fingerprint kit and then slipped in behind her, finding Terry Hirst spread out on the sofa, mopping his forehead with a dishrag.

"Terry!"

His eyes shot open and he bolted upright. "Jesus, Mark. Don't do that. You scared the shit out of me."

"How long have you been here?"

"Longer than you'd think. The way I heard it, no one's getting assigned private planes right now, but I called up and had one in ten minutes. I like to think somewhere a senator's mistress is standing on the tarmac wondering who stole her ride."

Beamon moved to make way for a man collecting fibers with a tiny vacuum. "And in all that time, have you found anything?"

"Found anything? Are you kidding? We found the proverbial jackpot. Haven't you heard? We've got the notes on Neal's initial development of the concept for the bacteria."

"Come on, it's never that easy."

"It is today. We sent copies to Steve Andropolous to see if he can use it to stop the spread. Doesn't look promising, though."

"So we've got notes but no author."

"Unfortunately, yes. But that's where it gets even more interesting," Hirst said, pushing himself from the couch and motioning for Beamon to follow him to the kitchen. "We know Neal left in a hurry — a couple of electrical appliances were left running and people who live off the grid just don't do that." He stopped and pointed at a large bloodstain on the kitchen floor. "There's more in the hallway. A whole trail of it, actually."

"Do we know whose it is?"

"Two different people. That's all we know at this point."

"So I was right."

"About what?"

"It's never that easy."

Hirst snorted and led Beamon out onto the porch, where there was a table containing a legal pad and a laptop computer. "It gets weirder. He bought a bunch of mailing lists from companies that make artificial rock-climbing holds and has been calling people from them to see if they were satisfied with the stuff they bought."

Beamon stared down at the list of names. "So, he sets the scene for a massive depression and then decides to go into the climbing hold business?"

"Seems far fetched, doesn't it?"

"He's already rich, right?"

Hirst nodded. "We have his net worth at about nine million, which until a few days ago was primarily invested in a mix of stocks."

"And now?"

"Mostly treasuries, precious metals, and companies specializing in renewable energies."

Beamon frowned. Once again, Erin Neal had proved that he wasn't a stupid man. Still, it was interesting that he hadn't moved those assets before.

"How many people has he called?"

"About a hundred according to his phone records."

Beamon tapped the pad on the table. "All the people on this list are women."

Hirst's mouth tightened. "Goddamnit!"

"What?"

"I missed that."

Beamon sat down and stared at the dark screen of the laptop. "Okay, so he's not interested in the companies, he's looking for someone — a woman who climbs."

"Aren't we all?"

"But he doesn't know her name or where she lives."

"We've talked to basically everyone he knows and there were several climbers — mostly friends of his former girlfriend, who I guess was into things like that. Some were even environmentalists, but we've cleared them all. Right now we're running down everyone he called."

"What about the laptop? Anything interesting there?"

"Password protected. We're going to send it to the eggheads at the NSA and see if they can get in. But I wouldn't hold your breath."

Beamon nodded.

"What are you thinking, Mark?"

"The climber angle. He's obviously gone to a lot of trouble to find this woman. But she's not a friend of his, because he doesn't know her name. And she's not a biologist because he'd be able to find her through that. She's not even an acquaintance — because you have connections to acquaintances. Common friends and such."

"So why's he want to find her so bad, Mark?"

"Maybe he met her briefly in a bar or something and never could get her out of his head. He knows the shit's about to hit the fan and wants another shot . . . no, that's stupid."

They sat in silence for a few moments before Beamon spoke again. "What if she doesn't want him to find her?"

"You mean she's actively hiding from him?"

A thin smile spread slowly across Beamon's face.

"What? You've got something," Hirst said. "I can tell."

"I want you to get the mailing lists for every climbing hold manufacturer in the country and get basic background on every woman on them. I want it by the end of the day."

"That's not possible, Mark. You're talking about —"

"If you have to, shut down every other investigation the FBI's doing and put the people on it. No excuses, Terry."

23

The plane's wheels hit the ground hard enough to throw Jenna into the back of the seat Jonas was duct-taped to. The German's flight plan had led them to a small Texas airfield and she peered through the windscreen as they taxied across it. There wasn't much activity, which wasn't surprising now that the government was starting to divert fuel supplies from noncritical uses such as private planes.

Jonas's phone began to ring for what she counted as the twenty-second time during the flight, but he didn't react. He just sat there, completely motionless, staring straight ahead in a way that made Jenna want to check the tape securing him.

"Teague again," she said, glancing down at the phone. "We should have called the police. They could have gotten here faster."

Erin shut down the plane's engine and twisted around to look at her. "But we didn't, Jen. The government's focusing on exactly what they need to — securing the water injectors and figuring out how to handle the effects of the fields that Teague's already hit. Splitting their attention and giving them something to grandstand about on TV isn't going to help anyone."

It was just another excuse — the last in a long line of rationalizations that had brought them there. The truth was that they had no idea what good calling the police would have done or what Michael Teague's ultimate plan was.

Then why hadn't she fought harder?

It was an easy question to answer if she could bring herself to look that far inward. She had her life back. No matter how precarious the situation, she'd escaped her self-imposed exile, Erin was with her, and she had a purpose again. Admittedly, that purpose was trying to fix a horrifying disaster that was entirely her fault, but after eighteen months of trying to think of a reason to get out of bed in the morning, she wasn't in a position to be choosy.

One call to the police, though, and it would all disappear again — this time forever. She knew that ultimately she had no future, but it was hard to part with the illusion so soon.

"Okay, Erin. It's your plan. What now?"

He stared through the windscreen with nearly the intensity of Jonas. "Skip the country and leave this to the government."

"Then why don't you? I told you I could handle this alone."

"By turning yourself in? That's just stupid, Jenna."

"But sitting here doing nothing is so brilliant?"

Jenna had Jonas's duffle over her shoulder with her hand inside, aiming the German's own gun at him as they walked toward a sparsely populated parking lot. Erin was carrying a similar duffle with his own gun inside.

"Where's your car?" Jenna said.

No answer.

With the exception of the flight plan, the only thing of interest they'd found in the plane was a set of keys — though Erin hadn't missed a single opportunity to point out that their existence didn't necessarily mean they would the find the car they belonged to. Just another excuse to head for the most convenient border at the highest practical speed. He'd probably only agreed to fly her there because Mexico was almost in sight.

Jenna counted three people in the lot and another two smoking in front of the private airport's office. She tried to tell herself that no one was paying attention, but every glance in their direction, no matter how brief, seemed to take on a probing quality.

"Tell us where your car is," Erin repeated at a volume that made Jenna glance back. The men by the office were now gazing lazily in their general direction. They perked up even more when Jonas stopped short and spun around.

"Keep going," Erin said.

The German pointed to the hidden gun. "Shoot me."

"Don't fuck with me, man. I swear I'll —"

Jonas moved forward at a speed calculated to be too slow to startle them into shooting but too fast for Erin to overcome his surprise and maneuver away. The gun was causing him to abandon his well-tested defenses in favor of a weapon that he wasn't sure he could bring himself to use.

Jonas took advantage of Erin's hesitation and swung a fist into the gash in his side, doubling him over and causing him to drop his duffle. The gun was exposed now for everyone to see, but at least he managed to keep hold of it as he tried to protect his ribs from another attack.

"Jonas!" Jenna shouted, pulling her own gun from her bag and aiming it at the German as he landed a vicious kick to Erin's chest, toppling him and slamming the back of his head into the asphalt. Her weapon seemed impossibly heavy, shaking in rhythm with her accelerating heart rate. She'd never purposely harmed anyone, but now she was aiming a gun at another human being.

Jonas ignored her, leaping forward and landing with one foot on Erin's wrist, pinning his gun. The blow to the back of Erin's head had obviously been as bad as it sounded and he was unable to react other than to swing a limp fist into Jonas's shin.

"I said stop!"

At first, her voice seemed too quiet to carry much authority, but there was something in her tone that made the German pause.

To Jenna's surprise, her hand had steadied, as had her heart. "If you don't back away, Jonas, I'll kill you."

She wished that she could have said that the words didn't seem to be her own or that they were the product of panic, but it wouldn't have been true. She meant every word. She wasn't going to let him hurt Erin anymore. Even if it meant pulling the trigger and having to stand there and watch the consequences of that action.

Jonas seemed to come to the same conclusion. He smiled thinly and stood upright, retreating a few feet before stopping again.

"Don't worry," he said. "We'll see each other again."

Erin had regained enough strength to begin sitting up and Jonas turned, sprinting across the now-uninhabited parking lot while Jenna watched him over the sight of her pistol.

"Are you alright?" she said, helping Erin to his feet and glancing back at the office. The two men were no longer out front, but she spotted one of them peeking through a window, talking quickly into a cell phone.

She grabbed the bag off the ground and supported as much of Erin's weight as she could as they rushed toward the lines of parked cars.

"I'm sorry," he said, haltingly. "I should have stopped him. The gun . . ."

She desperately pushed the UNLOCK button on the key fob as they continued forward. "It's not your fault, Erin. None of this is your fault."

The lights of a white Toyota compact flashed a few cars in front of them and they stumbled toward it. She shoved Erin into the passenger seat and ran around to the driver's side.

"You're bleeding," she said as she started the car and threw it in reverse, squealing the wheels as she headed toward the airport's exit.

He shook his head violently to clear it and pressed a hand to his side. The fabric of his shirt was matted with blood.

"I think it's stopped," Erin said, still sounding weak. "Your stitches actually held."

She threw the car to the left, slamming him into the door and getting them off the main road as sirens screamed in the distance.

"That's it, Erin. As soon as Jonas gets to a pay phone he's going to warn Michael. You have to call the guy running the investigation and tell him what happened."

He didn't answer her, instead opening the glove box and riffling through the papers inside.

She swung the car onto an even quieter street and glanced in her rearview mirror before rolling to a stop. "Call him, Erin. Now."

"No. We can find them. There's got to be something here." He continued going through the documents he'd discovered, but after a moment just let them fall to the floorboard.

"Erin . . ."

"Okay, I'll do it. But first we have to get you out of here. Get you somewhere safe."

It was a beautiful fantasy. She'd run somewhere sunny and unspoiled and he'd follow in a year or so. Then they'd spend the rest of their lives swinging in hammocks and drinking out of coconuts while governments collapsed, economies crumbled, and people struggled to feed themselves.

"Eventually, I'm going to have to own up to what I did," she said. "To explain."

He didn't seem to hear, instead fixating on a small screen in the dash.

"Erin? Are you listening to me?"

He didn't answer, but reached out and turned on the car's GPS.

"It couldn't be this easy," he mumbled as he touched a house-shaped icon on the screen.

A moment later the car was filled with the pleasant voice of a woman asking them to turn left at the next street.

24

"Erin . . . I'm so sorry."

His infamous temper had completely failed him and he just sat there, hands drooped across the wheel and head resting against the window. Static had drowned out the NPR story for a moment, but then the voices inevitably faded back in.

"That's a fairly strong statement," the interviewer said.

"I stand by it. The information comes from a well-placed source and we've talked to a number of people in the field to corroborate it. At this point, I feel comfortable saying that the government believes that the bacteria were created by Dr. Erin Neal for the specific purpose of destroying the world's oil supplies."

"To what end?"

"Neal's a well-known radical environmentalist who's written a number of papers and even a full-length book on the subject. The theme going through all of them is that environmental destruction is inevitable and unavoidable. Obviously, he found the solution he was looking for. A final solution."

"A final solution," Erin said quietly. Now they were comparing him to Hitler.

He threw open the car door and walked away from the vehicle in a vain attempt to escape the sound of the radio.

"Is there any word as to whether Neal is in custody?"

"I think we can assume that he hasn't been captured at this point. I should mention that he has a history of violence and should be considered quite dangerous."

He heard the passenger door open and watched Jenna's shadow come up behind him.

"Erin. I'll fix this. I swear I will."

He laughed. "How? How are you going to fix it, Jenna? If they think it's me, they've been through my house and they found all my data on that bacteria."

She put a hand on his shoulder and, despite everything, he couldn't pull away.

"I'll call Homeland Security and I'll explain everything. I'll tell them that it was me. That I stole it. I'll *make* them listen to me."

"And based on all your credibility, they're

going to just let me walk off into the sunset?" He pointed back to the car, where the interview was winding down. "Time to wake up and see the real world, Jen. I'm a radical environmentalist with a history of violence."

Her hand slid from his shoulder and she took a hesitant step back. "It wasn't supposed to happen like this. I was only —"

"I don't want to hear it right now, okay? I really don't."

He stood there, staring through the heat haze at a distant metal building and the abandoned oil derricks beyond.

"Do you think he's still in there?" Jenna said.

He shrugged. "If he gets cell reception, Jonas would have called him by now. Maybe they're long gone. Or maybe they're waiting for us."

He pulled the pistol from his waistband and gazed down at it for a moment before fixing again on the distant building. "All I know is if I'm going to crash and burn, I'm fucking taking him with me."

Since the building had no windows and only one flimsy door, they had few options. Jenna grabbed Erin's arm as he stepped in front of the door, but he pulled away and slammed a foot into it. It buckled and he jumped through, holding his pistol in front of him with both hands, a technique derived entirely from the hundreds of cop shows he'd watched as a kid.

Not that he expected it to matter much. Most likely, Teague and Udo were hidden and ready for him, their crosshairs lined up on his chest. But what else could he do?

Jenna slipped in behind him holding Jonas's pistol in a similar fashion, though as far as he knew, she'd never fired a gun.

The inside of the building was a jumble of tables, overturned chairs, and wrecked research equipment. Erin continued to search for movement, peering over the sights of his pistol as he swept it back and forth across the room. Everything was still, until he spotted Jenna moving along the wall to a door at the rear.

"What are you doing?" he whispered loudly. "Get back here."

She ignored him, continuing silently forward and then jumping through the door. He ran after her through the debris and found her standing in a similarly wrecked room with her gun now hanging loosely at her side.

"Empty," she said.

He took a moment to examine the interior of the warehouse more closely. It was even more torn apart than he'd first thought. Drawers were lying upside down on the floor surrounded by broken glass, microscopes looked as if they'd been beaten with hammers, and the door had been ripped off a large incubator at the back. The refrigerator looked undamaged, though, and he opened it, reaching for one of the beers at the back. German. Big surprise.

"What's with the drinking?" Jenna said. "I thought you'd given it up for good."

"Me too," he said, deftly using the edge of a counter to pop the top off.

There were three televisions still intact in the back room and he found the remote to one of them on the floor. He pressed the POWER button and was suddenly faced with himself. Or more precisely, a photo from his college yearbook — probably the only thing the media had access to at this point. Kind of ironic, really. All the people who had turned on him after his book was published were probably now closing ranks and telling the reporters to fuck off.

He launched the bottle in his hand at the television, smashing the screen in a spectacular spray of foam and sparks. But it didn't make him feel any better. Not even a little.

When he turned back into the main part

of the warehouse, he found Jenna tossing the beer she'd found in the refrigerator out the door.

"What the hell are you doing?" he said, running toward her.

"Someone left in a hurry," she replied, arcing the last bottle through the air and watching it shatter on the rocky ground outside. "All the computers have their hard drives torn out and the filing cabinets are empty. That pile of ashes we saw outside is probably what's left of their documents."

Erin stared through the door at the smashed bottles and then flipped a chair back on its feet. As he sat down, he could feel the adrenaline run out. "What were they doing here?"

"How should I know?" she said defensively.

He was about to remind her that she had started all this, but he'd already done that too many times.

"It's a lot of gear, Jen. And this place isn't exactly Teague's style. I seem to remember him preferring artificial waterfalls and Swedish models."

She looked around the building again, chewing her lower lip. "Maybe they haven't hit all the water-injected wells yet. Maybe this is where they were breeding the bacteria to finish the job."

"I don't know, Jen. I really don't."

She started to move toward him, but then stopped just close enough to be awkward. "So maybe this helped. Maybe we stopped him from doing any more. And now he's on the run."

Erin didn't answer. She closed the remaining distance, kneeling and resting her hands on his knees. "It's so good to see you again." She managed a laugh, but it seemed in danger of turning to a sob. "With everything that's going on, that sounded really stupid didn't it? But I never thought I'd ever be close to you again."

He wanted to reach out and wrap his arms around her. To kiss her. To make all this go away. But that was even stupider.

An unfamiliar ring tone filled the room and Jenna crawled over to a broken monitor, finding the source of the sound beneath it.

"Christ," she said, looking down at the cell phone's tiny screen.

"What?"

She put the phone hesitantly to her ear. "Hello, Michael."

Erin knelt next to her and she held the phone out so he could hear.

"It looks like I missed you again, Jenna.

I'm sorry for that. I would like to have had a chance to talk."

"About what, Michael? About what you were doing here? About Saudi Arabia?"

"That. And other things."

"Why, Michael? Don't you understand —"

"Because someone had to before it was too late. You know that as well as I do, Jenna, you just don't have the courage to face it. Hundreds of years ago, when people destroyed their environment, they died or migrated and the earth was able to heal. But now we've changed all that."

"Are you insane, Michael? How will this save anything? You'll starve the most vulnerable people in the world and cause the wealthier countries to switch to even dirtier kinds of energy to keep things going."

"Perhaps. Is Erin there?"

She hesitated for a moment. "Yes."

"Ask him if he's been following the news."

"Fuck you," Erin shouted, grabbing the phone. "Why don't you come back here and we can —"

"Stop!" Jenna said, snatching the phone back and looking down at it. "He hung up."

"Son of a bitch!"

Erin stood and paced back and forth across the room, randomly kicking at the debris. There was no denying it. Teague had won. He'd disappear and live the good life while they were hunted down and blamed for the disaster that he'd caused — the final nail in a coffin Teague had been building for him since *Energy and Nature* had been published.

"Calm down, Erin. Don't let him get to you like that. He's doing it on purpose."

Of course she was right, but it was hard not to get lost in fantasies of squeezing Teague's pale little neck until his head popped.

"There's no more time," she said. "We've got to make a decision. You know what I think, but it's your call. I got you into this and I'll do whatever you want."

Erin slowed, finally stopping behind one of the few tables in the room that hadn't been overturned. Running was still the smart move, but was it futile? His picture was probably plastered across every television screen on the planet.

He took a deep breath and let it out slowly. "I'm scared, Jenna. I hate to admit it, but I am. What'll happen to us if we turn ourselves in or we get caught? There won't be any lawyers. Or rights. Terrorists don't get those things. Terrorists just disappear."

"So you're saying we should run?"

He shook his head. "A few hours ago, I would have said yes. But now . . ."

"What?"

"This lab is set up for research, Jen. Not production. And Teague's a nut, not an idiot. He's not finished. He's still got something up his sleeve, and this place was the key to it."

"Then let's call the government."

"If we call the government, we either have to do it from the road or turn ourselves in. Either way — we're out of the picture. Think about it, Jen. If the government was smart, who would they call to figure out what was going on here?"

He could see that she knew what he was driving at but was reluctant to respond.

"Go ahead, Jen. You know I'm right. Say it."

"Fine. If they could have anybody, they'd call us."

25

Michael Teague turned in his seat to watch Jonas slip in through the van's rear door and kneel amongst the equipment they'd managed to salvage during their hasty abandonment of the research facility. The most important piece — a large stainless steel thermos full of their newly modified bacteria — was wedged between the front seats. The product of so much money, so much sacrifice, he wanted to keep it within reach.

Jonas squinted into a dusty window and examined the dark, swollen cut on his forehead in the reflection.

"Why are you with us?" Teague asked. "Not for your expertise in genetic engineering. Not because you have the money to finance any of this or the vision to keep it going. You're here because Udo told me you could handle situations like this — that you could deal with two unarmed PhDs, one of whom is a goddamn woman."

"Michael, be calm," Udo pleaded as his brother continued to examine his wound. "We've perfected the bacteria and cleaned out the warehouse. We had no use for it anymore."

"That warehouse isn't clean," Teague said as Udo slowed the van to stay at exactly the speed limit. "It would have taken days to sterilize it."

"You should have burned it," Jonas said from the back.

"You seem bent on attracting attention to us," Teague shot back. "If it —"

"It doesn't matter!" Udo shouted. "Erin is a wanted man and Jenna can't afford to expose herself. They'll likely run. And if they don't — if they do try to understand what we were doing there and they succeed — what will that produce? Nothing. It's too late."

"They won't run," Teague said. "And eventually they'll tell the government who we are."

"Jenna should never have left that boat alive," Jonas said. "There was no reason for it. No reason to risk this happening."

Teague spun in his seat and glared at him for a moment, but there was no real point to it. For the time being at least, Jonas was necessary. They had thousands of miles to drive, fuel availability was disintegrating, and the public's reaction was becoming increasingly hysterical. Carjackings and the siphoning of gas tanks — sometimes forcibly — were becoming commonplace. Without someone of Jonas's temperament to deflect problems, their van and its huge auxiliary fuel tank would be a tempting prize.

"If we take shifts driving, how long to get there?" Teague asked.

No response.

"Udo?"

The German redoubled his concentration on the nearly empty road, refusing to look at him. "We weren't expecting to have to leave on such short notice, Michael."

"What does that have to do with anything?"

"The van's tank isn't entirely full. I'd planned to have Jonas begin the process of filling it when he returned. There was still plenty of time . . ."

Teague blinked, his mind taking a moment to process what he was hearing. "Are you saying we're going to have to stop to get gas?"

"Right now, we have enough for about seven hundred miles, but —"

"Do you have any idea how long that could delay us?" Teague shouted. "The gas-rationing program is going into effect in a few days. We could be on the road for weeks — completely exposed."

"I don't believe it will be that long. We can use —"

"You don't believe? I don't give a shit what you believe!"

"There's no point in insulting me or Jonas, Michael. The situation is as it is."

Teague slammed his hand into the dash and turned away, staring out the window and trying to calm down enough to think.

In the face of the massive technological barriers to their plan's success and the logistical complexity of delivering the first version of their bacteria, he'd been forced to leave many of the mundane details to Jonas and Udo. As the situation continued to disintegrate and the American people became more desperate, though, it was increasingly clear that there were no mundane details. Every error was potentially fatal.

No. Udo was right. It didn't matter. The bacteria were finally a success and they'd been preparing to leave Texas for their breeding facility anyway. Getting to Canada would be difficult without a full complement of fuel, but not as difficult as everything he had accomplished so far. They would get there. And he would finish what he had started.

26

The Kroger lot was mostly empty, but Jenna still parked well away from the entrance. For some reason it felt safer.

"I'm going to run in and get some supplies. Do you want to come with me?"

Erin shook his head. "The post office is just around the corner. I'll go get in line. Come pick me up when you're finished. The sooner we get out of town, the better."

He reached for the door handle, but she grabbed his arm, trying to think of something to say — something that would make him understand everything that had happened to her since she had left. Instead, she found herself leaning in to kiss him.

He turned away but didn't get out.

"I'm sorry," she said. "Don't know what —"

"Forget it," he said, and shoved the door open with his shoulder. She watched him cross the parking lot and then the nearly empty street, finally closing her eyes when he disappeared around the corner.

"Stupid!" she said aloud, pounding the back of her head into the seat. What was she thinking? That with everything she'd put him through — and was still putting him through — he'd just jump back into bed with her? She wasn't thinking. That was the problem. Everything was spinning out of control, but instead of doing something about it, she was just sitting there getting dizzier and dizzier.

Jenna got out of the car and slammed the door, feeling the heat of the sun burn through her shirt as she stalked toward the store. The smart move was to just keep walking — he was better off without her. In an hour, it could all be over. She could be sitting in the nearest FBI office, signing an affidavit saying he wasn't involved.

But what good would that really do? Erin was right — the government wasn't going to take her word for it, particularly now that every detail of his life was being examined with microscopic intensity on every news show in the world. They'd throw him in the same dungeon she ended up in and send a bunch of mediocre scientists picked for their political reliability to figure things out. The bottom line was that, at least for now, Erin was stuck with her.

She passed through the automatic doors, but didn't feel the sudden chill she'd come to expect. The price of electricity had jumped, too, as the oil-intensive process of mining and transporting coal sky-rocketed. Cooling commercial buildings to arctic temperatures was obviously too expensive now.

But that was the least of it. She wandered around the store looking at partially empty shelves and the hastily changed prices. Private industry was adapting with typically cold-hearted efficiency. The grocery business was quickly abandoning its inefficient centralized distribution system and bringing in local seasonal products to minimize transportation costs. Fruits and vegetables from overseas were either nonexistent or exorbitantly priced. Even the cost of bananas from Florida had more than doubled. On the other hand, Texas beef was plentiful and cheap, as were the locally grown sweet potatoes and apples that were overflowing into empty bins that had once held imports.

According to yesterday's *New York Times,* Maine was glutted with lobster and it was selling for less than half the cost of hamburger. Who would have thought there would be a day when people couldn't afford a Big Mac and would have to settle with lobster Newburg?

"Thanks, dude," Erin said as a heavyset postal employee helped him heft the last box onto the ones already stacked on the dolly.

"That's all of them," the man said, wiping the sweat from his forehead and stepping back so that Erin could wheel the precarious stack of microscopes, incubators, and other research equipment through the door.

So far, so good. The baseball hat and glasses seemed to be enough to keep people from equating him with the photos they saw on television, and now all he had to do was figure out how to get these boxes into the back of Jonas's Toyota. He should have asked Jenna to get some rope to tie a few things to the top, but he was still having a hard time thinking clearly when she was around — partially because of the effort it was taking to hold onto his anger and partially because of the fear of what might replace it if he lost his grip.

By the time he managed to maneuver through the second set of glass doors, he was thinking about the kiss again. Or, more precisely, the attempted kiss. What had it meant? Anything? And how did he feel about it? The answer to that was typically complicated. His emotions were stacked like the boxes he was pulling — layer after conflicting layer.

"That's a lot of stuff you've got there."

He slowed and then finally stopped, but couldn't bring himself to look behind him at the source of the voice. "I don't suppose you'd believe me if I said this isn't what it looks like."

Mark Beamon strode alongside him, taking a deep drag on his cigarette and then blowing the smoke in Erin's direction. "Never heard that one before."

His eyes were nearly invisible in the shade provided by a wide-brimmed straw golf hat. Combined with the sweat-stained Polo shirt, wrinkled khakis, and Birkenstocks, the overall impression was "slow."

Erin took a step back and eyed a fence that Beamon wouldn't be able to get over without the assistance of a crane, but a quick look around put an end to any plan to run. The woman pushing a baby stroller a few feet away had a subtle wire running from her ear, as did a Mexican-looking guy working on the post office's sparse landscaping. A couple of heavily tattooed bikers at the end of the sidewalk were a little less obvious, but they were not paying attention with an intensity that was almost certainly calculated.

In the end, though, it was the man who'd helped load the boxes who finally clamped the handcuffs on him while Beamon watched from a thin strip of shade he'd found next to the building.

"I've really been looking forward to talking to you," he said, throwing an arm around Erin's shoulders and leading him toward a van parked along the curb just as Jenna eased into the lot. Erin shook his head subtly and she kept going, looping back to the street and disappearing down it. He was surprised at the relief he felt when she was gone.

"Every time I think I've got this thing figured out, I get another piece of the puzzle that doesn't fit." He lowered the volume of his voice. "For a while, as you get older, experience makes up for the loss of brain cells. I've been starting to wonder if I've crossed the line — if ten years ago, I wouldn't have wrapped this thing up a week ago."

The back of the van was windowless and probably over a hundred degrees, which in itself wasn't that bad, but combined with the gentle rocking and adrenaline, Erin was feeling increasingly nauseous.

Beamon pulled a cigarette from a nearly empty pack and put it between his lips.

"Would you mind not smoking, please?"

He lit it with a silver lighter that he snapped shut loudly. "My fiancée thinks I quit. The more miles there are between me and her, though, the less I can help myself. Don't get me wrong — I don't really have any illusions that I'm fooling her. You know how women are."

Erin scooted back along the van's floor, trying to get as far away as he could from the tendrils of smoke working their way toward him.

"And speaking of women," Beamon said. "How's your old girlfriend? What was her name? Jenna?"

Erin managed not to react, but then realized that no reaction at all was probably the most suspicious response he could have come up with. "What are you talking about?"

"All those climbing equipment mailing lists you were gathering up," Beamon said. "Intriguing. You know, I got hold of the rest of them and had my people sift through all the names. You know what I found?"

Erin didn't answer.

"Not interested? Not even a little bit?

That's okay, I'll tell you anyway. I found a very compelling woman living outside Bozeman, Montana. Jennifer Baker. Actually, I didn't find her — she was long gone by the time we got there. She has investments totaling about two million dollars that even my army of CPAs can't trace back to their source. She's got a fake social security number, no friends, no family, no medical or work history. Then, lo and behold, we start seeing charges on her credit card. Medical equipment, no less." Beamon thumbed behind him at one of Erin's boxes. "The kind you use to study bacteria."

"What's that got to do with me?" he said, knowing how stupid it sounded even before it came out of his mouth.

Beamon scooted toward him and pulled a small photo from his pocket. "It's from her driver's license. Not a great picture and obviously the hair's different, but I'd say that the reports of Jenna Kalin's death were a little premature."

Once again Erin made the mistake of not reacting and this time the smirk on Beamon's face made it clear that it was too late to backpedal.

"I'm thinking that means Michael Teague and the Metzger brothers are slinking around somewhere, too," he said, shoving the picture into his pocket and sliding back against the wall of the van.

"I guess you've got it all figured out, then don't you?"

"Come on, Erin. Look what's happening out there. Hell, look what's happening to *you*. I think it's time you told your story."

"What's the point? Everybody already knows I'm guilty."

Beamon took another drag on his cigarette. "I finally got around to reading your book. It was very . . . what's the word I'm looking for? Meticulous. I just don't understand how we got here. What did you hope to accomplish with all this? Come on . . . you people love going on and on about this crap, right? So go ahead. Make your case."

"I thought I had the right to remain silent."

"It'd be a mistake to believe that, Erin. You've managed to piss off all the wrong people. Actually, you've managed to piss off just about everyone." He pointed toward the doors at the back of the van. "Hell, if we stopped right now and I told the people on the street who you are, they'd tear you apart."

"Go ahead."

Beamon sighed quietly, but didn't press further. He just sat there and went through the rest of his cigarettes, ignoring his captive's profuse sweating and death-like pallor. When the van finally stopped and the doors were thrown open, Erin would have fallen out if two of Beamon's men hadn't been there to grab him and drag him toward the small jet parked in front of them.

The woman who had been pushing the baby stroller and the postman were just ahead, but they froze when a man appeared in the doorway of the plane. Beamon, looking perplexed, stopped dialing his phone.

"Who the hell are you?" he said.

The man jumped down to the tarmac, smiling condescendingly. He was wearing a gray suit — jacket and all — but wasn't perspiring.

"My name's not important, Mr. Beamon. I work for the CIA. And we're here to take custody of our prisoner." He reached into his jacket, prompting the postman to put a hand on his gun.

"Whoa!" Beamon said. "Everybody stay calm, okay?"

Erin tried to focus, but felt strangely detached as he watched the postman's hand move slowly back to his side.

"Look, I don't want to be rude," Beamon said as the man fished a piece of paper from his jacket and held it out. "But I don't really give a shit who you work for. Now get away from my plane."

"Read it," the man said, shoving the document into Beamon's chest as the jet's engines began to spin up. Erin peered over his shoulder, skipping the body of the letter and going straight to the signature line. Gerald Dunn. The president of the United States.

27

Mark Beamon shoved the door open and stomped across the office. "What the fuck's going on, Jack?"

"Calm down," Reynolds said, rising from behind his desk. "I —"

"Calm down? *Calm down?* You send the CIA to take my only decent suspect *and* my only way home and you want me to calm down?"

"Mark, you —"

"Do you have any idea how hard it is to get across the country right now? I called you about a hundred times, but apparently now that I've handed over the guy you think is guilty, I don't rate a call back. If the head of security at United wasn't an old friend of mine, I'd still be in Texas. And even with his help, I still spent the last two days and nights sitting in airports."

"Mark —"

"Then, when I finally do get back, I find

CIA guys all over my office."

"Are you through?" Reynolds said. "Can I talk now?"

Beamon had an overwhelming urge to throw something, but when he looked around, there was nothing valuable or breakable enough to bother with.

"You brought this on yourself, Mark. After overlooking all the leaks, now we find out that someone working for you is the one responsible, for Christ's sake —"

"You're the one who insisted I use Erin Neal, Jack. If you think real hard, you'd remember that I —"

Reynolds held up his hand. "I'm not going to sit here and play the blame game with you, Mark. All I'm saying is that I don't see how it could surprise you that the president wanted the CIA to get involved."

Beamon spun and walked as far from Reynolds as the office would allow, finally pressing his back to a wall and folding his arms across his chest. It was exactly what he'd known would happen from the very start — the politicians would panic and start thinking they knew better than him and the hundreds of trained investigators working for him. The question was what to do about it.

Since neither Reynolds nor the CIA had

so much as mentioned Jenna Kalin's name, Beamon assumed that the few people he'd told about her were keeping their mouths shut. He'd left her Visa and ATM cards alone and they were being monitored, but she obviously knew it. She bought what she needed and got the hell out before his people could react. And trying to track her phone had produced similar dismal results — she only turned it on briefly, probably to check messages, and always right as her Visa charge was going through. Not a stupid woman by a long shot.

"This is a huge mistake, Jack. These CIA guys aren't investigators. They —"

"You haven't set the bar very high, though, have you, Mark?"

"No one seems to remember that I figured out what was happening and got Erin Neal in a matter of three weeks."

"Not good enough, Mark. Not even close," Reynolds said. "Open your eyes, for Christ's sake. This country — the entire world — is starting to come apart at the seams. Businesses are closing their doors left and right, unemployment's skyrocketing, imports and exports that we're completely reliant on are disappearing, the markets are panicking. And the only thing everyone agrees on is that we're going to be hit the hardest because we're the most energy-intensive economy in the world. We could go from being the most powerful country on the planet to being one of the weakest in a matter of a few months."

"What's your point?"

"What's my point? What's my *point?* Tomorrow the president is going on the air to explain the coupon system we've come up with for gas rationing so that we can keep critical services going. And as far as we can tell, this isn't a short-term measure. It's permanent. How do you think that's going to go over with the American people?"

"What the fuck do I care, Jack? I'm not a goddamn politician. What I'm telling you is that you're making a mistake. The CIA's had two days. What have they given you?"

Reynolds didn't answer.

"I take that to mean 'nothing.'"

If there was anything he'd learned about Erin Neal, it was that he was one tough son of a bitch and that he'd do anything to protect Jenna Kalin. He needed to be handled with finesse that the CIA just didn't have.

Beamon took a deep breath, realizing that he wasn't going to win by escalating this confrontation. "Look, Jack, this is more complicated than it looks, and it's not going to respond to a bigger hammer. Is Erin Neal involved? Hell, yes. Did he do it? I'm not so sure."

"Are you holding out on us, Mark? Is there something you know that we don't? Because if I find out there is, I will personally crucify you."

Beamon ignored the threat — he'd taken worse from far more powerful people. "Let me talk to him, Jack."

Reynolds shook his head. "It's out of my hands."

"You've got —"

"I worked it out that you can stay involved in the investigation," Reynolds interrupted. "But you'll have no management authority. You'll answer to the Agency. Otherwise, you're out."

28

The noise was soft enough that at first Jenna thought she had imagined it. Still, she pulled the pistol from her lab apron and padded to the door. Her heart was pounding in her ears as she twisted the knob and jumped out into the blazing sunlight, gun shaking in front of her.

But Jonas wasn't standing there with the gleaming knife and dead smile she had expected. And there was no Homeland Security SWAT team slinking around in desert camo aiming machine guns at her. Just the hot, dusty wind.

Next time, though, maybe it would be different.

She was about to retreat back into the warehouse, but instead wandered across the cracked soil and sat down on a boulder.

She had so many things to worry about that government death squads and psychotic Germans barely broke the top five. Erin had been gone for more than three days without a word. The news channels were airing increasingly detailed descriptions of his life that now included brief mentions of her as his former girlfriend, but nothing about him being captured. He'd just disappeared.

And he wasn't the only one. The *New York Times* had broken a story about other environmentalists — many of whom she knew — who had been picked up by Homeland Security and were still missing. Other than the families, though, no one seemed to care. The American people were suffering more and more each day and weren't of a mind to block paths that might alleviate that suffering.

Resentment toward the Europeans and Asians, who were faring better because they consumed less energy than Americans, was growing but continued to be overshadowed by animosity aimed at Canada. The media was mostly at fault — missing no opportunity to juxtapose images of Toronto and Montreal's car-choked streets with the sparsely populated streets of America's cities, as well as creating increasingly elaborate graphs to depict the skyrocketing profits being generated from Canadian oil.

The stock market continued to tumble and unemployment continued to rise as it became clear that the U.S. economy had been operating at the very edge of collapse for years — desperately reliant on cheap energy and ever-increasing debt to stay one step ahead of disaster. The bread lines of the depression that had seemed so distant months ago were becoming a very real possibility.

Because of her.

She went back inside and sat down behind a microscope purchased at a children's hobby store, wondering again what she should do.

The guilt she felt about not turning herself in had been bad enough without having to wonder what had happened to Erin and the other environmentalists, but now it was becoming unbearable. Why hadn't the cops been there when she'd jumped through that door? The obvious answer was that Erin hadn't told them where she was. But why? Did he think the government would just throw them both in a hole somewhere and not believe a word they said? Was he doing it out of some kind of wildly misguided loyalty? Or worse, out of love? That would be the most awful thing she'd ever heard. For everything she'd done to him — everything she'd done to the world — she deserved whatever fate the government came up with. But so far, other people were paying the price.

The problem was that she didn't know his reasons and she couldn't decide whether to try second-guessing him. He had implied that the man leading the investigation — the apparently camera-shy Mark Beamon — was a fairly reasonable guy. Erin could tell him where she was whenever he wanted. So, for the time being at least, she was stuck.

Jenna picked up a sabotaged computer and tossed it through the door onto the teetering pile of debris she'd cleared from the warehouse. The lab was more or less in order again, with all the furniture upright and covered with improvised equipment. She assumed that the government had found Erin by watching medical equipment sellers, leaving her no choice but to provision the lab with hobby microscopes, petri dishes adapted from Wal-Mart containers, and incubators made out of toaster ovens. Even that had been a risky operation, though. Her credit card was undoubtedly being monitored and she assumed that the local police had a description of her and Jonas's car from the altercation at the airport.

Not that she would have to worry about either of those problems for much longer.

When it had become clear that the fuel shortage was going to persist, companies began passing their higher energy costs through to their customers — creating the first double-digit inflation in years and running her credit card up faster than she'd anticipated. Combine that with the fact that she was nearly out of gas and not exactly in a position to go pick up her ration card, it wouldn't be long before she was reduced to shoplifting and getting away on foot.

She walked over to one of her homemade incubators and peered inside. Despite a valiant effort, Udo hadn't been able to completely sterilize the lab before abandoning it. She'd found a bacteria sample in a small puddle of oil hidden by an overturned table. It had appeared dead at first, but she'd babied it, fed it, and watched over it. Now it was growing. Fast.

29

The darkness continued to amplify Erin Neal's rage, fanning it to a point where nearly everything else was almost completely swallowed. Even the pain.

He'd been blindfolded since he'd been forced onto the jet that had brought him to wherever he was now. How long ago was that? Days? Weeks? Without eyes, there was no way to see the light come and go, to measure the time he'd spent lying naked in a cold concrete cell or contorted into positions meant to break him. For the last hour, or two, or ten, he'd been bent over what felt like a metal railing, his left hand and right ankle handcuffed together at the bottom. A flow of icy water — somewhere between an energetic drip and a light stream — was falling from the ceiling, and no matter how creatively he used his limited maneuvering room, he couldn't get away from it or bring it to his cracked lips.

He yanked violently on his handcuffs for what must have been the thousandth time, but the effort was barely enough to even send a jolt of pain up his arm anymore. He was so tired. The fury that he'd spent so much time trying to control was about all that was keeping him going now. But even that was weakening.

He thought about Jenna, and, for one of the few times in his life, wished he could believe in God. If he did, he'd pray that she had just kept on driving — that she had crossed into Mexico and was on her way somewhere that no one would ever find her. His only regret was that he would never get a chance to give her the swift kick in the ass she had coming.

He didn't hear anything — he never did — but suddenly someone grabbed his hair and pulled his head back, erasing the imperceptible smile that thoughts of Jenna still had the power to create. There was no way to know how many of them there were — enough to make fighting pointless as the handcuff on his ankle was released and he was rammed face-first into the deep puddle he'd been standing in. The blood rushed from his head, making the darkness he'd been living in swirl sickeningly. He managed a weak, frustrated scream as he felt himself being dragged across the concrete, but that was all.

"Wake up!"

Erin jerked his face away from the smelling salts and opened his eyes, squinting against the light. It took a moment to focus, but he finally recognized the man sitting in front of him as the one who had taken him from Mark Beamon.

"Well, congratulations, Erin. You've made it through your first day. Not bad for a science geek."

Erin felt the breath catch in his chest. One day? It had only been a day? How —

He closed his eyes for a moment, forcing himself to calm down. Of course, the man was lying.

"One day? Already?" Erin said, testing the handcuffs securing him to a chair held to the floor by heavy bolts. "The battery in my watch must be dead."

"Funny," the man said, flashing a smile that suggested an addiction to tooth whitener. He had the buzz cut and clipped, efficient sentences of a military man, but there was a pale softness to him that made it all an obvious lie. His unimaginatively casual clothes seemed impossibly crisp next to Erin's battered, naked body — the impression of clean, dry warmth undoubtedly intended.

"Word is you're not stupid," the man said. "So you know what we want. We want to know what reserves you've hit, who was involved, and how to stop the progression of the bacteria. And make no mistake — you're going to tell us. Everyone does. It's just a question of how long."

Erin didn't answer. He wasn't so arrogant to believe that he wouldn't eventually succumb to the lack of sleep, the pain, the constant cold and hunger. How long before they were able to confuse him? To get him to say something he shouldn't?

It was possible that they already knew about Jenna and — to disorient him — weren't saying anything, but it was just as possible that they didn't and the difference between her getting away and getting gang raped in the cell next to him was how long he could hold out.

"What would it hurt to give us a name, Erin? The damage is done, right? You were too smart for us. What can we do now?"

Erin let out a short laugh, a string of blood-tinted spit extending slowly from his lip.

"Did I miss something funny?"

"You're already ramping-up production in

Canada's tar sands — one of the most environmentally disgusting processes ever dreamed up. And you've taken all the environmental controls off the coal industry. What are you so afraid of? A hundred years from now, your grandkids will be driving their SUVs through the smog and wondering what the sky looks like. Congratulations."

The man nodded slowly, obviously recalculating his approach. "Maybe they will. But what about the people living now, Erin? What have you done to them? Like you say, no one in the U.S. is going to starve over this. But what about Congo?"

"So if I tell you what you want to know, you're going to take the oil that's left and give it to the poor? Your goons have a lot more work to do before I'll buy that one."

"They have all the time in the world, Erin, and only you to focus on because we don't have anyone else. What about the other people involved? Maybe they're really the ones responsible and not you. Maybe you just got caught up in all this. But we have no way of knowing because you won't help us find them. I admire your sense of loyalty, Erin, but why should you suffer when they're sitting on a beach somewhere drinking cocktails? Do you think they'd do it for you?"

It was impossible not to think of Michael Teague and the fact that staying quiet about Jenna was keeping that officious little prick safe, too. On the other hand, every hour that went by made it harder not to start rooting for him. Fuck this guy and fuck the world.

The man reached into a bag on the floor and Erin tensed, but when his hand reappeared it held a laptop and not the pliers and scalpels he'd expected.

"Recognize it, Erin? It's yours."

Obviously they'd discovered that his password was a little harder to guess than his birthday.

"Why don't you help us get into this, Erin? As an act of good faith. And I'll return that good faith with a blanket, a mattress, and a hot meal. Help us stop this and maybe all that work in the tar sands, all that coal smoke, and all those dead African children won't be necessary."

"There's nothing in there that will help you," he said truthfully. "And when you find that out, where will that leave me and my new mattress? I don't think so."

"If there's nothing in here, then what do you have to lose? Why not take a chance and let me prove to you that my word is good?"

Erin looked directly into the man's well-groomed face. "Because of what *might* be in there. That hard drive could have everything you need to stop this and the name of every person involved. All right there less than a foot away from you. That's my little piece of revenge."

The man jumped from his chair and slammed a fist into the side of Erin's head. "Do you think this is a fucking game? Do you have any idea what we do to terrorists? No, actually, you don't. Those pictures you saw on TV from Abu Ghraib? That's nothing!"

Behind him a door opened and two men in military uniforms came in carrying a crank-driven generator with two wires leading from it. Erin wasn't paying much attention, though, instead focusing on the crotch of the man in front of him. It was hovering tantalizingly close and, though Erin's hands were hopelessly secured to the chair, his feet were free.

"Do you hear me, Erin? You won't fucking survive finding out what —"

He brought his foot up between the man's legs with every ounce of strength he had left, imaging that he could feel the testicles spectacularly and permanently exploding into useless blobs of flesh that would soon turn gangrenous.

His tormentor sank slowly to the floor as the two soldiers dove at Erin, one grabbing his legs while the other closed an arm around his throat. He barely noticed though, still fixated on the man taking shallow, labored breaths on the floor in front of him. It was an image that would sustain him for another week. Maybe more if he was lucky.

30

Nothing tangible had changed in the office, but still the atmosphere was almost completely unrecognizable. As Beamon started across the busy room, no one would look him fully in the eye — instead, his people subtly adjusted their trajectories away from him, or, if that failed, mumbled polite greetings before rushing off. He'd experienced the same thing before, of course, and always found it a little like being a ghost: invisible most of the time, but if he yelled "boo," about half the room's occupants would have heart attacks.

That awkward environment made the man threading his way through the crowd even more obvious. Not only did he seem to be able to see Beamon, but he appeared completely unafraid.

He couldn't have been more than thirty-five — a sharp-looking kid who made a production of glaring at the expensive watch on his wrist. Whether that was to indicate how busy he was or to suggest that Beamon was tardy for his walk of shame was unclear.

"Bob Oberman wants to see you."

"And where exactly would I find him?"

He pointed to the office that, until yesterday, Beamon had occupied and then examined his watch again. Not a Rolex — something more subtle. Maybe Cartier.

"Right away," he prompted.

Beamon nodded noncommittally and floated past the people who used to work for him, stopping briefly in front of a stack of boxes carelessly stuffed with his personal effects, before peeking into his former office.

He had to admit that it looked a lot better. Oberman must have had all his things moved over from Langley by jet helicopter. The furniture was well-polished and artfully arranged to maximize the small space. Every detail had been carefully attended to, right down to the wall of richly framed photos depicting him with various politicians and sports figures. Busy, busy.

The man himself, though, was nowhere to be found, so Beamon tracked down the box containing his coffee mug and headed for the break room. He'd barely managed to find the sugar when Terry Hirst came in and closed the door behind him.

"What the hell's going on, Mark?"

"I'm pretty much out, Terry. You aren't, though. This is about me."

"What are we going to do about it?"

Beamon shrugged. "Nothing."

"Look, I know you've had your differences with the Agency, but there *are* a lot of good people over there."

"The president seems to agree."

"Yeah, but the problem is that Bob Oberman isn't one of them. He doesn't know the first thing about investigations — he's a politician. And, frankly, kind of an asshole."

"Not my problem anymore, Terry."

"Then why are you here?"

It was a good question. To get his stuff? No, he could have just sent for it. Because he preferred his humiliations to be as public as possible?

"Did you get anything out of Jenna Kalin's house in Bozeman?" Beamon asked, finally.

Hirst looked relieved at his display of interest, no matter how mild. "Michael Teague's and the Metzger brothers' fingerprints. We also know that they flew in and out of a private airport near there. Jonas ended up in Tucson and we found his prints in Erin Neal's house. The blood in the hallway we think was Jenna's, the blood in the kitchen was definitely Neal's."

"Yeah? A falling out of former conspirators?"

"It gets better," Hirst said. "Apparently, there was a strange scene when Neal and Kalin got to the parking lot of the airport in Texas. They had a third man with them, but he ran off."

"A third man?"

"Positive ID from the witnesses. Jonas Metzger."

"And you say he ran off?"

"It seems that he attacked Neal and Jenna Kalin intervened by pulling a gun."

Beamon continued to stir his coffee absently. This wasn't any of his business. He should just pick up his boxes and get the hell out of here. And he would. In just a few minutes.

"What then?"

"They took off in a silver Toyota."

"Where to?"

"Not a clue. And nobody got a plate number."

"What about the APB?"

"Nothing. We sent descriptions of Teague and the Metzger brothers, saying they're wanted for something unrelated, but honestly the cops have their hands full right now and they're reducing their patrol miles to conserve fuel."

Beamon nodded silently.

"What now, Mark?"

He looked into Hirst's expectant face. "Look, Terry, the idea of handing Jenna Kalin and everything else over to Oberman is killing me. But this isn't a game. Are you reading the paper? The world's economy is falling apart, the Middle East is set to implode, and everyone seems to think that's just the beginning. I saw some guy on TV yesterday saying we're going to lead the world into a depression that makes the thirties look cushy. Unless someone decides to start World War Three first."

"You're making my point for me, Mark. We can't just walk away and leave Oberman to spin his wheels and kiss the president's ass. We have to —"

The door was thrown open and the same thirty-something who'd spoken to him earlier looked around the room suspiciously. "I thought I was clear that you were to wait in Bob's office until he has time for you."

31

Jenna Kalin bolted awake and grabbed for the gun next to the sleeping bag she'd wrapped herself in. The only light in the building was provided by the narrow crack beneath the door, and it cast everything into deep shadow, twisting the outlines of the lab equipment around her into shapes that threatened to come to life and attack.

She released the gun and stared into the sliver of light, looking for movement that might indicate someone outside. It remained steady and her breathing slowly returned to normal. Just like it did every morning.

She threw off the sleeping bag and picked her way through the semidarkness to the room at the back. A few blind jabs at the remote and the surviving television set illuminated the room.

It was almost always the same few stories now: The government had captured Erin

Neal, the "terrorist" behind the bacteria, and was making "significant progress" in unraveling his network. The generally peaceful demonstrations that had been going on in front of the Canadian embassy had finally turned violent and yesterday the police had used tear gas to disperse the crowd. The National Guard had posted people at gas stations to stop glutting — the latest slang word for filling your tank with more gas than your ration card allowed. The practice, now under control, had been starving critical vehicles, like fire engines and police cars.

Not that fuel availability had much of an effect on her now that her primary mode of transportation was the wildly overpriced bicycle and trailer she'd managed to buy. It wasn't the most convenient replacement for Jonas's car, but it was more practical than running around trying to buy black-market fuel in a vehicle that the police were probably looking for.

She flipped on the lights and wandered through the lab looking dejectedly at the makeshift equipment she'd been wasting her time with. Her improvised incubators had produced plenty of bacteria to work with, but so far she hadn't found a significant change in the way it behaved. It ate hydrocarbons and multiplied faster than she'd designed, but that was a relatively minor change that would be easy to bring about with selective breeding. Maybe she was being paranoid and this was nothing more than a production facility to supply bacteria for Teague's psychotic plans.

No, that couldn't be true. The facility was clearly not set up for production — it had been a platform for research. But research into what?

She opened the door to the refrigerator and stared at the half-empty containers of cottage cheese and lemonade. She'd put off the twenty-five-mile bike ride into town as long as she could. Although the idea of pedaling endlessly through the heat and using her credit card when her getaway vehicle had a top speed of fifteen miles an hour wasn't particularly appealing, the alternative was starvation.

Jenna pulled on a pair of shorts, filled a couple of water bottles, and swallowed the rest of the cottage cheese as she pushed through the door and into the sunlight.

The stack of debris leaning against the outside wall had continued to grow as she tossed the remnants of her finished experiments out into the elements to die. She stopped for a moment to balance the empty cheese container on top of a Tupperware dish full of hardened reddish sludge and thought of Erin.

She needed him back. Not only for his brilliance, but so that she could think clearly again. The not knowing was killing her, making it impossible to concentrate on anything but elaborate fantasies about the horrible things that could have happened to him.

But pretty soon it would be over. There were only a few more days' worth of tests she could do with her Wal-Mart lab. Hopefully, she'd hear from him, but if not, it would be time to start making her own decisions. To take responsibility.

She started toward the bicycle she'd left leaning against a boulder, mentally calculating her day. If she averaged ten miles an hour she'd be back in a little more than five hours — leaving her plenty of time to get some work done. Assuming she wasn't so tired she just passed out in her sleeping bag.

When Jenna got to within a few feet of the bike, she started to slow, her eyes fixed on the reddish reflection of the sun off the chain. She knelt, finding it difficult to breathe as she ran a hand across the hardened gunk that had clogged her gears.

A glance over her shoulder confirmed that the containers full of dried bacteria were more than forty feet away and burning beneath the full force of the Texas sun.

The bacteria weren't dead. They were air-borne.

32

"At least you work for the government and I work for a hospital. A lot of other people are just out of work," Carrie said, her voice muffled by her fidgeting daughter, who was too big to be sitting on her lap in small car.

"Em, sit still for God's sake!"

Beamon glanced in the rearview mirror at the four girls in the backseat and pointed at a minivan so crowded that the windows had to be open for everyone to fit inside. "Could be worse."

"Goloco-dot-org," Emory said.

"What?"

She was momentarily distracted by an extraordinarily fat couple coasting down the road on a tandem bicycle, so one of her friends spoke up. "It's a Web site where you can find people to carpool with, Mr. Beamon. You put in, like, your address and the address you're going to and what time and everything. You can even put in what kind of music you like. Then it hooks you up with someone going your way."

Beamon smiled. Were young people really limitless in their adaptability or did they just seem that way to him because he'd become such an old dog? He knew a lot of his friends worried about a world run by the next generation, but it seemed unlikely that they would do worse.

Why couldn't his genius have been in something positive like computers? The Google guys had made themselves billionaires by sitting around dreaming up ideas that made people's lives better, while he'd made himself a thousand-aire getting shot at and stabbed in the back.

"Why didn't you think of that, Em?"

"What?"

"Goloco-dot-org."

"Because I'm nine."

"I don't want to hear excuses."

When his cell phone rang for the fourth time in the half hour they'd been in the car, he reached into his pocket and turned it off.

"What did you just do?" Carrie said.

"Huh?"

"You just turned off your cell without even looking at who was calling."

He shrugged. "I've hardly seen you at all

over the past few weeks and I thought it would be nice to have a couple minutes without the phone."

Quiet snickers and whispers were audible from the backseat as Carrie peered around her daughter's shoulder. "That's nice. Thank you." It came out more like a question.

He'd finally made his decision just after three in the morning, though it hadn't been one of those confident, peaceful decisions that had him nodding off a few seconds later. The bottom line was that although it was certain Bob Oberman wasn't the guy to run this investigation, it was just as certain that trying to do an end-run around the government was going to turn into a disaster for him and the people still loyal to him. So he was on his way to see Jack Reynolds with a briefcase containing everything he knew. And then he was going to go back to his quiet little office at Homeland Security and watch the world fall apart.

Beamon pulled off the highway and negotiated the quiet streets as Carrie did the best she could to twist around in her seat. "Debbie, your mom's picking all of you up after school, right?"

"Yes, Ms. Johnstone."

"And, Em, you're staying over there?"

"Uh huh."

"Okay. You be good and help clean up the dishes after dinner. I'll be home around nine."

"Why so late?" Beamon asked.

"The hospital's changed over to longer shifts for everyone — the idea being fewer shifts means less driving. I —" She fell silent for a moment. "Oh, for God's sake . . ."

"What?"

She thumbed behind her and Beamon glanced at the flashing lights in the mirror.

The snickers from the back increased in volume as he eased to the side of the road and rolled down the window.

"Shhhhh," Carrie said as the two policemen approached on opposite sides of the vehicle. She wouldn't roll down her window or even look at them, though. Her hippie years at Berkeley had left her with a jaundiced view of law enforcement. Beamon often included.

"Sir, could you step out of the car, please?"

"Come on," Beamon said. "I know we shouldn't have two people in the front seat, but with everything that's going on, couldn't you cut us some slack?"

The cop, who was probably in his early thirties, appeared overly nervous about what was a fairly common infraction these days. "Sir, I'm asking you to step out of the car."

Beamon did as he was told, sighing quietly and listening to the snickering turn to strangled laughter as the girls slapped hands over each others' mouths.

"Please turn around and face the car."

"Are you kidding me?" Beamon said, pointing to an SUV that looked as if it had an entire high school basketball team in it.

"Turn around," the cop repeated. He looked reluctant, but his hand moved a little closer to his gun.

Beamon frowned and put his hands on the car, looking into the face of the even younger man standing by Carrie's window. He looked downright horrified.

Beamon wasn't frisked; instead, the cop went straight for the pistol beneath his suit jacket and relieved him of it.

"I can explain that. I'm an —"

"Yes, sir, Mr. Beamon," the other man said. "You spoke at my graduation from the academy. I want you to know how sorry we are about this."

The handcuffs clicked around Beamon's wrists and he was pulled away from the car as the girls pressed their faces against the window. They looked impressed.

Predictably, the passenger door was suddenly thrown open with enough force that the cop standing by it had to jump back to avoid being hit. Carrie shoved Emory off her lap and leapt from the car.

"Ma'am. You need to —"

"Don't ma'am me. What's going on here? Why have you handcuffed him?"

Beamon remained silent. Now they were in for it.

"Please, ma'am —"

"Don't tell me what to do! Look, this is America and we have rights here. I demand to know why you have him in handcuffs."

There was a brief silence before the man answered. "We don't know, ma'am."

"Carrie," Beamon cut in. "It's okay." He nodded toward the cop slowly backing away from his fiancée. "What's your name?"

"Joseph."

"Carrie, give Joseph the briefcase that was down by your feet and we'll talk later, okay? The girls are going to be late for school."

She glared at him for a moment and then reluctantly reached for the briefcase. "Is there someone I can call?"

He actually laughed at that. "I'm pretty sure there isn't."

The White House conference room was populated by the usual suspects, with the unfortunate addition of Bob Oberman from the CIA. He was standing confidently at the head of the table, his smooth patter stuttering perceptibly when Beamon was led in.

"The timeframe we're concentrating on now is around when Erin Neal originally worked for the Saudis."

"That's when you suspect he was turned?" President Dunn said.

"Yes, sir. We believe he converted to Islam when he was remediating a similar infection at a field called the Hawtaw Trend. So, combined with his well-documented environmental beliefs, we have a clear motivation to go along with all the other evidence against him."

"Who was the al Qaeda operative he said he was working with?"

"Ishmael Fedallah."

Beamon smirked as he took an empty chair at the table.

"Do we have anything on him?"

"Not yet, but we're working on it."

"Obviously, you've learned a lot from your interrogation, but have you gotten anything more practical?" Jack Reynolds asked. "Something we could use to strategize our economic response or stop the spread of the bacteria?"

"No, sir. Honestly, I think it's unlikely that

Neal would know exactly what was hit and when — he was there for scientific knowledge and, as you know, terrorist organizations are fanatics for compartmentalization." He glanced at Beamon. "But, as you said, we've made significant progress in the short time we've been running this operation. We already have a name, a motive, and an organization. It's just a matter of time now before we identify the rest of the people involved."

As Oberman fell silent, Beamon focused on the president, who looked understandably worried. The latest announcement from his administration was that the way people paid for energy was going to be restructured. The first units you bought would be extremely cheap and every successive unit would get more expensive. Great for a poor guy living in a six-hundred-square-foot trailer, but Dunn's conservative backers lived in large houses that needed serious heating and cooling.

The president studied the notes he'd scribbled before looking up at Beamon. "Bob tells us that some of your people have refused to contribute to what may be the most important investigation in history, and that you've been maneuvering behind his back. Is that correct?"

"Yes, sir. I suppose it is."

Obviously, it wasn't the expected response and the room fell into a church-like silence that Beamon figured he had better use before he found himself sharing a cell with Erin Neal.

"We — I — was continuing a line of investigation that I'd been pursuing before the CIA took over." He lifted his briefcase onto the table. "I was on my way to give it to Jack when I was . . . diverted."

"Are you insane?" Reynolds said in a tone clearly calculated to make everyone understand that he had had nothing to do with Beamon's actions.

The president held up a hand, silencing what would have undoubtedly been a long and overly theatrical protest.

"Mr. Beamon. In light of your reputation, I'm going to give you an opportunity to explain yourself."

In Beamon's mind, that translated to something like "The CIA hasn't given us anything we can use to rescue the people we count on to vote for us and we're getting desperate."

"The truth is, sir, I'm concerned that Bob isn't competent to run this investigation."

"And you are?" The CIA agent said, but

was silenced by another wave of the president's hand.

"And what makes you say that, Mr. Beamon?"

"Well, for instance, the fact that Ishmael and Fedallah are characters from *Moby Dick*."

Everyone looked over at Oberman, but for once he didn't have a response.

"Then you're saying that you don't believe Erin Neal is involved with al Qaeda?"

"That's exactly what I'm saying. In fact, I don't think he has much to do with any of this. I think he came up with the basic structure of that bacteria because he thought he could use it to clean up oil spills."

"Are you trying to tell us that this was an accident?" Oberman said.

"No, Bob. I'm saying he had a girlfriend. A woman who was also a very gifted biologist, but much more radical than he was. She had strong ties to the Arctic National Wildlife Refuge. She's the one who adapted the bacteria —"

"This is the dead one you're talking about?" Oberman said. "I think you need to look at the facts a little harder. We have solid dates on when the contamination was introduced, and it was *after* she died."

"She's not dead, Bob. She lives in Montana."

"You have proof of that?" the president said.

Beamon nodded. "She supposedly drowned along with a number of other radicals, but I think it's a fair bet that they're all still alive, too. And that they — not Erin Neal — are behind this."

A young woman slipped through the door at the back of the conference room with a telephone in her hand.

"What do you need, Sharon?" the president asked.

"I have a call for Mr. Beamon. It's Terry Hirst."

Beamon looked around him at the faces of some of the most powerful men in the world and then twisted around in his chair. "Could you tell him I'm busy?"

"I tried, but he won't take no for an answer."

"Excuse me a second," Beamon said, accepting the phone and walking as far as the room would allow before putting it to his ear.

"Terry," he said quietly. "I'm in with the goddamned pres—"

"Jenna Kalin's using her phone again."

"Can we get a bead on her? Who's

she calling?"

"Turn on your cell, Mark. She's calling you."

33

It was hard to believe that outside the relentless Mexican sun had turned the landscape into a burnt-out moonscape. Beamon shoved his hands in his pockets against the chill and dodged around a spray of water coming from a rusted pipe.

The CIA's short-lived control of his investigation was over and they had done their organization proud by disappearing so quickly and completely that it was almost as if they'd never been there. Of course he hadn't had the opportunity to see it with his own eyes and had to rely on reports from Terry Hirst, who had called to thank him for the elaborate cake with the CIA seal and "Good Riddance" printed across it. In the background, the noisemakers that came free with the cake had been clearly audible.

Petty and childish? Sure. But that kind of behavior helped him forget the expanding scale of the disaster he was once again presiding over.

"What is this place?"

Beamon refused to look at Jenna Kalin, who had looped an arm through his as though he could protect her from the stained cinderblock walls and broken-down industrial machinery disintegrating into puddles on the floor.

The truth was, he didn't know. Some kind of abandoned Mexican factory purchased by the CIA as a base for the games they liked to play but preferred not to have reported in the news.

"I asked you not to come, Jenna. It's not too late for you to go wait outside."

She didn't answer, redirecting her gaze to the two men escorting them, trying to stare them down from behind. One was the CIA agent who had taken custody of Erin Neal in Texas and the other was an anonymous and typically no-nonsense man in an army uniform.

Before picking Jenna up, Beamon had demanded a signed letter from the president saying that she would be remanded to his sole custody and would not be turned over to any other authority. Not worth the paper it was printed on, of course, but at least everyone was clear about where he stood on the subject. And so far, things were going relatively smoothly. No one had commented when he'd brought her back to the office for coffee or put her up in a nice hotel room with minimal security, though he understood that it was giving ulcers to the few White House staffers who didn't already have them. Interestingly, it seemed to be bothering her, too.

They stopped at a metal door secured by a padlock of almost comical dimensions and waited for the soldier to open it with the key hanging around his neck. The door swung slowly on rusted hinges and Beamon winced as Erin Neal came into view.

He'd obviously been cleaned up, but the carefully arranged hair and well-pressed clothes only highlighted his swollen face and blood-filled right eye.

The fury that was etched so deeply into his face faltered when he saw Jenna, and he sagged forward against the handcuffs securing him to his chair. As Beamon suspected, his impressive ability to resist the CIA's interrogators had been the product of only one thing — protecting the woman he still loved.

"Oh, my God," Jenna said, rushing through the door and kneeling next to him. "What did you people do?"

The two men escorting them were completely unmoved by a scene that, in Beamon's mind, encompassed the few things worthwhile in mankind — courage, compassion, love. No matter how misguided and destructive Jenna's actions had been, there was still something to admire there.

"Erin! Say something. Are you alright?" She was having a hard time getting the words out as tears began running down her cheeks. "This is my fault. It should have been me. I should have stopped when I saw them at the post office. I should —"

"How did they find you?"

"I turned myself in."

"No . . ." he said weakly. "Why would you do that? Do you have any idea what I've gone through to keep you out of this?"

"Erin, you don't know what's happening. I had no choice. But I said I wouldn't talk to them until I saw you."

Beamon took a key from the CIA man and stepped behind Erin's chair, a dull jolt of adrenaline surging through him. He wasn't looking forward to this.

Jenna didn't seem to notice he was there until she heard the key sliding into the handcuffs. Suddenly, her eyes cleared. "Wait! Don't do —"

But it was too late.

She was knocked to the floor when Erin

leapt from the chair and spun, swinging his elbow toward Beamon's head.

Despite anticipating the attack, Beamon was unable to duck in time. The room suddenly went blurry and he felt his knees collapse as the elbow connected and the open handcuff cut a deep gash in his face.

By the time Beamon hit the concrete, Erin had grabbed the small table in the center of the room, though what he planned to do with it was unclear. The soldier running at him guessed wrong, raising his arms to protect his face and instead getting hit in the shins. He quickly found himself tangled up in the table legs, sliding on his stomach across the wet floor. Erin leapt in the air and came down with one foot on the back of the soldier's neck. The man went limp, but fortunately there was no sound of crushing vertebrae accompanying the blow.

The CIA man obviously hadn't expected his enforcer to have any trouble with an injured, sleep-deprived biologist, and was only now going for the door. Beamon was still struggling to balance himself on all fours as Erin ran forward and blocked the room's only exit.

"So there is a God after all," he said before driving a fist into the man's soft midsection. The agent doubled over and Erin grabbed his face, forcing him upright and ramming the back of his head against the cinderblock wall. The crack was a little too loud, and Beamon pushed himself to his feet, realizing that he'd made a serious mistake.

He lurched forward, but then collapsed onto all fours again. When he finally managed to look up, Jenna had jumped onto Erin's back.

"That's enough!" she shouted, snaking an arm around his neck and locking her feet around his waist. The CIA man appeared to be out cold, suspended only by Erin's hand clamped onto his throat.

"Erin, you're going to kill him!"

He pulled the man's head forward so he could drive it into the wall again, but Jenna managed to stop him by tangling her arm in his.

"Let go of him!"

He did as she said and the unconscious man slid to the floor. Jenna slowly disengaged from him, keeping one arm around his neck until she was sure his surrender wasn't just a ploy.

Beamon scooted back against the wall, listening to the shouts and pounding coming from the other side of the door. Erin didn't seem to hear the racket, though, and turned toward him. Only a chair and a 120-pound woman were between them now, which wasn't terribly confidence inspiring.

"Mark says he didn't have anything to do with this," Jenna said. "And I believe him."

The rapid rise and fall of Erin's chest began to slow and Beamon tried to shake the remaining cobwebs out of his head, but succeeded only in spattering the wall next to him with his blood. He smiled painfully. "Do you feel better now?"

"What the fuck are you grinning about?"

Beamon shrugged. "It never occurred to me that you'd win."

34

Michael Teague eased the van forward another two feet and came to yet another stop. Behind him, the line of cars they'd been sitting in for the last eight hours extended as far as the eye could see. In front, though, the Canadian border was tantalizingly close. So close, in fact, that he didn't bother turning his engine off and instead left it idling wastefully.

It had taken two weeks to complete a drive that they should have been able to do in a single push. Of course, the blame for that was primarily Udo's, but his failure to keep the van's tank full had turned out to be only the beginning of their problems.

With Erin Neal in custody, it was almost certain that Jenna was also in the hands of the government. She would never leave her beloved Erin to suffer a fate meant for her. And if that was the case, Teague had to assume that the authorities knew all about him and the Metzgers.

So now they had to worry about being recognized, which forced them to use the back roads where police were scarce and supplied with only enough fuel to react to emergencies.

That made getting their own fuel much more difficult. Now eBay had a section dedicated to the trading of gasoline and other petroleum products, but in rural areas, people needed their fuel rations to cover the distances necessary to live. And even if you were able to find sellers, they were often many miles away — creating a situation where you had to use a half a tank of gas to buy a full tank of gas.

"Another one," Udo said, pointing through the windshield at a car pulling past the border station and being directed to return to the United States.

The escalating cultural tension between America and Canada, combined with the fact that most Americans were crossing the border just to buy gas that they'd take back and sell, had caused a steady tightening of border security. Two days ago, though, there had been a shooting at a Canadian gas station by an American citizen and it had been the proverbial last straw. In the time they'd been waiting to cross, about four out of five cars had been turned back.

The truck in front of them pulled up to the gate and Teague watched the border guard lean in the window. No more than thirty seconds went by before he motioned the driver to return to the U.S.

Teague's foot hesitated over the accelerator when the guard waved him forward. Would they have photos of them? Had Jenna discovered that they'd modified the bacteria to thrive in the open elements and spread by air and water? If so, what would the governments of the world not do to capture them? And if they were captured, what would they not do to punish them?

This was the last hurdle. Once they were across the border, fuel would be available and they could make it to their facility south of the Athabasca tar sands in one long push. Then he would change the face of the world forever.

Teague glanced over at Udo, who had grown a haphazard beard and was wearing a baseball hat with "Yellowstone" embroidered on it. Jonas was even less recognizable. His long hair was now close-cropped and he'd been force-feeding himself for the entire drive, gaining almost twenty pounds, which effectively softened the frightening intensity that made him so distinct. Teague, for his part, had shaved the top of his head into an enormous bald spot and dyed what was left of his hair nearly black. A set of distractingly out-of-style glasses rounded out what he hoped was an effective disguise.

The wind coming through the window turned the sweat on his forehead cold as he pulled up and held three fake Canadian passports out the window.

"Would you all get out of the vehicle, please?"

"What's the problem?" Teague asked, concentrating on appearing relaxed as he opened the door and stepped out. Udo did the same, and Jonas followed, squeezing his new bulk between the front seats of the van.

"What was your business in the U.S.?"

"Vacation. We were just driving around touring when all this happened," Teague said in an easy, friendly tone. "We were in Florida when the shit really hit the fan. I mean, how much farther could you get from home and not fall in the ocean?"

The border guard examined him suspiciously and then turned his attention to the Germans. Jonas had rubbed his eyes to make them as red as possible, and he coughed energetically into his hand. They'd spent their interminable drive working on Udo's already light accent and he would be fine answering general questions, but Jonas was hopeless. The best they could come up with was a bad case of laryngitis.

"Could you open the van, please?"

Teague walked around the back and did as he was asked, pulling the doors open to reveal a calculatedly messy interior. They'd dumped the medical equipment they took from the lab and replaced it with clothing, brochures, coolers, and guide books. The guard crawled inside, pushing things around and then suddenly froze.

"Something wrong?" Teague asked, his heart rate rising despite having anticipated this.

"There's an extra fuel tank," the man said, anger audible in his voice as he jumped back down to the pavement.

"We had that installed in Louisiana so we could make it back across the U.S.," Teague said. "It's easier to buy in one big lump than to try to go looking for twenty gallons every day."

The guard was obviously unconvinced. "There's no rule against you coming in with the tank," he said. "But we have regulations about how much fuel you can take back into the U.S. If you fill that up and try to cross back, you're going to have serious problems."

"Are you kidding me? We're never going back. Do you have any idea what it's like to drive a gas-guzzling van with Canadian plates across the U.S. right now? We're lucky we didn't get shot."

Still looking skeptical, the guard opened the driver's door and leaned inside. He searched the glove box and floor, finally settling on the large stainless steel thermos wedged between the seats.

Teague watched nervously as he tapped it with a fingernail and then reached for the lid to twist it off. Even though Teague knew there was a hidden locking mechanism that would make it impossible, he found himself holding his breath until the guard gave up and turned back to him. "What's in this?"

The future, Teague thought as he leaned in the door and turned the thermos around to display the Starbucks sticker on the front.

35

"Real equipment," Jenna said, dragging a hand across a tangle of stainless steel and plastic as she followed along behind Beamon. The lab was state of the art — every surface polished, every gadget carefully built into a table or wall, every computer brand new.

"After a couple of weeks of sleeping on the floor and working with toaster ovens, this must look pretty good," Beamon said.

She shook her head slowly. "I should have called you sooner. I shouldn't have waited —"

"There's no point in dwelling on 'should have,' " Erin said.

"He's right," Beamon agreed. "Besides, if you'd called me right away, you'd have probably ended up in the hands of the CIA and then we'd be nowhere right now. So mark it up to a bad decision that came good."

"Erin! Jesus, man. Thank God you're finally here."

Steve Andropolous pushed his way past two men in lab coats and ran across the crowded room, but stopped short about ten feet away.

"Hi, Steve," Jenna said quietly.

"Jesus . . . they told me you were alive, but I don't think I really believed it until this second." He started forward again, gaining speed before colliding with her and wrapping her in a bear hug. "The idea of you out there alone in the ocean . . ." He sniffled loudly. "Going under and fighting your way back up. And then going un—"

"It's okay, Steve." She patted him on the back and then tried gently to break his grip. "I'm alright."

He finally released her, taking a step back and redirecting his teary gaze toward Erin and Beamon. "What the hell happened to you guys?"

The cut in Beamon's cheek had been neatly stitched, but now seemed to demand an elaborate pirate costume. Erin's face was intermittently swollen and bruised, and his right eye was still blood red, though the doctor said it looked worse than it really was.

"I could really use some good news," Beamon said as Andropolous gave Erin an equally energetic if not quite so emotional embrace.

"Good news?" he said, looking vaguely startled as he released Erin and stepped back. "There is no good news. I only have 'really bad' and 'totally fucked up.' Come on, I'll show you."

Jenna tried to keep her eyes on Andropolous's back as they followed him through the lab, but it was impossible not to notice that the people around them stopped work as they passed. Were they just curious or did they know that she was responsible for all this? Was there accusation on their faces?

"Did they send you all my data?" she asked.

"We got *everything,*" he said. "Seriously, they disassembled the whole building you were in and shipped it along with a few hundred tons of the dirt it was sitting on. It's all sealed in an airplane hangar a few miles from here."

"And what have you figured out?" Beamon asked.

"Mostly that Jenna was right — no big surprise there, I guess. The bacteria she designed has been heavily modified to survive in the open elements and to spread easily."

"Any idea how long it can survive outside?" Erin asked.

"Nope. We haven't managed to kill it yet. We've got samples in all kinds of different conditions: we're starving it, freezing it, subjecting it to high levels of solar radiation. Nothing works. It seems to have the ability to go dormant in really adverse conditions."

"How long can it stay that way?"

"I'd guess a long time."

"How long?" Beamon asked. "A week? A month?"

"Probably years."

"Christ," Erin said quietly.

"So let me get this straight," Beamon said. "If this stuff gets out, it could travel around the world, getting into oil-production facilities and fields without any human help at all, and people will end up pulling their cars around with horses."

Andropolous didn't answer, and Jenna was finding it increasingly hard to breathe. Erin finally spoke up.

"You're thinking too small, Mark."

"Small? That's small?"

"It's true that engine fuel is an oil derivative, but they also rely on petroleum products for lubrication. If your car runs out of gas, no big deal, right? But if it runs out of oil, it's history. Now extrapolate that out. Think of the huge turbines that generate our electricity. Or water pumps, or windmills. Now consider the petrochemical industry that makes our pharmaceuticals. And —"

Beamon held up a hand. "I get the point."

"That's just the bad part," Andropolous said hesitantly. "You haven't heard the really fucked up yet."

"You've got to be kidding me," Beamon said. "How the hell could it get worse?"

They turned a corner and stopped in front of a floor-to-ceiling glass wall, behind which was Jenna's bicycle. Andropolous tapped a few commands into a keyboard and a large monitor came to life.

"What you're looking at is a magnification of the bike's seat."

Jenna backed away until she bumped into a table, but Erin stepped closer, peering at the screen.

"You can see the pitting where the bacteria's eating it," Andropolous continued.

Erin took a deep breath and let it out slowly. For the first time, he looked scared.

"Am I missing something?" Beamon said. "What are you telling me? That in a couple years our main form of transportation is going to be squeaky bikes that are really uncomfortable?"

"It's not just the seat," Erin said. "That type of plastic is in everything. It's what we use to insulate wires, to build parts for machines, to make clothing. If these bacteria get out, you can pretty much say goodbye to everything — the electric grid, the Internet, phones. You name it, it's gone. We're talking about plowing fields the same way we did a thousand years ago. It —"

"Stop," Beamon said, grabbing both Erin and Jenna by the backs of their collars and shoving them into an empty room at the far end of the lab.

"This isn't the bubonic plague," he said, slamming the door behind them. "It's oil! You're exaggerating, right? Trying to make a point?"

Jenna felt the malaise that had taken hold of her suddenly disappear and she began pacing the length of the room, her stride turning almost violent as she moved back and forth. "That son of a bitch! That crazy son of a bitch!" Her breath came faster and faster, until she had to put a hand on the wall to stay upright.

"Are you alright?" Beamon said, sounding sincerely concerned. Erin disappeared through the door and returned a moment later with a paper bag. He dumped a sandwich and some chips onto the floor and handed the bag to Jenna, who began breathing into it.

"She does this," he explained to Beamon. "She'll be okay."

Beamon watched her slide to the floor, the bag expanding and contracting rhythmically as her ability to focus slowly returned.

"You were about to put this in perspective for me," he said, turning to Erin.

"Yeah . . . look, if this was something like bubonic plague you could probably expect about a twenty percent kill rate. This is going to be a lot higher."

"Higher? Than a disease? I don't —"

"Think about the way we live now, Mark. There's something like three hundred million people living in the U.S., about one percent of whom have any idea how to grow a vegetable or tend a farm animal. Most people have no survival skills at all; and, besides, the country isn't set up for that kind of lifestyle anymore. Let me put it this way: What happens here in D.C. if the grocery stores stop getting food for even a couple of weeks and there's no gas for you to go somewhere food *is* available? How would you feed yourself?"

Beamon thought about it for a moment. "My fiancée has a garden. I guess I'd eat a lot of squash."

Erin nodded. "Is there a fence around it?"

"No."

"And how many of her neighbors know about that garden but don't garden themselves?"

"I don't know. A lot."

"Okay. How many of them would you be willing to kill when they got hungry and came after your squash?"

Beamon didn't answer.

"Now let's cut off everybody's power. No more refrigeration. Do you know how to build a root cellar? Could you can the vegetables your fiancée is growing? Do you have enough to last the winter? And even if you're one of the few people who can say yes to all those questions and you have a whole lot of guns, how are you going to stay warm? But you're one of the lucky ones — you can heat with wood. Where are you going to get that wood and how are you going to transport it to your house?"

Once started, Beamon's mind began working through the never-ending ripples that would be caused by the sudden destruction of the world's oil supply and no matter how he twisted it, he came to the same conclusion Erin had: in a few years there would be a couple of million survivors in the U.S. working individual sustenance farms. He thought about Carrie and Emory. About his friends and what was left of his family. About the chaos and violence that they'd be thrown into.

"Mark, are you still with me?"

"What if it does get out? Can you kill it?"

"Maybe if it was confined to a small isolated area. I suppose it's possible."

"But what if it isn't confined?"

Erin shook his head as Jenna pushed herself to her feet again.

"Better?" Erin asked.

She nodded.

"This isn't a convenient time for the end of the world. I'm getting married next month," Beamon said, starting to feel uncharacteristically panicked. "I'm going to have a goddamned family. Look, you chased Teague out of his facility a couple of weeks ago, right? That would have to slow him down."

"Probably not as much as you think," Jenna said. "He wasn't set up to breed that bacteria on a large scale there. He must have another facility somewhere."

"Something closer to the target," Erin added.

"What target? I thought the whole world was the target."

Jenna shook her head miserably. "You've got to understand that you can't just go out and throw a few handfuls of this stuff into the wind and expect it to spread all over the globe. You'd have to start with a lot of it and then dump it somewhere it could get a good foothold in nature."

"And how would you do that?"

"How the hell would I know? I didn't —"

"Jenna," Erin said, putting a hand on her shoulder. "Calm down. Mark isn't accusing you of anything. But you did work with Teague. Maybe you know something and don't even realize it."

"Well, I don't. I hadn't even seen them for almost two years until he showed up on my doorstep. I —"

"Enough," Beamon said. "This isn't getting us anywhere. Sometimes when I'm in a situation like this, I put myself in the shoes of the guy I'm chasing. If you were him, how would you do it? How would you release this stuff?"

They fell silent for a few moments before Erin spoke up. "Could he put it down a water injector and let it build up in a reserve?"

"Underground doesn't really work," Jenna

said. "Sure it'd spread, but how would it get released? The minute we found it, we'd cap off all the wells. What you really need is a big, open pool of oil."

"What if I blew up an oil tanker," Beamon said. "That would cause a big spill and then I could just fly over it with a crop duster."

"Too complicated and too short-term," Erin said. "It'd be easier just to go to Russia and dump it on the oil fields they've got leaking all over the place."

"Still, it seems like you'd need more scale," Jenna said.

They both fell silent again for a moment.

"That only leaves one thing," Erin said.

Jenna nodded. "Canada."

"What?" Beamon asked. "What about Canada?"

"It's perfect," Jenna said. "You've been watching television, right? Canada has the tar sands — oil-permeated sand dunes that cover tens of thousands of square miles. Plus, they're fuel self-sufficient, so you can still get around."

"And they speak English, so it wouldn't be that hard for him to blend in," Erin said.

"So that's it," Beamon said. "If they can get it to take hold in the tar sands, it would spread."

Erin nodded. "Assuming they could breed enough of it and release it over a wide enough area, the stuff would go nuts. And then the wind would take it and that's it."

36

President Dunn actually laughed, though it seemed likely that it was because he had no idea how else to react. He was the only one in the room standing, frozen at the head of the crowded table.

"You're talking to me about the end of human civilization? Do you hear how ridiculous that sounds?"

Mark Beamon cleared his throat, feeling the weight of what he knew continue to settle on his shoulders. "Not exactly the end of human civilization, sir. The end of *industrialized* human civilization. According to the people I'm talking to, we'll see a die-off of somewhere in the neighborhood of sixty percent of the world's population, with a lot of variation depending on where you live and how you live. Obviously, if you're a sustenance farmer in New Guinea, you're not going to be all that heavily affected."

"And if you're an American?"

"We're on the other side of the equation — a heavily armed population that's completely reliant on energy for just about everything."

"And who exactly are these people you're talking to?"

"Erin Neal and Jenna Kalin."

"The ones responsible for all this," the president said. "Where are they?"

Beamon had briefly considered bringing Erin and Jenna to this meeting, but it seemed more likely that they would turn it into a circus rather than provide useful information. "They're at the lab —"

"You've given them access to our facility?"

Beamon sighed quietly. There was no time for this. "I put them in charge of it."

Not surprisingly, that prompted Jack Reynolds to speak up. "Mark, doesn't that seem a little stupid? I mean, get them involved, let them consult, but —"

"Come on, Jack. Erin had nothing to do with any of this, and I'm convinced that Jenna just wanted the Alaska fields shut down — something that wouldn't have had any consequences beyond cutting oil company profits from a hundred billion a year to ninety billion."

"Are you willing to bet your life on that?"

the president asked.

"I think I have, sir."

The room went silent as the president lowered himself unsteadily into his chair. "What you're telling us creates . . . complications."

"I'm not sure I understand."

"You're certain they're going to use Canada's tar sands to spread the bacteria?"

"No, not certain. It's by far the most obvious target, though — a huge amount of exposed petroleum with strong winds blowing across it. It could be as simple as flying a crop duster over the area or driving a tanker truck along one of the roads through it."

"But at this point, you don't think they have the bacteria available."

"We're working under the theory that they're currently producing the bacteria at a facility somewhere in Canada."

"So we still have time?"

"We're working under that assumption because the alternative is . . . well, let's just say we're not thinking about the alternative right now."

"Then your recommendation is that we warn the Canadian government and have them secure the area."

"Absolutely."

The president turned to a man in a military uniform. "How would that affect your plans?"

He crossed his arms, an act accompanied by the quiet clink of medals. "Obviously, a heavy Canadian military presence in the tar sands area would complicate things and could present some logistical problems — none of them insurmountable, though. Canada's military capabilities just aren't that substantial and the element of surprise is on our side."

Beamon's brow started to furrow, prompting Jack Reynolds to grab him by the arm and pull him to the back of the room. "Not a word, Mark. This has nothing to do with you or your investigation."

"What the hell are they talking about, Jack? Are we going to war with Canada?"

"We've been able to hold things together so far, Mark, but I don't think even you know how close the country is to complete economic collapse. Canada has the largest petroleum reserves in the world and there'll have to be some fair distribution system that doesn't involve them driving around in gold-plated Humvees while the American people starve."

"Are you fucking kidding me, Jack? We're —"

"There's a ninety-nine percent chance that this is all going to get done through diplomatic channels, Mark. But it makes sense to have a contingency plan — and that's all we're talking about here. Stay focused on what you're doing, okay?"

Beamon opened his mouth to reply, but then fell silent as the president stood again.

"If Mr. Beamon here is right and we don't stop the release of this new bacteria, would we have a nuclear option?"

A man Beamon didn't recognize shook his head. "We've done simulations with conventional biological attacks and found that it's more likely the blast would accelerate the spread."

"So we have no ideas at all as to what to do if we don't find these people in time?"

Silence. No one even looked at each other.

"What about provisions to keep the government operational?"

Reynolds tugged on Beamon's arm to bring him back to the table, but Beamon just shrugged him off. The more distance the better as far as he was concerned.

"Relocation to NORAD would probably be most viable."

"And would that provide adequate protection?"

The man didn't answer immediately, and

Beamon found himself staring intently at him. It was bad enough that when faced with an unprecedented human disaster, the politicians' focus turned so quickly to saving their own necks, but what was worse was that it might work. Instead of repopulating the world with doctors, farmers, and craftsmen, it would be repopulated with lawyers, politicians, and generals.

"NORAD was designed to withstand a very different kind of attack, sir."

"But a biological attack was one of them."

"Yes, but a biological attack on *humans*. We'll put our top people on it, but the facility was built with state-of-the-art materials — the kind that would be susceptible to these bacteria. It could very quickly turn into a dark hole in the ground."

"This needs to be a top priority — I want to know later today what kind of retrofitting can be done to adapt it."

"We'll do our best, sir."

The uncertainty in the man's voice cheered Beamon up a bit. If he was going down, he sure as hell wanted these assholes to go down with him.

The president seemed confused for a moment, but regained his resolve before speaking. "Based on Mr. Beamon's recommendation, we're going to warn Canada about the possibility of a bacterial attack on their tar sands, and we'll just have to revise our attack plan accordingly." He looked in Beamon's direction. "As much as I hate to say it, our future — everyone's future — is in your hands."

37

"It is Erin and Jenna's doing," Jonas said, leaning between the seats of the four-wheel-drive vehicle they had transferred to. "You know this."

Teague ignored him and gunned the vehicle over a decaying log, bringing them out of the dense trees and into a small clearing dominated by a camouflaged metal building a little larger than the one they'd occupied in Texas.

Even Jonas fell silent when he saw it. While it wasn't particularly impressive or unique, it represented the end of years of work and sacrifice and the beginning of the most significant transformation the earth had undergone since the extinction of the dinosaurs. But this transformation wouldn't be precipitated by a meteor or climate change. It would be their doing.

The scent of pine was strong as Teague threw open his door and stepped into the thick mud. He thought it fitting that he was taking these final steps surrounded by pristine wilderness and silence. It would be a constant motivator — a reminder of the state he would return the world to. The vulgar beach houses would be washed away, the empty streets of Manhattan would crack and heave as the buildings slowly crumbled onto them. Bison herds, miles across, would roam the plains again.

Udo was already reaching for the canister of bacteria when Teague leaned back through the door to retrieve it. The German backed away, allowing Teague to pull the thermos from between the seats. The wind immediately turned the metal cold in his hands, and for some reason that, too, seemed fitting.

When Teague entered the building, the generators and lights were already on and Jonas was standing in front of a television watching the latest reports on the situation that so concerned him.

"The tar sands are completely protected," he said. "There are patrol planes and satellites taking pictures. All the roads in have been blocked by the army."

"What difference does it make?" Teague said, putting the canister on a table covered in a thick layer of dust. "We're a hundred miles from the edge of the tar sands."

"But they're close," Udo interjected. "They're working out the details, Michael."

"They're too late."

Udo glanced at his brother and shook his head subtly. They'd obviously been talking about this privately.

"I understand your feelings about Erin Neal," Udo said. "But it would be a mistake to underestimate him or Jenna. They are brilliant people, Michael. And we looked up this Mark Beamon on the Internet. He has a similar reputation in his own field. They know us, they know the bacteria, and they've already calculated that we'll use the tar sands to —"

"And yet here we are," Teague said angrily. "Despite Jenna, despite Erin Neal, and despite the best Homeland Security has to offer."

"But —"

"Enough!"

He took the thermos from the table and walked to the center of the room where a thick pipe rose from the concrete floor.

Ten feet below ground it was connected to an old pipeline that traveled hundreds of miles north to an abandoned oil extraction facility in the middle of the tar sands. Before it was mothballed, the pipeline had transported oil to a much larger system that crossed the border into the U.S.

The part of the pipe that snaked beneath the tar sands now contained a mix of oil and fertilizer that would increase the growth rate of the bacteria exponentially. Once introduced, his creation would spread uncontrolled until it filled the entire length of the pipe. Then it would only be a matter of releasing it.

"Michael!" Jonas yelled. "Come here."

He ignored the shout until Udo seconded it. "Michael, please! You must see this."

Teague let out a frustrated breath and walked toward the television, stopping suddenly when he saw the screen filled with a photograph of him speaking at Yale. The volume came up as photos of Udo and Jonas joined his on-screen, but Teague wasn't listening.

They were deep in an unpopulated stretch of the Canadian wilderness, far from the area the government was focusing on, and far from anyone who could identify them from those photographs. Once again, he was one step ahead.

"They aren't saying anything about Jenna," Udo pointed out. "We were right. She must be working for them."

Jonas slammed the remote on a table and

rushed through a door at the back of the building, but Teague paid no attention, continuing to watch his image on the screen.

He would have liked another month of anonymity but, in the end, it wouldn't matter. He'd always planned for this to come out — for the world to know who had done this and why. Humanity would know that they had brought this on themselves with their reckless campaign to destroy millions of years of creation in the hollow pursuit of meaningless comforts.

"This is a dangerous time," Udo said. "The bacteria will grow quickly, but until it reaches critical mass, everything we've worked for is vulnerable."

Teague could hear the clang of metal behind him and he walked to the back of the building, leaning a shoulder against a doorjamb to watch Jonas free the chain wrapped around a heavy steel cabinet.

"What is it you think you're going to do?" he asked as Jonas pulled a rifle from the cabinet.

"I'm going to correct our mistake. I am going to kill Jenna and Erin Neal."

"How do you propose to find them? They're working with the government in the United States."

"I will make them come to me."

Teague nodded silently. Jonas, like the other weapons in that cabinet, was a useful tool. There was no way to predict exactly the path society's collapse would take and how quickly or violently it would happen. And in the face of that kind of uncertainty, someone like Jonas could be useful.

On the other hand, he was becoming increasingly difficult to control. At first, Teague hadn't been concerned because Udo seemed to hold sway over his brother. But now, he was afraid the relationship was having the opposite effect, that Jonas was making his older brother more defiant.

Perhaps this was for the best. If he kept Jonas here, his anger and frustration could further contaminate his brother. And for what? An unpredictable enforcer who would almost certainly not be needed.

What would happen if he let the German go? Perhaps he would succeed in dealing with Erin and Jenna — and although getting rid of them was probably not critical, it certainly would eliminate one of the most prominent threats to them. On the other hand, if Jonas failed, it would likely be the end of him, and that had the potential to solve a number of other nagging problems.

Teague turned and walked back to where Udo had attached the thermos to the top of the pipe jutting from the floor. It looked like some kind of modern sculpture — the graceful stainless curves of the thermos gleaming against the dirty rust of the industrial pipe.

Udo held out a large wrench and Teague took it, sliding it around the valve release and throwing his weight against it. For a moment it didn't move, but then it submitted, sending the bacteria into the pipe in a barely audible rush.

Finally, it was done.

38

The wind blew the hair across Jenna Kalin's face, but she didn't bother to push it away, instead letting it fill her mouth and eyes along with the foul air.

She stood alone at the crumbling edge of a large concrete reservoir, hands shoved deeply into the pockets of her down jacket, and watched clouds swirling over the endless oil-soaked dunes. Canada's tar sands, now universally seen as humanity's savior, would more likely be the cause of its demise. And once again, it was her fault.

The rusting industrial building a quarter mile away had been one of the first facilities to extract oil from the area — washing it from the sand, collecting it, and then transporting it to far away refineries. As technology had improved, though, it had become obsolete and finally was abandoned to decay in what had once been a vast emptiness stretching from horizon to horizon.

The first helicopters to land had been filled with Canadian special forces, who quickly secured the area but found no one. Now, two hours later, the landscape was dotted with helicopters and people were everywhere — studying derelict pipes and machinery, taking soil samples, shouting into satellite phones.

The initial sweep confirmed their worst-case scenario. Not only were Michael and the Metzgers not there, but it looked like no one had been for years.

Did she really think it would be this easy? That she could swoop in and save the day? No. But she hoped she would. And other than Erin, hope was all she had anymore.

She squinted into the distance, finally finding him standing behind a partially collapsed trailer to keep out of the wind. He was kicking at the ground, head down, while Mark Beamon talked heatedly with someone she didn't recognize.

They'd decided to leave her alone, mostly because neither seemed to know what else to do. Erin made the occasional awkward attempt to make her feel better, but he still couldn't decide whether to comfort her or to strangle her. The funny thing was that strangling her would have probably been better for both of them in the long run.

Their feelings for each other had the potential to further complicate an already impossible situation. The truth was that she didn't have much of a future. Maybe no one did.

Mark Beamon waved to her and she reluctantly started picking her way through the industrial debris littering the ground. The wind died down and as she got closer she slowed, trying to pick up what was being said.

"Look, I don't know what you want from me," Beamon protested. "I —"

The man in front of him cut him off. "Do you know how difficult it was to get you this kind of access, Mark? To get our people to cooperate with you at all? Your press is telling the world that we're hoarding our oil and trying to starve you. Our embassy's been attacked. And do you know what your government's doing?"

"Nothing," Beamon said. "I know. But it's just the press. They say what sells papers. What can we do?"

"Your president could get on television and tell the American people everything we're doing to try to help. He could —"

"Bullshit, Carl. How long have you and I known each other? More than a decade? And I don't remember ever thinking you were stupid. Politicians love diversions, and you're the diversion du jour. As long as the American voters are pissed at you, they don't have time to get pissed at the people who actually got them into this."

Beamon looked relieved when Jenna finally reached them and he put a hand on her shoulder in what she knew was an honest attempt to be reassuring. "Jenna, this is Carl Fournier. He's my counterpart here in Canada."

Fournier didn't offer his hand, instead folding his arms and staring at her with an expression too opaque to read. He was much more imposing than Beamon — probably six foot four — with a narrow waist, well-defined features, and a precision haircut that seemed impervious to the elements.

"And what if we don't think that your government standing by doing nothing is good enough?" he said, looking at her, but talking to Beamon.

"You've got to be kidding me, Carl. You're giving me an ultimatum? Now? If this bug gets loose, the few Canadians that are left will be living in caves and hunting moose with spears."

"You don't make it easy, though, do you, Mark? It's not enough for you to come here and start making demands when the relationship between our countries is at an all-time low, but you bring the woman responsible. How do you think that looks to the people I work for?"

As far as Jenna was concerned, the Canadian's reservations about her were completely justified. Even she couldn't completely understand why she was still roaming around free. When she'd asked, Beamon told her not to look a gift horse in the mouth, but the complete silence on the matter was becoming increasingly eerie — as though someone was lurking just out of sight, waiting for the moment she was no longer useful.

"I'm not trying to bark orders, here," Beamon said. "I'm offering my help. And all the PR crap aside, so is the American government."

"Oh, right. You've been so generous in offering military assistance to secure our energy reserves. Seems a bit convenient, though, doesn't it? I wonder how hard it would be for us to get those reserves back if we accepted your help?"

Beamon didn't immediately answer, his unwillingness to deny Fornier's accusation clearly not an oversight. "What's the bottom line here, Carl? Do you think I'm here to screw you?"

Fournier considered the question for a moment. "You personally? No."

"Then can we move on?"

Fournier's expression suggested that he knew he had no choice but to cooperate, and he turned to Erin. "You've searched the building. Have you learned anything at all?"

"That there's nothing here."

"Well, that's helpful, isn't it?"

"There are a few old factories like this in the tar sands," Beamon said, cutting Erin off before he could respond. "What makes this one unique is that it was bought by a company we can't get a handle on. The deeper we dig, the more confusing the ownership gets. Basically, a classic front corporation."

A fighter jet screamed overhead, drowning out even the wind, and they all looked up as it angled north and began to climb.

"Are you sure you didn't miss anything?" Beamon said as the sound of the engines faded.

Erin shook his head. "Look around you. The place is falling down. There's no power, no containers left that aren't rusted through, and even if they weren't, they aren't big enough to do what Michael needs to do."

"Maybe we're totally wrong," Jenna said.

"Maybe he is in Russia. Or maybe he's come up with something we haven't even imagined. I mean, he's had years to think about this. We've had a few days. We're wasting our time. We don't have a chance . . ."

She fell silent when Fournier's phone began to ring. He turned his back and moved out of the shelter provided by the trailer.

Beamon put his hand on her shoulder again. "You've got to do me a favor and forget the past. You can't change it and it's just going to cloud your judgment. If Teague wins, you'll most likely get your opportunity to die horribly and pay for your sins. Until then, though, I need you to stay focused."

She nodded, but couldn't bring herself to look at either Beamon or Erin. "You're right. I'm sorry."

"Don't be sorry. Just keep it together, okay?"

"Okay."

"Mark!" Fournier shouted, jogging back up to them a bit out of breath. "The company that owns this place just rented a building in Calgary and had a bunch of lab equipment shipped to it." He slapped his hands together and rubbed them against the cold. "We've got them."

39

"We have people stationed here and here," Fournier said, pointing to a couple of blurry figures on the screens lining the inside of the van.

Beamon tried to adjust himself into a position where Erin's elbow wasn't digging into his ribs, but could barely move in the confines of the vehicle. "That's it? Two people?"

"It's the best we can do, Mark. It's more or less an industrial area with no sidewalk and a street that doesn't go anywhere. If it was suddenly full of pedestrians, it would be obvious. Just getting these cameras in place was a nightmare."

"Which building is it?" Jenna asked.

"The green one on the right. It used to be a veterinary clinic and a lot of the medical infrastructure is still inside, so it's ideal for Teague and his people. None of the neighbors have seen anyone go in or out, but they admit they haven't been paying much attention."

It started raining, the heavy drops ringing against the top of the van and partially obscuring the images.

"Any sign of life inside?" Erin asked.

"Nothing at all," Fournier said. "But with the shades closed there's no way to be certain."

"Then what are we waiting for?" Jenna said. "They could be in there right now. Why are we just sitting here?"

Beamon watched the rain running down the rear windows of the van, once again trying to come up with a plan that didn't involve getting everyone killed. And, once again, drawing a blank.

"Okay," he said finally. "Send your guys in."

"We're a go," Fournier said into his walkie-talkie.

Screens that had been blank suddenly came to life as the helmet cameras of men waiting a block away were switched on and began following their careful progress toward the target building. The two people Fournier had in the street moved as casually as they could in the direction of the vet clinic, their slow pace somewhat forced in light of the rain. If Beamon was right, though, it wouldn't matter if they went in with a high school marching band.

"This is Team Leader. We're in position," came a voice over the van's speakers.

Beamon shrugged. "Go ahead."

Fournier's men were better than he had expected. The two people in front rushed the door, kicking it in on the first try as a group of well-placed men with assault rifles swept out to cover them. The sturdier rear door was collapsed with a battering ram only a few seconds later, and a number of the screens took on the dim, jerky feel of a computer game as the tiny building was efficiently searched.

"We're clear," came the voice over the speakers. "There's no one here."

"Shit!" Fournier said as Beamon leaned back against the wall of the van and glanced over at Erin and Jenna. Her head sunk into her hands and she stared at her feet, trying to control her breathing. Erin seemed far away — as though he'd given up on all this long ago and was trying to find another way out.

"Did you get the stuff I asked for, Carl?"

Fournier nodded. "But I'm not sure they're going to be able to walk."

"This is stupid," Jenna managed to get out

358

before enough rain got in her mouth to force her to swallow. "There could be something in there that'll tell us where Michael is. We don't have time for this!"

Fournier attached the back plate to the body armor she was wearing and her knees sagged dangerously. It was soaking wet, adding to the weight, but in the end, the rain was a gift from God. One of the few Beamon had received lately.

"Better safe than sorry," Fournier pointed out.

Erin grimaced as shin guards were strapped to his legs. "Yeah, if we were expecting a fucking air strike. If this is so dangerous, why isn't Mark wearing any of this crap?"

The light, police-issue vest Beamon had on looked anemic beside the full military armor covering Erin and Jenna. With the unfortunate exception of their heads and a few joints necessary for movement, they were more or less bulletproof — assuming normal bullet varieties and muzzle velocities, of course. But what choice did he have? A tank would be a little obvious.

"Walk for me, Jenna. Let's see how you do."

She scowled, but did as he asked, teetering unsteadily alongside the van. She looked a bit like an old wind-up children's toy, but by the time she turned and started back, her gait wasn't much worse than his had been after letting Carrie talk him into playing tennis.

"It'll do."

The car stopped about twenty yards from the veterinary clinic and Jenna threw the back door open, swinging her legs to the ground only to find herself stuck. The weight of the body armor had been manageable, but the addition of the fireman's jacket that Beamon insisted she wear to cover it up put her over the edge.

She started to take it off, but then felt Beamon's foot in her back. With that less-than-gentle nudge, she managed to haul herself onto the pavement and stand there swaying unsteadily in the strengthening wind. Fournier was a few yards away, talking heatedly with a uniformed man holding the leash of a Labrador retriever.

"What've we got?" Beamon said, joining Fournier as Erin came around the car and took a position next to Jenna. Not too close, she noticed, but not as far away as the day before.

"We've run a check for incendiary devices, but didn't find anything."

"Incendiary devices?" Erin said. "Bombs? Why would there be bombs?"

"Relax," Beamon said. "There are certain procedures we follow in situations like this. That's just one of about fifty." He glanced back at them through the rain, the relaxed smile on his face looking less reassuring than it did desperate. Not all that surprising after listening to their bleak prediction for the future. Or, more precisely, the lack of one.

"Okay, let's get you to work," Beamon said, motioning them forward. "See if there's anything in there that can help us."

Erin started toward the building, moving quickly, but Jenna had to break into an awkward jog in an effort to catch up.

"Jenna, wait!" Beamon shouted. "Don't run!"

Other than that warning and the rain, no sound preceded the explosion of pain in her left shoulder blade. She pitched forward, her increased weight magnifying her momentum as she crashed into Erin's back. He managed to turn and get a hand beneath one of her arms and would probably have been able to keep them from falling if it hadn't been for a second impact from behind.

Erin went down first, partially sinking in a

361

deep puddle as she landed on top of him. A moment later, Beamon's weight came down on the both of them and she realized that he was responsible for the blow that had actually sent them to the ground. She was aware of shouting and a barrage of gunfire that turned the raindrops into flashing crystals. But it all became increasingly distant as her mind focused on the seemingly impossible task of getting air into her lungs.

At first she thought it was because of Beamon's weight pressing down on her back, but then realized that had nothing to do with it. The reason she couldn't breathe was that she'd been shot. She was dying.

The police closed in on a Dumpster with the lid thrown open and she saw someone firing a gun from inside, causing small chunks of asphalt to explode around her. She paid no real attention, though, trying to move into a position from which she could see Erin. Since the bullet's impact had nearly lifted her off her feet, she doubted she had much time left.

A hand grasped the collar of her coat and she felt herself being dragged slowly across the wet pavement. A moment later, someone — Erin she guessed — grabbed her wrist and nearly ripped her arm from its socket in his effort to help get her to cover.

Another flash from the Dumpster and Erin toppled forward, landing hard and not moving. The image of his still body sent a surge of adrenaline through her powerful enough to overcome her slow suffocation. She managed to get hold of his coat and crawl on top of him in an effort to protect him from the gunfire.

"Goddamnit, Jenna!" she heard Beamon shout. "Let go! I can't pull you both!"

But she continued to spread herself out across his back as her peripheral vision slowly went blank.

"He shot himself," Fournier said, showing a phenomenal grasp of the obvious as Beamon peered into the Dumpster at the body of Jonas Metzger. His changed appearance and the blood splattered across his face should have made him difficult to identify, but his eyes gave him away. Even staring sightlessly into the dark sky, they had lost none of their fanatical intensity.

"Shit!" Beamon shouted, and kicked the side of the Dumpster. It felt so good that he did it again. And then he found he couldn't stop.

"Mark, are you alright? You should try to —"

He held up a hand, silencing Fournier, and then limped off toward an ambulance idling in the middle of the parking lot.

The rain had stopped and Jenna was lying face down on a stretcher with a couple of paramedics hovering over her. Erin hadn't been hit as cleanly and was sitting on the wet asphalt a few feet away.

When he spotted Beamon, he jumped to his feet and rushed forward, only stopping when he found himself staring into the barrel of Beamon's pistol.

"You son of a bitch! You knew! You knew that he was going to try to kill us!"

"Not now," Beamon said, looking down at Jenna and feeling a flood of relief when she lifted her head.

"You alright?"

A weak nod.

"I want a fucking explanation," Erin said, his anger overcoming his judgment as he took a step forward.

"Oh, come on, Erin. Teague knows we're all over the tar sands and then suddenly he uses the same front company that owns a building we know about to deliver sinister-sounding lab equipment here? A little obvious, don't you think?"

"So you put us out as bait?"

"Yeah," Beamon said, keeping his gun

trained on Erin, who was now shaking with rage. "But I felt bad about it."

40

The pounding on the door matched the pounding in Beamon's head, both in volume and tempo, but instead of getting up, he leaned back in his chair and put his stockinged feet on the bed. The empty bottles from the room's minibar were lined up on the table next to him, starting with bourbon, moving to gin, and ending with vodka. The beer bottles were yet unopened.

Instead of stopping, the banging on the door intensified until it was impossible to ignore.

"It's not locked for Christ's sake! What?"

It was immediately thrown open and Erin stalked into the room with Jenna in tow. He spun her around by the arm and yanked up the back of her shirt. "Have you seen this?"

The bruise was reminiscent of a sunrise, almost black in the middle, radiating out to purple, red, and finally fading to yellow as it passed beneath her bra strap.

"That's a good one," Beamon said, leaning over to fish a beer from the minibar. He held it out to Erin, but the peace offering just made him angrier.

"I notice you're not shot," he said, dropping Jenna's shirt. "What if he'd aimed for her head?"

"Head shots are unreliable. You'd be surprised how often the bullet just deflects off your skull."

"That's it? That's your fucking explanation? Head shots are unreliable?"

"And the part about your skull deflecting them."

Erin lurched forward, but Jenna saw it coming and stood between the two men. "Forget it, Erin. Okay? It doesn't even hurt anymore."

An obvious lie, but told convincingly enough to save Beamon from getting his ass kicked again. He opened the beer in his hand and took a pull. "A few days ago, you were standing around telling me that billions of people are about to die. Today you're complaining about a little bruise. I played the hand I had, Erin."

"You could have told us."

"What would have been the point? You'd have said yes."

Erin opened his mouth to protest, but

367

instead just flopped down on the bed and propped himself against the headboard.

"Are we going home?" Jenna asked, taking a seat in the only other chair in the room. Judging by her expression as she sat, her back not only hurt, it hurt a lot.

"These guys are here, not in the States," Beamon said, feeling a twinge of guilt for hanging them out as targets. Fortunately, it was numbed by the alcohol. "There's nothing left for us at home."

"What about your fiancée and her daughter?"

"You sure I can't interest either of you in a beer?" he said, pretending he hadn't heard. But he could see from Jenna's expression that she wasn't going to let it go.

"On the surface, oil getting cut off sounds so trivial," he started. "But then you sit down and really start thinking about it and . . . I guess I'm not sure what I would say to them. 'Sorry I couldn't figure this thing out, but maybe you'll be one of the lucky ones — maybe you'd die in the violence and not slowly starve to death.' "

"It's not your fault, Mark. It's mine."

"It's fucking Michael Teague's fault!" Erin shouted. "End of story, okay? If he wanted us dead bad enough to send Jonas, it means he hasn't finished this thing. We've still got time. Now, what are we going to do with it?"

Beamon shrugged.

"Well, now we know that the shell company you've been looking at is definitely connected to Michael," Jenna said. "What about its other assets?"

"We're working through that," Beamon said. "But beyond the factory out in the tar sands, there isn't much. Actually, there's almost nothing. We're pulling the facility's engineering and architectural plans and we'll let you have a look when we get them, but since you've been over it in person, I doubt that'll go anywhere. We're digging into the backgrounds of Teague and the Metzgers to see if there's anything in their past that could lead us to them, but the chances are somewhere between slim and none. Fugitives disappear all the time and if they're smart and have some resources, they're damn hard to find — even if you have years to look. And if I understand you, we don't have years."

Jenna shook her head miserably.

"So as near as I can tell, the only thread we have left to pull is how Teague is going to breed enough of this stuff that it can get a foothold in the tar sands. And you two seem to be the world experts on that."

Erin sunk a little farther into the pillows he'd propped behind him. "You give us too much credit, Mark. Why would either of us have ever given any thought to how you'd breed tons of bacteria in secret?"

"This Teague guy isn't some kind of Einstein. Mostly a businessman with a background in computers, right? And you said Udo is middle of the road as biologists go. So if they've figured it out, why can't you?"

"Maybe we've already stopped him," Erin said. "Maybe cutting off access to the tar sands did it."

"Then why go through all that trouble to kill you?" Beamon said.

"Vindictiveness?"

Beamon shook his head. "He exposed a lot and lost one of two people working for him. There's more to it than that."

"Okay," Jenna said. "Then he hasn't finished this thing and he's scared we're going to figure it out before he can. That means we have a chance."

Erin pulled a pillow over his face and spoke through it. "Maybe he's overestimated us. I mean, even if he could breed it and if the tar sands were wide open, how would he deliver it? You're talking about tanker truck loads of the stuff spread out over a huge area to get the effect he's shooting for."

Beamon drained his beer and reached for another. The alcohol was making his head feel like it was full of gauze, but that's about all. The pounding was still there, along with the fear and guilt.

"As I see it, there's only one bright spot in all this," Erin continued. "I may starve. I may even get burned at the stake by a bunch of Mad Max rejects. But at least I know that whatever happens to me is going to happen to Teague at the same time."

Jenna's brow furrowed a bit as Beamon popped the top on the bottle in his hand.

"What?" he said.

"That's not right," she said.

"What's not right?"

"Michael Teague isn't Jonas. For him, a lot of this is about power and feeling superior." She leaned forward in her chair until the pain in her back stopped her. "I've known him for a long time and I can tell you that there isn't anything he believes in enough to die for. I'm not even sure there's anything he'd suffer for."

"What choice would he have?" Erin said. "He's setting something in motion that's going to be impossible to control."

"No," she said, her voice gaining a certainty that Beamon hadn't heard before. "Think about the times you met him, Erin.

He doesn't feel anything but disdain for people. He considers himself above them. The worst thing that could possibly happen to him would be to die anonymously — just one of a million people who died on any given day. No, he'd be prepared. He'd sit there and watch everything fall apart from a distance."

"Yeah," Erin said, pushing the pillow from his face and sitting upright on the bed. "He'd sit there and tell himself that we brought it on ourselves and that this is the price we pay for not listening to him."

Beamon set his beer down on the table and blinked hard, trying to concentrate through the fog he'd so carefully constructed with the well-stocked minibar. "But that's impossible, right? I mean, based on what you've told me, there's no way to hide from this."

"There is if you knew it was going to happen years in advance," Erin said. "There's still solar, wind, maybe hydro. But with all metal parts and synthetic lubrication."

"But not a house," Jenna said. "More of a compound. It'd have to have a good water source and fields where you could grow food and run livestock. Somewhere well away from civilization. It'd have to be pretty inaccessible and defensible because the people who worked on it would know it was there."

"And in a good climate," Erin added. "You wouldn't want to have to heat it and cool it, and you'd want a long growing season."

Beamon fumbled in his pocket for his cell phone. "There can't be that many people who could design and build something like that."

"There aren't," Jenna agreed, the excitement creeping into her voice. "And between Erin and me, we probably know most of them."

41

They had been hiking since dawn and the fatigue in Michael Teague's legs nearly caused him to collapse as he jumped from a small boulder into the deep brush below. All around him, the trees rose tall and thick, blocking the view of the dark clouds that had been intermittently drenching them for the past six hours.

Udo was twenty yards ahead, moving with surprising speed through the tangled ground cover that carpeted the ten-foot-wide corridor cut years ago when the pipeline they were following was installed.

They'd watched the news of Jonas's death the night before, Udo concentrating on the television and Teague concentrating on his reaction. Surprisingly, he'd watched for just a few moments, not even waiting for the end of the story before disappearing into the back room. When he reemerged hours later, he'd asked Teague to join him outside where they'd conducted an awkward and bloodless ceremony that consisted of Udo talking about his brother's conviction and sacrifice. It had lasted less than five minutes.

Although Udo's reaction was opaque and conflicted, Teague's wasn't. Of course, he was disappointed that Jonas had once again failed to put an end to the threat that Jenna and Erin posed, but the German's suicide could hardly be considered a negative outcome. Admittedly, he had been useful over the years, but it seemed likely that he would have become more and more of a liability as the world began its next chapter. Together, the Metzger brothers had the potential to be difficult to control.

Udo began to slow, searching the ground, and finally dropping to his knees as Teague caught up.

"It's here, Michael."

Teague dropped his backpack and handed the German a small shovel, which he used to carefully uncover a metal valve. He pulled a plastic vial from his own pack and opened the valve to fill it.

They were close to twelve miles from their building, and the fluid was thick and black, seemingly unaffected by the bacteria they'd introduced. As expected, the farther they traveled away from the initial contamination, the lighter the bacterial loads became.

Just how much lighter, though, couldn't be determined until Udo returned to his lab and made precise measurements. With that information, he would be able to extrapolate just how long it would take for the entire pipe to fill and give them a time-frame for release.

And when that day came, they would fire the hundreds of small charges they had placed along the length of the pipeline, letting the bacteria drain into the tar-soaked sands, where it would thrive and be carried by the wind until it blanketed the entire planet.

42

"So what do you think?" Mark Beamon shouted into the microphone attached to his headphones. Jenna and Erin were in the back, faces pressed against the helicopter's windows to better see the lonely cluster of buildings spread out beneath them.

"It looks right," Jenna said as Beamon motioned for the pilot to make another pass.

"It's a thirty-five-acre inholding surrounded by BLM land. We're about twenty miles from the nearest dirt road and another thirty from the nearest pavement. The terrain to get up here is pretty rugged. If you're not flying, the easiest way to do it would be to follow the river on foot, but you're looking at a pretty grueling multi-day hike with no trail."

"One thing's for sure," Erin continued. "Somebody spent a hell of a lot of money here. Look how much forest they had to clear to put those pastures in and to make the land arable."

Their altitude gave them a clear view of the neat, efficient partitioning of the land — fenced areas held horses and livestock, with other sections hosting various crops. In the center of it all was a low adobe building topped with solar arrays and surrounded by several smaller outbuildings and barns. Most interesting, though, was the tall stone-and-earth wall that surrounded the entire area. Beamon followed the curving lines, trying to calculate its length. There must have been miles of it.

"Can we get a little closer to the river?" Jenna said, and the pilot responded with a nausea-inducing dive.

"See right there, Mark? That small dam is microhydro — it generates electricity. And this area of California is perfect, climate-wise."

It did look perfect. Idyllic, even. The sky was an intense blue and air blowing through the cockpit was a pleasant eighty degrees. The entire scene had exactly the suspiciously utopian feel that Beamon had expected.

He pointed down and the pilot dropped the helicopter into the dirt next to four others. The rotors kicked up a swirl of dust that seemed to go completely unnoticed by a lone figure running at them with a familiar half-lope, half-waddle.

"Mark! What, did you stop for breakfast?"

Beamon climbed out of the helicopter, crouching against the downdraft as he ran alongside Terry Hirst. "What've you got?"

"A lot," he replied, leading Beamon to the main building as Jenna and Erin followed. "This is quite a spread."

"Do we know who owns it?"

"Nope. The paper trail runs in circles — just like in Canada. I will tell you this, though — it's totally self-sustaining."

"I didn't know you were an expert."

"I'm not. I'm taking the word of the people living here."

"There were people here?" Beamon said, not sure why he was surprised. Livestock and crops didn't tend themselves.

"We talked to all of them individually and got the same story from everyone. They were hired before the place was even built for their expertise in alternative power and agriculture. They oversaw the construction and they've spent the last couple years taking care of the place and working out the bugs."

"Do you think they're involved?"

"Nah. They're all pretty rabid environmentalists, but not crazies like Jonas

Metzger."

"So they were willing to talk?"

Hirst grimaced. "You can't get them to shut up. They're all feeling pretty smug with everything that's going on in the outside world right now."

They passed through the heavy front doors of the main building and into an expansive entryway where a mosaic of the sun covered most of the floor. The temperature inside was a good ten degrees cooler and the only light was provided by a chandelier hanging over a bulky wooden table. The overall impression was a kind of hippie version of *Lifestyles of the Rich and Famous*.

"The ultimate survivalist spa," Beamon commented.

"The place doesn't suck," Hirst agreed. "I mean, they've got pretty much all the creature comforts here — the walls are something like five feet thick, so it never gets hot, and they have lots of well-placed glass to keep things warm and light in the winter. Nice stereo system, computers, a great kitchen with a huge wood-burning stove —"

"But we don't know for certain that it's Teague's," Beamon interrupted.

Hirst shook his head. "I don't think there's any way we can be absolutely sure unless we put it on TV and see if anyone claims it."

Erin jumped up on the table in the center of the room and grabbed the chandelier with both hands, hanging his entire weight on it. There was a dull cracking sound and a moment later, it pulled free, covering him with a shower of sparks and tiny chunks of the ceiling.

Beamon wasn't sure how to react and he leaned into Jenna. "Is this another one of his tantrums?"

She shook her head and indicated that Beamon should watch as Erin yanked down some wires and examined them.

"It's Teague's."

Beamon squinted at the wires, but they didn't look all that remarkable to him. "This is pretty important, Erin. Are you absolutely certain or are you just speculating?"

"Look at the electrical insulation on these. It's cloth. This stuff's been obsolete for decades. The only thing it had going for it is that it wouldn't be affected by the bacteria."

Beamon nodded silently and then wandered back outside into the sunlight. Another helicopter was coming in and he watched it land.

"Forensics people from San Francisco," Hirst explained.

Beamon watched them drag equipment out onto the ground for a few moments before pulling a phone from his pocket.

"You won't get a signal," Hirst said, holding out a satellite phone. "Try this one."

"You've got eight hours," Beamon said as he dialed. "Go over everything you can and make arrangements to take whatever you don't have time to look at."

"What happens in eight hours?"

Beamon ignored the question, listening to the phone ring before being picked up.

"General Vance's office," the woman on the other end said.

"Hi Kelly — it's Mark Beamon. Put Chuck on. I need a little favor."

"Come on!" Beamon shouted as Erin and Jenna ran toward the helicopter spinning up behind him.

"This is the most incredible place I've ever seen!" Erin said as he helped Jenna into the back. He was a bit breathless, but Beamon wasn't sure if it was from the run or all the eco-gadgets he'd spent the day poring over.

"It's all state of the art and purpose-built. Even the solar panels are sealed in a way that won't let the bacteria damage them. There are three all-metal windmills lying at the edge of the forest. I assume they're going to set them up on high ground as soon as the government collapses and stops monitoring the use of public lands."

"Strap yourself in," Beamon said as the sound of the blades grew louder.

"Did you catch the gun room, Mark? There's enough stuff in there to take over France. It seems like Teague isn't inclined to share."

Beamon twisted around in his seat and held out a video camera. "Do either of you know how to work this thing?"

"I used to have one kind of like that," Jenna said. "But I'm no expert."

"You are now. We tried to get the press in here, but they didn't have enough fuel to make the trip and I didn't have time to find them any. So we're just going to have to film it ourselves."

"Film what ourselves?"

He pointed to the east at a formation of fighter jets just coming into view.

"What are those for?" Jenna asked.

"Are you filming?"

She shrugged and searched for the camera's ON switch as their pilot turned the helicopter to give her a better view.

"Okay, I've got it," she said. "But I still don't see —"

Flame burst from the side of one of the

jets and Beamon smiled as the missile impacted the roof of the main building. Two horses that had resisted every effort to run them off wisely started galloping toward freedom.

"Jesus Christ!" Erin shouted, pressing his face against the window. "What the hell are you doing? That place is —"

"Don't stop filming!" Beamon shouted as one of the barns was hit, shooting solar panels high enough in the air to force their pilot to retreat to a safer distance.

"Are you responsible for this?" Erin said, looking almost panicked. "Do you have any idea —"

"Hell, yes, I'm responsible. Pretty wild, huh?"

The missile impact with the microhydro dam was dead center and it sent out a wave high enough to flatten most of the cornfield.

"Nice one!" Beamon said, clapping energetically. "Isn't it amazing how when they shoot those things —"

"Are you nuts?" Erin screamed. "Do you have any idea what went in to building a facility like that? What an incredible piece of engineering it is? There's technology in there that I've never even seen — that nobody's ever seen. Stuff that we're going to need if Teague manages to release that bacteria."

"No," Jenna said, sounding increasingly depressed as she zoomed in on the drowning corn. "What good would it do, Erin? There's no time. Mark's right."

"What the hell are you talking about, Mark's right?"

"You know as well as I do that Michael's watching the news. When he sees this — when he sees that he's going to end up like everyone else, do you think he'll still go through with it?"

Erin leaned into the glass again and watched the fire spread into the trees. "I guess not. I mean, I see what you're getting at, but couldn't you have just filmed your guys swarming all over it?"

Beamon shrugged. "I guess I could have, but it wouldn't have been anywhere near as satisfying."

43

Michael Teague stumbled again, this time over nothing but his own feet. His hips were deeply bruised from the weight of his pack, creating a dull throb that was starting to eclipse the pain from the bleeding blisters on his feet.

He had spent a sleepless night out in the elements, snow collecting on his sleeping bag as he listened to the wind and Udo's rhythmic snoring. He could still feel the effects of that, too, in his bone-deep fatigue and the knot in his lower back.

Udo, though, seemed unaffected by any of it, his pace even more grueling than the day before. When he dropped out of sight over a small rise, Teague felt a moment of panic at being left alone in the endless wilderness. He forced his shaking legs forward, using his hands for balance as he tripped up the hill, and finally brought the German into view again.

"Udo! Slow down!"

He didn't seem to hear, jumping off a large boulder and once again disappearing from sight.

"Udo!"

The German didn't reappear, but the sun broke through the clouds and illuminated a clearing a few hundred yards ahead. They were finally back.

In the open, the wind was a palpable force, pushing him forward and slamming the open door of the warehouse repeatedly against its metal siding. Teague raised his hand to keep the dirt out of his eyes and ran inside, struggling to close the door behind him.

They'd left the heat on and the warmth began to penetrate his heavy clothing, causing his skin to burn and itch as though it didn't remember what it was like not to be wet and half frozen. Udo stripped his pack off and began lining up the samples he'd taken next to his microscope.

"How long until you know?" Teague asked, pulling off a glove and fumbling to turn on the television.

"Not long."

The German's voice had lost its animation since Jonas had died, and now Teague wondered if it was ever really there. Had his brother's suicide changed something in Udo, or had Jonas's brooding presence just made everyone seem exuberant by comparison?

"That's not an answer."

"It will take a few hours to examine the samples and another hour to calculate the optimal date for release. Is that better?"

Teague nodded and began removing his jacket, turning his attention to the television and a man making suggestions on how to cut back on skyrocketing food costs and still get a balanced diet.

He flipped to Fox, which was airing an interview about an attempted carjacking in Miami that had ended in a half-hour-long gunfight. Another turn of the channel brought him to some shaky overhead footage of a spreading wildfire.

Several buildings had been consumed, but it was impossible to see detail with the flames leaping around their burned-out husks. He was about to go get something to eat when he realized that the scene was strangely familiar.

"It isn't clear exactly what started the fire," the disembodied voice of the newscaster said. "And we haven't been able to get any updated information beyond the fact that it's now under control."

Teague remained motionless, his exhausted mind having a difficult time grasping what he was seeing. The camera pulled back, revealing what was left of a pattern that he recognized as the one he had so painstakingly designed — the main house, the stables, the storage barns. The only thing not burning was part of the cornfield that had been inundated by his shattered dam.

It wasn't possible. The buildings were made primarily of earth and concrete, with gravity-fed fire sprinklers. Even if the fire systems failed, there was still no way to account for this kind of destruction.

It became harder and harder to breathe as he realized that it wasn't an accident. His refuge had been purposely destroyed.

Teague took a hesitant step backward, but bumped into something that stopped him. He spun and found Udo staring up at the screen.

"It's all gone," Teague stammered. "Everything we built. How? There was no connection between us and that property. I was so careful . . ."

Udo didn't acknowledge that he'd even heard; instead, he just turned and walked back to his microscope while Teague tried to process his new reality.

It wasn't possible. He'd spent more time on that facility than any other part of his plan, parceling out the design and manufacture to companies all over the world, creating a paper trail that led through an endless maze of blind alleys and dead ends, switching contractors various times during construction so that no one would have the full picture. He'd been so meticulous, so confident in his preparation, that there had been no need for a backup plan.

He looked over at Udo, who was calmly putting an oil sample on a glass slide. Did he understand what had just happened? What it meant? They had no protection at all from the collapse that the bacteria would cause. The facility they were standing in had enough heat, electricity, and food for a few more months, but that was all. There had been no reason to supply it further.

They would lose power like everyone else. The truck that brought them there would fail, cutting them off. Their food would run out and Canada's bitter winter would descend.

He reached for a chair and sat, leaning his elbows on his knees and holding his head in his hands. This building would become their tomb. They would die there of starvation and cold, alone and anonymous.

No.

He stood and walked unsteadily past Udo into the back room. The gun cabinet was unlocked and he reached inside, pulling out an automatic pistol. He had money, various identities, passports. He could call Homeland Security, tell them about the pipeline, and then disappear into Canada, which, with its undamaged reserves, not only would be untouched by the massive economic fallout his water-injected bacteria was continuing to cause but would quickly become one of the wealthiest countries in the world. It would be a life on the run, but if he was careful, it could be a comfortable one.

Teague took a deep breath and let it out slowly, staring through the open door leading into the main part of the building. He'd been so close — only days from changing the world on a level that no one had ever even conceived of before. Only to be stopped by the blind luck of some government hack.

When he passed back through the door, the German was no longer sitting at his microscope.

"Udo? Where are you?"

No answer.

He continued forward slowly, his gun

hand behind his back. Although Jonas had been more outwardly aggressive, it would be a mistake to assume his brother was any less committed. There was little doubt in Teague's mind that Udo intended to follow through with their plan and then just sit down in the snow to die. He would never agree to stop, and even if he did, he would become a liability — someone Teague would have to support and worry about for the rest of his life. No, it was time for him to join his brother.

Teague moved carefully around a divider wall, but Udo was still nowhere to be found. The radio control to the pipeline bombs was built into a low table bolted to the floor and Teague knelt beside it, grabbing the cables that fed it with a sweating hand. Once it was destroyed and Udo was out of the way, he would drive the truck back to civilization and disappear. As soon as he was satisfied that he was safe, he'd call the hotline number that was running across the bottom of nearly every television screen in the world and tell them how to find this place.

The pain in the back of his head flared suddenly and unexpectedly, robbing him of his balance and sending him pitching forward. He could see the shards of glass falling around him before everything lost focus and he smashed onto the concrete.

His disorientation was more the result of fatigue and surprise than the blow, and the sensation of his cheek being cut by the glass on the floor cleared his head, but not before he felt the gun being pulled from his waistband. He spun, swinging an arm wildly behind him, but it was far too late. Udo had already stepped back to a safe distance and was aiming the pistol at his chest.

"My brother is dead. I have no home. No friends. No life at all. I gave it all up. For this."

"Udo, stop!" Teague begged, holding a hand out in front of him while he got slowly to his feet. "I wasn't going to hurt you. You know that I wouldn't do that. I was trying to help you. If we keep on with this, we'll both die. We don't have any protection at all. We'll be like all the others."

"Yes," Udo agreed. "Just like all the others."

"But none of this is our fault! We tried to protect the world. We tried to warn people."

"Not our fault? Are you certain, Michael? How are we different? How much was destroyed to build our houses? Our cars? Our clothing? No, we're not innocent in this."

When Udo pulled the hammer back on

the gun, his eyes turned into a lifeless facsimile of his dead brother's.

"No! Don't kill me," Teague shouted, putting his other hand in front of him and taking a step backward. "I swear I wasn't going to hurt you. You have to believe that."

Udo came around behind him and shoved him forward with strength that seemed impossible for his thin frame. He pressed the gun into the back of Teague's neck as they walked through the main lab and into the back room.

This time, when the pain flared in Teague's head, it was immediately followed by a numbness that collapsed his knees. His vision swirled sickeningly, but he could still hear the rattle of the chain being removed from the gun cabinet and feel the cold of the links as they closed around his neck.

"Think about what we've accomplished, Michael. Think of the importance of it." The lock snapped shut and Udo took a step back. "And think about Jonas."

44

Erin Neal slipped into Jenna's room and then stuck his head out the door to look down the empty hall. He kept expecting to see guards, but there were none. Just an empty, silent corridor. Was Mark Beamon stupid? Or maybe he was really clever. Sure as hell he wasn't the trusting type.

"Erin, what is it?"

He closed the door quietly and turned to look at Jenna for a moment before walking to the minibar for a beer. He wasn't ready yet.

"You want a drink?"

She shook her head.

His knock had obviously woken her, leaving her staring at him through reddened eyes, wearing nothing but the Canada T-shirt she'd bought from the hotel souvenir shop. Her hair was different now and didn't tangle around her face the way it used to when she was awakened from a deep sleep.

But it was still Jenna. Here. Alive.

"It's after midnight," she said. "Did you think of something?"

"No."

Her look of disappointment wasn't doing much for his confidence, and his heart was pounding uncomfortably. He pointed at the bed in the center of the small room. "I just want to talk. Why don't you sit down?"

She eyed the mattress nervously and then shook her head. "I'm fine."

He forced an easy smile, but silently cursed himself. He hadn't intended that as the clumsy come-on it had sounded like. This was going downhill fast and he needed to turn it around.

"Okay. Here's the thing. I want you back."

He managed not to wince at the sound of his own words. Smooth.

"What?"

"Did I stutter?"

Oh, good. Anger. That was going to work.

Fortunately, even after all this time, she knew him well enough to just let it go. "I guess I'm saying that I don't understand why."

It was a reasonable response, but he wasn't sure how to deal with it. There was a simple truth here — that he'd always loved her and screwing him over while destroying the world as he knew it wasn't enough to change that. Strange but true.

"I've met a lot of nice enough women since you've been gone, but they all seem a little crazy and a little boring. You're just crazy."

Instead of the smile he'd hoped for, her expression turned despondent. "No offense, Erin, but you obviously don't get out much. After everything that's happened, I'm the best you can do?"

"Do you mind if *I* sit down?" he said, easing into the room's only chair and clutching his beer like a security blanket. "So that isn't an answer."

"I don't remember a question."

"You're going to make me say it, aren't you? Will you come back to me?"

"I . . . I don't know," she said, beginning to pace across the room. It caused her T-shirt to drift up and expose the bottom of her underwear. Blue.

It was strange what triggered memories — sometimes nothing more than a smell or a brief glimpse of something completely trivial. For him it was dumping his laundry into the washer and not seeing those stupid blue panties.

"Say it, Jenna."

"Say what?"

"You're obviously thinking something. Say it."

"I'm thinking how much I've lied to you. And since I've gone so far down that road, whether I should just keep on going."

"Yeah, it's worked out so well."

She stopped and turned to face him. "Are you sure you want to hear this?"

He wasn't, but he nodded anyway.

"Okay. I loved you when we broke up and I still do. My feelings never went away. I'm not sure they even faded any. No matter how much I tried to forget my life before."

Suddenly the constriction in his chest that had been there so long disappeared. He took the first deep, unfettered breath since she had disappeared, feeling the air fill parts of his lungs unused for almost two years.

"Whenever I was away from Bozeman, when I didn't think anyone was watching, the first thing I'd do is find a place to get on the Internet and Google you. At first, there was always something new, but as time went on there was less and less. I knew I was the cause of that. It's what I woke up thinking about every morning and what I was thinking about when I finally went to sleep every night." She looked down at the floor and let out a short laugh. "Listen to me. I'm standing here talking like I'm the victim."

Erin didn't know what to say. Or maybe he was just afraid he'd say the wrong thing. He had the distinct sensation that he was balancing on the edge of a razor.

"How many boring, crazy women?" Jenna said, breaking the silence.

"What?"

"Since me."

"I'm embarrassed to say."

Her expression turned enigmatic, the impenetrable mask he'd come to read as a moment when she didn't know how to feel.

"More than fifty?"

"I wouldn't be embarrassed to say that. Three. And none lasted more than two weeks."

"I'm so sorry, Erin."

"You?"

"If it's any consolation, that's three more than me."

It occurred to him for the first time that as bad as his life had been over the past couple years, hers hadn't been any better. At least he'd had the freedom to pursue happiness if he'd chosen to. She'd been trapped on all sides.

"Why'd you do it, Jenna? Why would you get involved in something like this?"

"I don't think you could ever really understand, Erin. You're all about studying minute details and weighing alternatives. I —"

"You're a scientist, too. A good one."

"But not a perfect one. A human one. I have beliefs and things I love beyond reason. I walked into this with my eyes open. I *wanted* to be part of this. And now I regret the hell out of it. But I still remember the feeling."

"If you'd have just thought about —"

"I know, I know," she interrupted. "I read your book fifty times. You're just terribly smart — every footnote in place, all the logic perfect, all the research unassailable. But sometimes truth can't be distilled down to a bunch of equations."

He shook his head. "Two plus two equals four, Jen."

"That's not the way the world works, Erin, and that's why you've never quite fit into it."

They fell silent again, but this time it was Erin who broke it. "So does this mean we're back together?"

Her eyes widened. "Have you been paying any attention at all to what I've done? To the fact that there probably won't be a future for any of us?"

"Now who's being overly logical?"

She turned and looked through the sheer curtains at the lights beyond. Erin stood and came up behind her, sliding his arms around her waist and pressing against her back. The city seemed strangely bright after the electricity rationing in the U.S.

"There's not much we can do now," he said, feeling her warmth sink into him. "Maybe blowing up his place in California will stop him. Maybe it won't. Either way, it's time to think about what's next."

"Next?"

"I have a lot of money that may not be worth the paper it's printed on in a few months. We could buy a floatplane, load it up with supplies, and head to Alaska. If Teague follows through with this, then we can wait it out there for a few years."

She pulled away, but wouldn't look at him. "Until everyone's dead, you mean? Until Mark and his new family have starved or been murdered?"

"There's no reason for us to die, too."

"You mean there's no reason for *you* to die. There's every reason for me to."

"What good would —"

She turned and pressed her mouth against his, silencing him. When she pulled away, the look of surprise on his face finally got him that smile, sad as it was.

"Maybe for one night, we could pretend none of this ever happened. Do you think that's possible anymore, Erin?"

45

Stepping from the relative quiet of the hotel hallway into the chaos of the commandeered conference area was disorienting. But then, just about everything felt disorienting to Erin that morning — the sunlight that had cut through the blinds to wake him, Jenna's naked body draped across the mattress next to him. Even his own face in the mirror. Something about it seemed different, but he wasn't sure what. Maybe everything. Probably nothing.

Jenna gripped his hand as they nudged past the conservatively dressed men and women darting around the room. It seemed that overnight Beamon had managed to move his entire staff over the border to Canada. No small feat these days, and an indication that he still had the government's support, though there was no telling how long that would last.

They stopped behind a man securing

computer cables to the floor and Jenna tapped him on the shoulder. "Excuse me. We're looking for Mark Beamon."

He pointed toward a storage room at the back and they started for it, Beamon's angry voice becoming audible when they were still twenty feet away.

"Jesus Christ, Jack! What are we talking about here? You said I had a free hand and I used it."

Erin slowed. "Maybe this isn't a good time, Jen. We should go."

"Go where?"

He didn't bother to resist as she dragged him forward, increasing uncertainty paralyzing him.

The problem was that he seemed to have lost his ability to read Jenna. He'd been shocked to find her still there when he woke up that morning, and wasn't sure if it was just because she didn't have anywhere to go or if it was something more.

What he was certain of, though, was that at least for a few hours, it had felt like none of this had happened. Now he just had to convince her that they had a shot at a future. Not a normal one, of course. Maybe not even a long one. But a future nonetheless.

"Jenna, we really need to think through

whether there's anything we can do at this point. Could we just go somewhere and talk for a little while?"

She ignored him and continued into the tiny room where Mark Beamon was pacing around a table with nothing on it but a single speaker. He glanced up at them, but otherwise didn't acknowledge their presence.

"A free hand doesn't mean the authority to call in a fucking air strike on U.S. soil!" Jack Reynolds said through the speaker. "What the hell were you thinking doing something like that without talking to me first?"

"Talking to you about what, Jack? It's not like I killed anyone. Hell, we had the fire out in a couple hours. What's the god-damned problem?"

The concern on Jenna's face was visible as Beamon continued to circle the table, stooped in a way that made him look shorter than he was. He obviously hadn't shaved that morning and the red of his eyes suggested that the half-empty bourbon bottle on the floor hadn't been shared with anyone.

"You're asking me what the problem is? You used the U.S. military to blow up an important piece of evidence!"

Beamon rolled his swollen eyes. "We needed to make sure that Teague knew he didn't have anywhere to run."

"Then why the hell not just send video of our people going through it?"

"I thought blowing it up would have more emotional impact," Beamon said.

The next few words Reynolds uttered were unintelligible, choked with a rage that Erin couldn't figure out. He hadn't agreed with the decision, either, but there was no denying the twisted logic of it.

"Do you have any idea how complicated the economic coordination of this thing is now, Mark? And you can multiply that by a thousand if you let this son of a bitch release the modified bacteria. The government could have used that facility as a command center."

Beamon's lip curled and his face darkened to the point that Erin almost felt compelled to back away.

"If you think I'm going to watch Carrie and Emory die while you and your political cronies hole up in California with a bunch of high school cheerleaders, you're seriously mistaken, Jack."

The speaker went silent for a few seconds. "Did I just hear you right, Mark? Are you implying that you did this to keep that facility out of the hands of the U.S. government?"

Erin felt his eyebrows rise. As near as he could tell, that's exactly what Beamon had said. And people thought *he* had a temper.

"You can take it any way you like, Jack."

Another brief silence. "I want you on a plane back to the United States, Mark. Now."

Beamon calmly lifted the speaker and held it a few inches from his face. "Why don't you come up here and get me?" Then he ripped the cord out of the wall and threw the speaker on the floor. When he turned back to them, there was a pleasant, if strained smile on his face. "So you two look well rested this morning."

Erin glanced over at Jenna and realized they were almost touching. The mandatory two-foot buffer that had existed between them was suddenly gone and it was apparently obvious.

"We're okay," Jenna said. "But you look horrible. Are you all right?"

"Couldn't be better."

He slid up on the table behind him and then lay back, his legs dangling off the side as he stared at the ceiling.

"It looks like you've got half the FBI up here," Jenna prompted. "Are you getting anywhere?"

"No."

He closed his eyes and for a moment Erin thought he might have stopped breathing.

"Mark?" The alarm in Jenna's voice suggested she had the same impression.

"What?"

"You've got a hundred people out there. They must be doing *something*."

He shrugged without moving from his position on the table. "We've gone through all the stuff we pulled out of the place in California, but there isn't anything that we can use to find Teague. Whatever you want to say about him, he's not stupid. I've got virtually every biologist on the planet trying to figure out how he's going to grow and transport these bacteria, and we're getting absolutely nowhere."

The door opened and Terry Hirst poked his head in. "Mark, I just got a call from the States. Apparently you've been fired and I've been put in charge."

"Congratulations."

"What do you want me to do about it?"

"I don't care."

"Okay. I'll just ignore it. But I think everyone would appreciate it if you'd get off that table and think of something."

The door closed again and Beamon's head

lolled in Erin and Jenna's direction. "The tar sands thing was a good idea, but I think he outsmarted us."

"What do you mean?" Jenna said.

"It was a red herring. They bought that facility to throw us off. And now it's too late for me to relocate my people to Venezuela or Russia. I fell for it."

Jenna crossed the small room and took hold of Beamon's hand. "We haven't lost, Mark. We can't. You understand that, right? We can't."

"I'm out of ideas, Jenna. All I can think about now is Carrie and Em. But even with everything I know, I can't come up with a way to save them."

When they finally left the room, Beamon was still lying motionless on the table, now with his eyes closed. Erin hoped that he was asleep — he looked as if he needed to turn off for a little while. As much as he hated to admit it, the old government hack had grown on him and he didn't like seeing him sink into despair. But what could he do about it? Things had gone too far.

"He's right," Erin said, leaning into Jenna's ear as they waded back into the sea of suits outside Beamon's door. "Teague's won."

She jerked to a stop, but he'd anticipated

it and put a hand on her back to keep them moving forward. "There's nothing we can do here, Jen. If there were, I'd stick it out. But there's not. We still have time to get that floatplane and set ourselves up, but we have a lot of work to do."

"I thought we resolved this last night."

"I don't think we resolved anything last night. Look, I know you don't think you deserve to survive, but have you really thought this through? It's not going to be the smart people who make it, or the compassionate ones. It's going to be the people who are willing to stick a spike in your eye for a box of stale Oreos. I don't —"

"Erin! Jenna!"

Terry Hirst jogged over to them. "How's Mark doing?"

"I'm worried about him," Jenna said. "He's just lying there on the table."

"Does he look like he's thinking?"

"He looks dead."

Hirst sighed quietly and pointed to row of boxes lined up against the wall. Each was labeled in bold letters, the one on the end marked ERIN/JENNA.

"We've got ideas on how this stuff could be grown coming in from all over," Hirst said. "I've had synopses of the most promising stuff put over there for you. Could you go through them and see if you can give me some kind of priority? A lot of them seem a little far-fetched and I can't afford to waste manpower."

"Of course," Jenna said, just like Erin knew she would.

"Great. I also threw in some stuff we got on that facility in the tar sands. Maybe you could flip through it and see if anything jumps out at you." He slapped Erin reassuringly on the back and then rushed off toward a group of Mounties that had just come through the door.

"Jenna, seriously," Erin said, hovering behind her as she dumped their box out onto the floor. "We need to get the fuck out of here."

"Then go," she said, dropping to the carpet and sorting through the seemingly endless papers and reports.

"You're a smart woman, Jen. But sometimes your judgment sucks. Staying here is as good as committing suicide."

She dropped the papers she was holding, and for a moment her eyes clouded. "You're right. You're always right."

"Let's not start that again. We —"

She put a hand over his mouth, silencing him. "I'm being serious. We both know we're not going to find Michael in time and we both know that I'm not going to run away from something that's my fault. So maybe it's time for you to get your plane. There's no reason for you to get caught up in what's going to happen."

He pulled her hand away. "No. We're staying together. If you stay, I stay."

"Why do you have to be so difficult? Why can't you just let me do what I have to do and not pile more and more on my conscience?"

He yanked a rubber band off a set of architectural plans for Teague's tar sands facility and smoothed them out on the floor. "Don't try to make this my fault, Jen. You could save me, but you're not willing to live with a little guilt. It's not worth it to you."

She swung a fist into his chest as hard as she could, but he barely felt it as he focused on the plans spread out in front of him. "What the fuck is that?"

The seriousness of his tone was enough to silence her, and she twisted around to see what he was pointing to. "What?"

He ran a finger along a line that led south from the building to the edge of the page and then flipped forward to a drawing of a partially buried half-meter pipe topped with a valve wheel. "We went over every inch of that place. Did you ever see this?"

46

The Canadian streets hadn't emptied like in the U.S., forcing Mark Beamon to drive up onto the sidewalk to get around a slow-moving minivan. Jenna grabbed the dashboard and glanced into the backseat where Erin was hunting for a seatbelt.

"Carl!" Beamon shouted into his cell phone. "We're headed your way. We're going to need a flight to the tar sands and some of your special forces guys. Yeah . . . no, I'm serious. Hold on."

He handed the phone to Jenna and turned to concentrate on driving into oncoming traffic.

"Hello? Mr. Fournier? This is Jenna Kalin."

"What's happening there, Jenna? Are you in a car?"

The sound of a siren started behind them and she twisted around to see a police cruiser closing in. Beamon thumbed toward it and then pointed at the phone.

"Uh, yeah, we are. There's a police car trying to pull us over and I think Mark wants you to do something about it."

"Hold on."

The phone went silent for a moment and then he came back on the line. "Can I assume you've found something that might help us?"

"We think so," she said, raising her voice to be heard over the wail of the siren. "We just got a copy of the original plans for the building in the tar sands. There's a pipeline that runs south from it for a few hundred miles before connecting to one of the major lines going into the U.S. It was probably abandoned when the company folded."

"So? You went over that building — we all did. No one has been there in —"

"The inlet for that pipe is gone," she said, cutting him off. "Why would someone bother to remove the inlet to an abandoned pipeline?"

"You tell me."

The siren suddenly stopped behind them, replaced by the sound of a horn. Beamon slammed on the brakes to let the patrol car pass and Erin reached around the seat to grab Jenna before she could be pitched into the dashboard. She flashed him a grateful smile, but he didn't look happy — as though he was angry about having to save her again. Or was she just reading too much into everything he did now?

"Jenna?" Fournier prompted. "Are you still there?"

"I'm sorry . . ." The police car passed them and the siren started again, cutting a swath through the traffic in front of them. "When they bought that building, we think they capped off the pipe, filled it with oil, and then hid the outlet. That's their incubator. All they have to do is dump in a bunch of bacteria, let it fill the pipe, and then somehow perforate it where it goes through the tar sands."

"How long would it take?"

"I don't know," Jenna admitted. "Maybe they've already done it. But maybe not. We need your patrol planes to fly along the route of that pipeline. We're guessing that they built some kind of structure over the point where they've cut into the pipe — a place where they could introduce the bacteria and wait for it to spread."

There was a long silence over the phone.

"Mr. Fournier?"

"Why should I do this, Jenna? The more I'm involved with you, the more I wonder if you're still working with Teague — if your job is to keep coming up with plausible leads and making us chase them."

"I don't know. Are you saying you have something better to do?"

47

The gun cabinet was wide open and only ten feet away, but it might as well not have existed at all. As Teague pulled hopelessly against the chain locked around his neck, he felt the rough metal coax a little more blood onto his stained collar.

He looked at the bottled water and energy bars Udo had left him, at the pipe he was locked to, at the metal walls that separated him from the cold, empty miles of Canadian wilderness. And finally, he looked through the open door of the room he was trapped in.

Udo had been sitting in full view for most of the day, but a little over an hour ago he disappeared. Teague could still hear him, though, and strained to decipher the sounds, to understand what was happening. Was the German preparing to blow the pipeline charges? Had it already been done?

Teague pulled on the chain again, but his

strength was gone. Even if he could free himself and reach the weapons, Udo was armed as well and undoubtedly only feet from the detonator button.

The sound of approaching footsteps prompted Teague to stand, ignoring the leg cramps brought on from sitting so long on the concrete floor.

"You don't have to kill me," he said as Udo took a position in front of the weapons cabinet. "I'm not a threat to you. I swear I —"

He fell silent when the German pulled his pistol from his waistband and threw Teague the key to the lock around his neck.

"What do you want?" Teague said, looking down at the key and wondering what it represented. Freedom? Death?

"I want you to do what you set out to do, Michael."

Teague turned the key in the lock and the chain fell to the floor, but he didn't move.

"I'm not going to kill you, Michael. You're afraid, and that is understandable. I feel these same things. As did Jonas. But we must master our fear, yes? We mustn't let it control us. Have you thought about this?"

Udo motioned toward the door with his pistol and Teague walked slowly, feeling the muscles in his thighs beginning to loosen.

The German's tone suggested that he hadn't yet released the bacteria, and that meant there was still an opportunity stop this. But how? There was a time when he would have been certain he could overpower the unassuming biologist, but now he was certain the opposite was true. Now he knew that it was Udo and not Jonas who had been the strong one.

"You have worked so hard and given so much to this cause, Michael. What you said before is true — without you, none of this would have been possible."

They skirted around the wall dividing the room and Teague stopped in front of a laptop resting on an otherwise empty table. At the bottom left of the screen was a square representing the building in which they were standing. A red line ran from it, crossing a narrow green band depicting the forest and then traveling into the murky brown of the tar sands.

Near its end, the line faded from red to yellow, depicting the section of the pipeline that was not yet fully contaminated by the bacteria.

"How long?"

"A few hours. Its growth is exponential."

Teague glanced over his shoulder to find Udo only a few feet away, his gun pointed loosely at the floor. He seemed hypnotized by the almost imperceptible expansion of the red line.

"Have you done the final bomb-test sequence?" Teague asked, concentrating on keeping his voice steady. Udo, like his brother, was a fanatic. He was obviously having a difficult time understanding Teague's change of heart and seemed to want to rationalize it as a momentary lapse instead of the reasoned reaction it really was.

"I haven't," the German said. "I thought that should be your honor."

As Teague ran his hand over the computer's keyboard, he fantasized about smashing it on the floor. But it would be pointless. The connection was wireless and they had backup computers — something he himself had insisted on.

Teague tapped in a few commands and sixty small blue dots appeared along the pipeline. For a moment, he thought they'd failed, but then the dots began turning green as each sent a ready signal back to the computer.

"They're all go," Teague said.

Udo stepped up behind him and stared down at the screen. "So many years of work. So many sacrifices. But we're finally here."

Teague grabbed the laptop and spun, swinging it at the surprised German's head. It connected hard and Udo crumpled to the floor, the gun skittering across the room and bouncing off the far wall.

Teague lunged toward it but Udo grabbed his pant leg, forcing him to reach out for the table to keep from falling. He tried to free himself and discovered that it was easy — the blow had weakened the German to the point that all he could do was watch helplessly as Teague walked casually across the room to retrieve the gun.

"I'm not going to die like this, Udo. I'm not going to die like all the others."

By the time he'd picked up the pistol and turned, the German was back on his feet, but swaying unsteadily.

"What do you matter, Michael? What do I matter? This is about the survival of the planet — maybe the only one of its kind in the entire universe. If we don't —"

Teague shook his head sadly. "I gave up everything for this — my career, my home, my position. But I'm not going to give up my life."

He raised the gun and Udo backed away until he bumped the wall behind him.

"I'm sorry," Teague said. "I admire your conviction, but in the end that's your problem. You're blinded by it."

He pulled the trigger and the gun clicked quietly.

Suddenly, Udo seemed to be able to stand under his own power without difficulty. His eyes turned dark and his voice took on Jonas's quiet monotone. "I'd hoped you'd be able to put your fear and selfishness behind you in the face of something as great as this. That after you had calmed down, we'd be able to finish this and walk into the wilderness knowing that because of us it would survive. Always."

Teague pulled the trigger again, and again, it clicked. He moved right, but Udo moved with him, blocking the only path to the weapons cabinet on the other side of the building. He recognized the knife that Udo produced as one of Jonas's — a long, silver blade with deep serrations across the back.

"You never truly understood, did you Michael? After all this, you never really believed."

48

The full moon created a colorless haze over the top of the forest, making it indistinguishable from an ocean as it rolled beneath them. With no lights or detail to fix on, Erin finally turned away from the window and looked around the helicopter's cramped cabin. Jenna was sitting next to him, dressed in black fatigues, her gloved hand clinging tightly to his. The others were dressed exactly the same, but it was still painfully obvious who was who. The Canadian commandos all wore the same robot-like expression, their gazes fixed sightlessly on whatever was directly across from them. Mark Beamon's belly was straining at clothes not really designed for the committed nonathlete and his sweat-glazed face hinted at either motion sickness or a hangover.

The helicopter began to slow and Carl Fournier stood, holding a steel rail above him for balance. His voice reverberated in

Erin's ear-phones. "This is as close as we're going to get without them hearing us. Let's move!"

The soldiers jumped to their feet in unison, rocking the helicopter nauseatingly as they threw the doors open to the cold wind. Erin squinted into it as two men tossed ropes out into the darkness, anchored them to harnesses at their waists, then flung themselves into space. It seemed like less than a second before the ropes went slack and Fournier pointed in his direction. "You're next!"

Erin shook he head. "Fuck that. You go."

"I'm staying up here to coordinate air cover. You agreed to this, Erin. There's no changing your mind now."

Jenna got up and pulled him to the open door, looping the rope through his harness before doing the same herself. "Just relax, Erin! It's going to be fine."

At least, that's what he thought she said. With the wind and the sound of the rotors, it could just as well have been "It's only two hundred feet to the jagged rocks, but don't worry, that rope was made by the lowest bidder."

It wasn't that he was afraid of heights in a classic sense — he piloted planes without any problems. What he didn't do, though, was climb out onto the wings when they were in flight.

Jenna grabbed his shoulder and gently pulled him backwards, letting the stretch of the rope take him out into the helicopter's powerful downdraft. His footing became increasingly precarious as Jenna lowered herself onto the helicopter's skids. She grabbed him again, this time by the back of the harness and gave it a yank — causing his feet to slip and his shins to slam into the edge of the platform.

"Goddamnit," he shouted, but all he could hear was the wind.

Jenna took hold of his rope and tried to feed some through to put distance between them and the rotors, but he pushed her hand away. He was perfectly aware that he was dangling in space beneath a man-made hurricane and that the ground would be a much better place to be. Slipping away from the relative safety of the massive chopper to dangle in the darkness from an invisible thread, though, wasn't as easy as he'd hoped.

He loosened his grip a bit and dropped gracelessly, his unwillingness to completely abandon the helicopter causing him to keep his feet on the skids and flip himself upside down. Unfazed, Jenna grabbed one of his ankles and used her weight to right him as she slipped by and disappeared.

He followed hesitantly, refusing to look down until his feet hit the branches of a tree — the next best thing to solid ground as far as he was concerned. Instead of just pushing away from it and rappelling neatly the rest of the way, he climbed through the branches and then slithered down the trunk.

"Good job," Jenna lied, running up and helping him out of the harness. He glanced up and saw a round shadow descending a little too fast. It hit with the sound of a sandbag, though with the addition of a breathless stream of obscenities.

"Mark! Are you alright?" Jenna shouted, running toward the prone figure as Erin followed.

"I'm great," Beamon said as he untangled himself from his rope. "Just fucking great."

When he was free, the helicopter began to move away, leaving them in silence. At first, it was as though the soldiers had disappeared, but on closer inspection, Erin saw the last two melting into the tree line to the north.

"Doesn't look like the end of the world, does it?" Erin whispered.

The three of them were lying amidst the

densely packed trees, looking out at a metal cube of a building glowing in the moonlight. It had taken almost four hours of hard hiking to get there and Beamon was flat on his back, his breath coming in short gasps that hung like fog in front of his mouth for a moment before being torn apart by the wind. The cut across his cheek that Erin had given him had opened up and blood was spreading dramatically as it mixed with sweat.

Jenna didn't answer, instead concentrating on the building with an intensity born of knowing that it was their last chance. It was exactly what they'd been looking for — a camouflaged building straddling the pipeline they'd found, miles from the heavily secured tar sands.

With the exception of Erin and Mark, there was no sign of life anywhere. No light bled from the building's only door, and there was no sign of the soldiers she knew were methodically surrounding the clearing.

"This is it," she said quietly. "It has to be."

Erin turned toward her but it was too dark to see his expression. The desperation in her voice was obvious, even to her. She couldn't bring herself to consider that this might be another of Teague's clever diversions or that they might be too late.

With so much darkness and silence, it would be too easy to lose herself in the consequences of her stupidity and naïveté. Too easy to imagine the machines grinding to a halt, the people abandoning the cities in search of food and security, the chaos that would ensue when they discovered those things no longer existed. And, finally, the horrifying brutality and death as people fought to survive in a world that no one had ever imagined. Except Michael Teague.

"He's in there, Erin. I know he is."

"There's no way to be sure, Jen. I mean, I hope he is, but —"

A voice crackled through their earpieces, cutting him off.

"One in position. No windows or doors." Pause. "Two in position. No windows or doors." And so on until everyone was accounted for.

Beamon rolled onto his belly and shimmied in their direction, stopping alongside Erin. "This is it, then — the only way in or out. Are you sure about what we can expect inside?"

"It'd be a pretty simple operation," Jenna said. "They'll have cut into the pipe and there'd be an outlet somewhere in the building. I don't think they'd need much of a lab

— a microscope, some slides. Stuff like that. And if we're right that they've planted bombs along the pipeline, there'll be a way to detonate them. I'd guess a laptop based on the way Teague likes to do things."

Beamon nodded and spoke into his radio. "We're going. If anyone inside doesn't do exactly what you say, shoot first and we'll ask questions later."

"Wait a minute . . . ," Jenna said as the men surrounding the building confirmed that they'd heard and understood. "We aren't a hundred percent sure this is even the right building. It could be —"

"It could be what?" Beamon said. "You've been telling me for the last week that if I don't stop this thing, billions of people are going to die. That doesn't really put me in a position to take risks, does it? If this turns out to be a Boy Scout camp, we'll just have to hope they can follow instructions."

"You can't —" Jenna started, but Beamon was already on his feet, moving cautiously into the clearing, his pistol held in front of him.

"Stay here," he said. "I'll be back."

She watched the soldiers close in on the door and managed to push herself to her knees before Erin grabbed her. "You heard him, Jen. We're supposed to stay here. You'll just be in the way. I'm serious."

His tone and the weakness of his grip suggested that he knew he was fighting a losing battle. She shrugged him off and followed Beamon across the clearing, glancing back and trying to wave Erin off as he started after her.

By the time Beamon noticed them, the soldiers were on each side of the door placing charges on the hinges. He stopped and grabbed Jenna by the back of the neck. "Goddamnit!" he whispered loudly. "I told you to stay!"

"You might need us. We know —"

"Yeah, but I need you *alive,* okay? Now just stay here."

She did as she was told for just long enough to give him a solid lead, and then she started forward again, reaching the building and slipping along it to take a position behind a black-clad figure toting a submachine gun. Another man was holding up his fingers in an elaborate countdown. When he got to three, everyone looked away as a flash lit up the trees around them. She could feel the heat as the door was violently ripped from its hinges and the men disappeared inside.

She felt Erin clamp a hand over her shoulder, but again she pulled away, running through the still-burning hole in the side of the building.

"Nobody move!" she heard someone yell as the soldiers fanned out across the concrete floor. Beamon was partially obscured by smoke, hanging back with his pistol thrust out in front of him and letting the special forces people do their jobs.

Jenna's eye caught a sudden movement to her right and she watched helplessly as a man raced from behind a set of shelves stocked with canned food and equipment.

"Udo! Stop!" she screamed, but it was too late. The first bullet hit him in his right shoulder blade, causing his body to twist violently but not knocking him down. After that, the drone of gunfire filled the building. Udo kept lurching forward, the impacts of the soldiers' rounds seeming to add to his momentum as he tried to get to a laptop on a table near the wall.

"Mark!" she heard Erin shout. "The computer! He's going for the computer!"

At first, Jenna wasn't sure he had heard, but he adjusted his aim and, a moment later, she saw a portion of the laptop's screen explode. It slid a few feet, but didn't fall even when Udo slammed into the table and collapsed on top of it.

Ignoring the bullets flying around her she

ran toward the German, unable to believe he was still moving — his shirt was completely shredded and barely covered the pulverized flesh that had once been his back.

She'd made it nearly halfway when someone hit her from behind, knocking her to the floor and dragging her from the path of the bullets still filling the air. She struggled to get free, but this time Erin wasn't so easily dissuaded. He'd pulled her almost back to the door they'd first come through when the building suddenly went silent. No more gunshots. No voices. Not even footsteps. She looked back to see everyone in the room standing motionless, staring at Udo's body. He was still draped across the table, but now had one dead hand on the keyboard of the shattered laptop.

"Don't shoot!"

She jerked around in the direction of the familiar voice and saw Michael Teague through an open doorway she hadn't noticed before. He was kneeling on the floor with one of the Canadian soldiers aiming a gun at his head.

"Don't shoot!" he pleaded again, moving as far from the man covering him as the chain around his neck would allow.

"Goddamnit!" Beamon yelled, his voice echoing through the building as he slid the laptop from beneath Udo's lifeless fingers. "Do you think he got to it in time?"

"It's still running," Erin said. "You just shot the screen."

"Fuck!" Beamon's shout was loud enough to startle a few of the soldiers sweeping the building.

Jenna's earpiece crackled to life again, this time with the voice of Carl Fournier. "Mark! What's happening in there? We have reports of explosions along the pipeline."

Jenna felt her legs go weak as Beamon slammed a fist into the laptop. It couldn't be. Not after all this. They had been so close.

She turned and ran unsteadily into the room at the back, grabbing Teague by the collar and throwing him onto his back. "How much bacteria was in the pipe? Tell me how much!"

"I tried to stop him," he said, not resisting when she grabbed the chain and pulled him back into a sitting position. He wouldn't look at her, instead staring down at the empty cans of soda and food wrappers surrounding him. "I tried . . ."

Jenna concentrated on softening her voice. "We know, Michael. We know you wanted to stop him. But you have to listen to me now. How full was the pipe?"

"At least ninety-five percent. Probably a

hundred."

She backed away unsteadily, looking up at the man covering Teague and, for a moment, actually considering grabbing the gun and killing him herself.

"Michael! The valve you used to access the pipe. Can it still be opened?"

Teague's eyes narrowed at the sound of Erin's voice, but he nodded.

"Everyone out!" Jenna said, running into the main part of the building as Erin crawled onto the pipe outlet jutting from the floor.

She grabbed Mark's arm and pulled him along as she crossed the room. "That's a two-foot-diameter pipe," she explained. "We're going to open it and try to relieve some of the pressure to slow down the leaks where those charges went off."

"Won't that just move the problem from there to here?"

"Some of it. But there's no oil here — it should go dormant pretty fast. Now, you have to listen to me. You need to set fire to the forest around this building and then to the building itself."

"What about where the pipe was perforated?"

"You'll have to use toxic chemicals that'll penetrate the sand," Erin said, using a wrench he'd found to pry out the pin locking the valve. "If I don't make it out of here, talk to Steve Andropolous. He'll know what to do."

Beamon hesitated for a moment, but then pointed to the man holding a gun on Teague. "Get that chain off him and let's get the hell out of here."

"We didn't bring bolt cutters," the soldier replied. "We used detonators on the door and planned on doing the same on any locks we found."

"Can you shoot it?"

"Risky. The bullet could ricochet . . ."

"Fuck it," Beamon said. "Leave him."

"What?" Teague said. "You can't leave me here."

Beamon just shrugged and everyone started filing out.

"Wait!" Teague shouted. "I can help you! I know everything about these bacteria. I can help stop it."

But they were already through the door, the sound of approaching helicopters already audible.

"Jenna!" Teague yelled. "I tried to stop Udo. You know that. You have to get me out of here."

She ignored him and climbed onto the pipe next to Erin. "I can do this myself. Go

435

with Mark."

He grinned and shook his head slowly. "Remember our first date? What a disaster it was?"

"What the hell are you talking about? Erin, you've got to get out of here."

Beamon's voice came over her earpiece, but he wasn't talking to them. He was calling in the air strike.

"Kind of fitting, don't you think?" Erin said as they heaved on the large wheel controlling the valve. "I mean, that our last date would turn out this way?"

The wheel turned a few inches and a narrow stream of reddish sludge shot from the pipe, arcing nearly thirty feet in the air before spattering across the building's far wall. After the initial movement, the valve loosened and soon the stream was pounding the wall hard enough to dent it. The onslaught sounded like a huge waterfall, but it wasn't loud enough to cover up the distant explosions as Canadian Air Command planes set fire to the forest around them.

They jumped off the pipe, both slipping and splashing down into the sludge. Jenna struggled to her feet and wiped her eyes, only to see Teague pulling desperately on his chain as his creation flooded around his ankles.

He shouted noiselessly at her and she took a hesitant step toward him, but Erin grabbed her and pulled her in the direction of the glow coming through the hole in the side of the building.

Outside, the smoke was already thick, driven by the predawn winds. She put her arm in front of her face and breathed through the fabric of her sleeve, but it didn't help. Erin kept pulling her along, but soon slowed and finally stopped when he realized what she already knew — there was nowhere to go. She turned in a slow circle, watching the flames dancing across the tops of the trees and the fighter jets continuing to fire their rockets at a distance calculated not to send the bacteria into the air.

When she finally came back around to Erin, she saw the flames reflected in his eyes and knew that she'd finally done it. She'd finally killed him.

"It would have been so much better for you if we'd never met."

She couldn't tell if he was smiling or if it was just a trick of the shimmering light.

"After spending the last two years mourning you and the next ten minutes waiting to catch on fire, you'd think I'd feel that way.

But I don't. As insane as this sounds, I still think my life was better with you than without you."

The smoke between them was becoming increasingly tangible and she moved in closer, sliding her arms around him. There wasn't much more time. She was already feeling dizzy from lack of oxygen.

"I want you to know something," she started, but fell silent.

"What?"

A shadow in the smoke that she'd taken for a hallucination became more and more defined as it came up behind Erin. It almost looked like . . .

"Hey!" Mark Beamon shouted. "I hate to spoil the moment, but if you follow me there's still a chance we might make it out of here."

EPILOGUE

Erin Neal tilted his face into the New Mexico sun and closed his eyes for a moment, causing his bicycle to arc lazily toward the edge of the empty road. The sky was a perfect uniform blue and the air was cool and still. He'd almost forgotten there could be days like this.

After he and Jenna had escaped being burned alive in Canada, he'd stayed on for a while — spending seven months living in freezing cold tents and metal sheds, doing unimaginably horrible things to the earth. No procedure for dumping toxic chemicals on pristine wilderness had been ignored — he'd used helicopters, tanker trucks, fire-suppression planes. There had even been some talk of blimps until they'd discovered they didn't do well in those kinds of cross-winds. In the end, he'd single-handedly created an ecological disaster area that would have made even the Soviets cringe.

Now the world was playing a waiting game, spending billions testing soil, air, and groundwater for even the slightest trace of Teague's bacteria. If, in a few years, none had been found, the Canadians would team up with the U.S. and Europe to begin the multi-trillion-dollar project of removing God knew how many cubic yards of dirt and safely disposing of it. How that was going to be accomplished no one was quite sure.

Erin stood on the pedals and propelled the bicycle up a hill that opened into a sweeping view of the massive research complex at the end of the road. Small houses topped with solar panels dotted the desert around it, connected by a web of narrow dirt streets. The price of oil had settled at about four hundred and fifty dollars per barrel, making paving economically unviable unless it was absolutely necessary.

In the distance, he could see their resident farmer running his tractor across a field that provided much of the food for the two hundred and fifty or so people who worked there. It had been a battle to get that done — the government still liked to throw money around for no reason while waxing rhapsodic about nonexistent security concerns — but in the end it was much more economical than transporting all their food in with gas at twelve dollars per gallon.

His little agricultural project was just one example of myriad changes the world had undergone in the past year and a half. Of course, there was the initial panic when it had sunk in that the forty percent reduction in world oil production was going to be more or less permanent. That was the way it always went, though. It was human nature to be absolutely certain that every deviation from the status quo was a sign of the apocalypse. But it was also human nature to adapt when those changes became inevitable.

After years of becoming increasingly smaller, the world seemed to explode in size almost overnight. Most of the airlines were gone now that a coach ticket overseas cost a third of the average American's substantially diminished salary. Imports and exports had pretty much dried up as well, and military adventurism on any scale was no longer tolerated by voters now painfully aware of just how much fuel a little skirmish abroad could suck up.

And so the United States had turned inward, going back to local manufacturing and food production, creating new technologies for conservation, and focusing more and more on electricity generated from coal and nuclear. The economy was finally starting to stabilize, though it was clear that it would do so at a substantially lower level. Many stores were open only three days a week now, and the skyrocketing number of people telecommuting had caused a massive crash in commercial real estate and the auto manufacturing business. Ford and GM were just now getting back on their feet — with substantial government help — refocusing their business on catching up with Toyota in electric-vehicle technology.

Although life had changed for everyone, people actually seemed grateful that they had enough to eat and a roof over their head. The glass is half empty sentiment that seemed to have taken hold in America was gone and people realized that things could be a lot worse. Even the media had done an about-face — focusing on stories about can-do people and technological successes instead of sensationalizing the worst humanity had to offer.

Erin coasted down the back of the hill, weaving from side to side to keep his speed below the point where his lunch would blow out of the basket secured to his handlebars. In front of him, a chain-link gate began to open and a guard in crisp fatigues held up a hand in greeting.

"Nice weather, huh, Doc?"

He smiled as he pedaled by. "You've got the best job in town today, George."

Erin ignored the nearly full bike rack, gliding through a set of automatic glass doors and across the building's lobby — one of the very few benefits of being in charge. Most of the people around him were only vaguely familiar despite his best efforts to put names with faces, and he was forced to surreptitiously read their name tags when returning their greetings.

Jenna had always been in charge of that — using her nearly photographic memory to keep him out of trouble at conferences and presentations. Whenever someone he swore he'd never seen before walked up to them, she'd smile and say "Bill! We haven't seen you since Buenos Aires!" Or "Susan! Last time we saw you, you were eight months pregnant! How *is* little Max?"

But she wasn't here now. She'd been whisked out of Canada the day after the fire and he hadn't seen or heard from her since.

Mark Beamon had assured him — and continued to assure him during their heated weekly conversations — that she was fine and that he was doing everything he could for her.

That had worked for a few months, but Erin's anger and frustration had finally exploded and he'd made it clear in one of those conversations that if Jenna didn't reappear in a hurry, he was going to walk.

Beamon, whose droopy-dog sincerity could be shockingly reassuring, convinced him that it wasn't time yet to play that card. But now, after many more months of silence, it was getting to be time to act on his threat.

He was still the world expert on this type of biological attack, and they desperately needed him to direct the research into a way to counteract Teague's bacteria, should it resurface. But that might not always be the case. It was impossible to know when some kid twice as smart as him would suddenly appear out of MIT's basement, or the government would relax enough to put some congressman's brother in his chair. He needed to spend his political currency while it was still good.

Erin coasted into an empty elevator, turning his bike in a well-practiced maneuver that allowed him to push the button for his floor without getting off. When the doors opened again, he pedaled out into the hallway, but then came skidding to a halt when Mark Beamon appeared from a bathroom.

"I take it that since you're running the place, you don't see any reason to set your alarm," he said, wiping his damp hands on his slacks.

All their communication had been via phone or email since Beamon and Jenna had left Canada together. Why was he here? Traveling from D.C. to New Mexico wasn't exactly trivial anymore — even for the government.

"Erin? You alright?"

"You look good," Erin said, managing to shake off his surprise but sounding stupid anyway. It was a true statement, though. Beamon's hair had continued to thin, but his eyes were clear and his tan skin hung tighter to his cheekbones than last time they'd seen each other.

Erin had received an invitation to Beamon's wedding a while back, though there was no way he could get away to attend. Instead, he'd commissioned a local D.C. artist to sculpt an enormous fountain with cherubs peeing into a pool. Not cheap, but what did you give a man who had everything?

"Marriage seems to agree with you."

"I can't complain. Thanks for the fountain, by the way. Gives my backyard a little class."

They both fell silent, just standing there, looking at each other. There was little doubt this visit was about Jenna, but Erin wasn't sure he wanted to hear what Beamon had to say. What if something had happened to her? What if they'd decided that after what she'd done, she was never going to see the light of day again? What if Beamon had been lying to him and they'd put her somewhere like the place they'd sent him? What if —

"Do you have any coffee?" Beamon said finally.

"Yeah, sure. There's a pot in my office."

Beamon looked around admiringly as he followed. "Quite a spread you have here. They tell me you run a whole city."

"It's more of a town," Erin said, still finding it impossible to bring up Jenna as his stomach slowly tied itself in knots. "You know, just the employees. And there's a town council that handles most of the details."

His secretary glanced up from her computer as they walked in and tapped a calendar on her desk. "You've got a congressional oversight teleconference in two hours, Erin. Do you have all your budget numbers together?"

He shook his head absently and reached for the knob to his office door. He couldn't avoid the conversation forever. "So why are you here, Mark. Where is —"

Jenna pushed herself off his couch as he entered, an uncomfortable smile spreading across her face. "You wouldn't know where a biologist could get a job around here, would you?"

Her eyes were a little glassy as she crossed the office and threw her arms around him.

For a moment he couldn't speak, suddenly realizing that he'd never really believed he'd ever touch her again.

"Are you . . . are you okay? Where have you been?"

"Prison," she said.

He stared furiously at Beamon, who had passed by them and sat down behind the desk that dominated the room.

"Oh, don't look at me like that. Get her to tell you about it."

"It wasn't that bad."

"Not that bad?" Beamon said. "It had goddamned tennis courts."

"It did," she admitted, taking Erin's hand and leading him to the sofa. "Mark came and visited me every couple of weeks."

"Does this mean you're out? You're free?"

He looked over at Beamon. "Is that what this means?"

He grinned as he opened the desk's drawers and examined their contents. "It turns out that the government's thirst for blood was satisfied by the gruesome deaths of Teague and his German friends — particularly the fact that Teague drowned in his own creation. Even a congressman isn't too dense to see the poetry in that."

"Do you know for a fact he drowned?"

"No, but it makes a great story," Beamon and Jenna said in unison and then both laughed.

"There's also a general feeling that you need to be kept happy," Beamon continued. "And then, of course, Jenna can be a lot more valuable here than working on her net game in prison."

"Here?" Erin said, still unable to fully process what he was being told. "You're going to stay here?" He'd never even dared to consider that. His best-case scenario had been to walk off the job and negotiate a comfortable spot for Jenna on some desert island in return for toiling his life away in New Mexico. This seemed too good to be true.

Beamon crossed the room and Jenna stood to give him a grateful hug. He shook

Erin's hand and headed for the door, but stopped before he reached it.

"Don't ever do anything like this again, okay?"

ABOUT THE AUTHOR

Kyle Mills lives in Jackson Hole, Wyoming, where he spends his time biking, rock climbing, and writing books. Visit him online at www.kylemills.com.

The employees of Thorndike Press hope you have enjoyed this Large Print book. All our Thorndike and Wheeler Large Print titles are designed for easy reading, and all our books are made to last. Other Thorndike Press Large Print books are available at your library, through selected bookstores, or directly from us.

For information about titles, please call:
(800) 223-1244

or visit our Web site at:
http://gale.cengage.com/thorndike

To share your comments, please write:
Publisher
Thorndike Press
295 Kennedy Memorial Drive
Waterville, ME 04901